The Accidental Wife

SIMI K. RAO

Kando Books

Editing: Brittiany Koren/Written Dreams
Cover art design/Layout: Ed Vincent/ENC Graphic Design
Cover photographs © Shutterstock

Category: Mainstream Fiction/Romance

Dear Reader,

Namaste! I hope you enjoy reading ***The Accidental Wife***. I certainly enjoyed writing it for you. It's a story that stems from listening to personal accounts of my friends living in India and abroad, as well as my own experiences as a physician. I use some words and phrases from Hindi and other languages, so I thought a glossary might be helpful. You'll find the glossary in the back of the book. Please feel free to post a review of this book, and to check out my first book, ***Inconvenient Relations*** which was released in 2014. Feel free to contact me on my Facebook group page at this link: https://www.facebook.com/groups/simikraoreadersandfriends

Thank you,

Simi K. Rao

Dedication

For my mother. I am what I am because of you.

Prologue

"Another beer to calm the nerves?" A distant cousin who Rihaan had never the pleasure of meeting before, suggested with a knowing smirk.

This was followed by a loud burst of laughter. It was close to midnight, but the party had just begun at the usually serene Mehta abode in South Delhi. "Rihaan doesn't need anything to cool him down. He's going to be a full-on man tonight! Can't afford to disappoint *bhabhi*, right?" This was promptly followed by another outburst of mirth.

Rihaan submitted to several friendly thumps on his back, returning them with the obligatory wry smile that could be interpreted any which way they desired. He didn't care about their opinions.

It was true, he hadn't let a single drop of alcohol pass through his lips. Not because he was anxious to perform well on his wedding night and impress his new wife. On the contrary, he wanted to keep all his faculties intact so he could confirm the suspicion that had been gnawing at his brain ever since the wedding ceremony. And with each moment that passed, his unease had grown steadily.

Unable to bide his time any longer, he stood up and went toward his room paying no heed to the numerous whistles and catcalls that followed in his wake.

Thrusting the door wide open he strode toward the marital bed. It was bare except for his bride's wedding finery that lay in a neat pile in one corner. His heart now thudding at a frantic pace inside his chest, he scanned the vicinity, fervently hoping his concerns were for nothing.

He approached the wide open balcony door, and his pulse slowed down slightly. Perhaps he'd just been imagining it all?

A girl stood there leaning against the railing, her face upturned toward the full moon. On hearing him approach, she turned around. "Finally! I've been waiting like forever!"

He frowned, straining to decipher her features obscured by deep shadow. "Deepika?"

"Naa…, not Deepika." She stepped forward into the light, a bright smile illuminating her strikingly graceful features.

His heart sank. *Not Deepika.*

"I am Naina—the girl you married. Goodbye, Rihaan."

Wishes and Demands

New York City, two months ago

Rihaan Mehta was a confirmed bachelor, at least he had been determined to be one. Until now.

He had several reasons why—the most significant being his independence. To not have a girl nagging him day and night asking about his whereabouts or harrying him to present himself at home at 6 p.m. sharp was a convenience he treasured. He pitied his dad who was probably so accustomed to being henpecked, he wouldn't know what to do if he was left alone for a day. Rihaan enjoyed the freedom to do what he wanted when he wanted to.

He was also urged toward bachelorhood because he'd never really appreciated an inclination toward the fairer sex. No girl had ever been able to bowl him over with her charms, though not for the lack of trying; many had. He just hadn't been adequately stimulated by what he called superficial accoutrements. Nor had he felt the need for feminine company, except on rare occasions when he'd been obligated to have a date on his arm. His work provided him with all the company he desired and he couldn't be happier; he loved what he did.

Six months ago, after graduating *summa cum laude* from the very demanding and rigorous neurosurgical residency program at Mass General/ Harvard Medical School, Rihaan had joined as the youngest associate at one of the busiest neurosurgical practices in New York City. And he had distinguished himself so well that today his chief had offered to make him partner. *Partner?* He was delighted and would have been flying on cloud nine, ten, or maybe even eleven, if it hadn't been for the untimely demands of his mother.

His parents, Shashank and Shobha Mehta of the 'famed' Mehta clan of New Delhi, along with their two children Rima and Rihaan had immigrated to the United States more than twenty years ago, defying the expectations of the elders. His father was ambitious. He had undertaken to spread the Mehta business beyond the *desi* shores by establishing one of the biggest and finest jewelry chains abroad. And where best to commence such a venture but the Big Apple? Shashank had kept his word, accomplishing what he said he would, thus making the entire family proud.

But Rihaan, instead of joining his father and continuing with the family business tradition, had opted for medical school to become a *dimaag ka doctor* (head doctor). No, not a doctor who deals with mad people, but one who wields a *chaku* and a *churi* (knife and scalpel) to fix them. Everyone, including his favorite uncle, Rajbir, had shook their heads in disapproval.

"We don't care for such mumbo jumbo," Uncle Rajbir had said. "Business *mein kya kharaabi hai?*" (What's wrong with business?)

But on a bitter cold day when Mama and Papa Mehta saw their defiant son felicitated as one of the best to have passed through the hallowed grounds of the famed Harvard university, they couldn't check the flood of joyous tears from flowing down their ruddy cheeks.

From then on, Rihaan had been given free rein. When he chose to relocate to a tiny rental in the city and give up the luxurious trappings of the family's huge suburban villa, pleading inconvenience, his father gave his grudging assent. Then, when he opted to stay away from the many communal *pujas* and parties his mother threw (mostly in the hope of finding a suitable daughter-in-law for herself) Papa Mehta looked the other way. And when Rihaan pruned his visits home to one weekend every other month, often less, his parents could only hope he perceived their distress. Rihaan thus succeeded in slowly, but surely distancing himself from the crazy chaos of his massive family, except for those occasions he was required, such as his sister, Rima's wedding and then later, the *naamkaran* of her child.

Finally he was at peace.

But this state of affairs was intolerable for Shobha. He knew his mother felt cheated. She had voiced her opinion often enough. How many years had she spent yearning for someone she could order around the house, and who would wait upon her hand and foot. How long had she hankered to be the *Saas* to beat all *Saases*.

But Rihaan wouldn't oblige her. Despite her lining up hundreds upon hundreds of suitable girls (handpicked by her of course) he wouldn't bow his hard head down and give in to her wishes, causing her to mutter often in his presence, 'What a waste of a handsome face and six figure income to boot!'

One day during his last visit, she threw in her final salvo and served him the ultimatum in typical Bollywood style. *"Shaadi ke liye tayyaar ho jao nahin toh tum mera mara muh dekhoge."* (Get ready to marry or you'll see me on my death bed.)

He didn't stay over that weekend.

"Do you think she is serious?" Rihaan asked his father while he was being shuttled to the local subway station. Rihaan hated driving, particularly in New York, where a car is considered a handicap. He preferred the subway or his faithful bicycle, which he rode every day to and from work come rain, snow or shine.

Shashank guffawed. "No son, she won't kill herself. But she'll certainly kill you if you don't bring her a *bahu!*"

Shashank was very loud for not so large a man. Rihaan, who towered above him at more than six feet, had inherited his lanky genes from Uncle Rajbir.

Rihaan chuckled. "Guess that is one reason why I don't wish to get hitched. Because no girl deserves to be a victim to mom's ministrations, no matter how well intentioned they may be. I'd rather stay single."

His father voiced his opinion sagely, "You say so now. But soon you will change your mind."

"Why? I can see how happy *you* are married to Mom!"

Shashank turned to face his son. "In all seriousness, I'm as happy as I will ever be. *You* could be even happier."

Rihaan eyed him skeptically. "I don't get it."

Shashank continued with a patient smile. "You are young. You have everything going your way—choice of education, job, respect, incredible success. But for how long? How long can you sustain this pace? Life comes with its share of unpleasant surprises."

His expression grew somber. "I was like you once, Rihaan—young, dynamic, impatient, indestructible. I didn't need anybody, didn't want anybody. But then *papaji* coerced me into tying the knot. Now, when I think about it, I'm glad he did. Though, perhaps I'd have preferred a less forceful woman." He erupted into a loud laugh. "Anyway, that is beside the point. I'm as happy as I ever will be."

Shashank glanced at Rihaan. "What I mean is, that a time will come when you'll find an empty space inside that can only be filled with love. Mark my words." And on that cryptic note he pulled to a halt.

Rihaan adjusted the ubiquitous backpack on his shoulder. "I'll think about it Dad," he said, before nodding goodbye and walking away. But he didn't intend on doing any such thing. He'd said so just to humor his father.

That night, Rihaan tossed and turned restlessly in his narrow, single bed, whereas typically, he'd have fallen fast asleep as soon as his head hit the pillow. His mother's threat along with his father's pearls of wisdom were raising a clamor inside his mind. He'd have to do something. He knew his mother wouldn't rest without seeing him wearing that noose called matrimony. But by no means was he willing to forsake his entire future by assenting to one of her favored picks. Those women were all unbearable— each and every one! Yet he couldn't see a way out.

Swearing, he kicked off the sheets and swung his long legs off the bed. A shuddering chill shot straight through his spine as his feet came in contact with the cold hardwood floor. Gripping the edge of the bed to steady himself, he shot a glance at the digital clock—morning already, and the chances of sleep fading rapidly into oblivion. Might as well get a move on.

Rihaan rented a one bedroom apartment in the posh Upper East Side of Manhattan. He had secured it at a bargain as the owner who happened to be a close friend, had just got himself hitched, thereby being pressed to move to larger quarters. Rihaan loved the place, even though many would consider it slightly cramped. But for him it was perfectly convenient, located at an ideal distance from the park and a half-hour to forty-five minutes at most from work.

Pulling on a pair of worn out sweats he'd had since college, and his dependable trainers, Rihaan grabbed his bicycle and headed out toward Central park.

He pedaled down 5th Avenue, which at this early hour looked very unlike its jazzy self, and swung onto one of the numerous paths leading into the Park. There, after docking his bike, he took off at a brisk-paced jog. This was his daily routine. The unencumbered spaces and crisp, clean air helped keep his brain robust and operating in top gear for the rest of the day.

It was late autumn. Soon, very soon, a glittering white powder would descend from the skies and cover everything in a blanket of snow—a pristine, flawless layer of crystallized water vapor—one of the most beautiful scenes nature could offer. Rihaan contemplated, as his breath steamed in front of his face, of what the winter would bring. Passing a few other travelers like himself, he nodded to a couple of nameless yet familiar people he recognized seeing before: a young man exercising his playful boxer and an elderly gent with his wife out on a leisurely stroll, their faces serene and blissful.

He then came upon another couple voraciously making out on a bench, even in this bitter cold. They continued undeterred as he ran by. He snickered. *Idiots! Wait till she springs the surprise!*

Abruptly, he found his steady momentum disrupted as a memory flashed in his mind. His feet came to a jarring halt and he had to grab onto a red oak to keep from pitching flat on his face—the effect of the recollection was so great, it gave him a mini stroke every time.

The occasion was his high school prom night, and not a happy occasion at all. Cindy, the prom queen had dared him to a kiss and he'd obliged quite willingly. And then in the girls' bathroom, in a tiny stall, his raging hormones had taken over. Egged on by a few slugs of beer, one thing led to another. Thank heavens someone had barged in at the right moment—or else.

"Phew!" Rihaan slid down onto a bed of bright red leaves.

Cindy had been pregnant and the perpetrator had dumped her, making him, Rihaan, the dumb, rich fall guy.

Ever since he'd sworn off girls. "I'll never let that happen to me again. Ever!" He blurted out the words to no one in particular, not caring if anyone had heard him. But all he saw was the spectacular image of the skyscrapers reflected in the calm waters of the lake, where two white swans were taking a lazy turn. *Bloody couples everywhere!*

His pager came alive, springing him out of his reverie. It was from Lenox Hill ED. He reached for his cell phone in his back pocket, but didn't find it there.

For a brief moment he was caught in a panic, thinking he'd omitted it in his rush to leave that morning. But then he located it deep inside his right sock, though he had no clue how it made it there. He called back.

"Hi Rihaan. This is Jasmine Walsh. A very good Monday morning to you!

I think we can use your help here."

"Hi, Jazz. Morning to you, too. What's the matter? I thought you ER docs had everything covered," Rihaan responded with a grin.

Jasmine Walsh was a fiery red-headed Irish woman who had attended med school with him, and he didn't let go any opportunity to tease her. She was known for her short fuse. But not today.

"I thought we were until this fifteen-year-old rolled in with a bullet in his back," Jasmine said. "His friend accidentally shot him while playing with his father's gun."

"That's horrible. Tell me you're joking! What the hell were they doing playing with guns so early in the morning?" Rihaan asked.

"Having a party, I guess." Jasmine sighed. "The parents are out in Cancun celebrating their 20th anniversary or some such thing, so the boys chose to have their own bit of fun. Lot of booze, drugs and horseplay with guns. That's all I know. Anyway, when can I expect you? I've already assured the hysterical mom that you are the best hope her kid has."

"Thanks for tooting my horn, especially when I haven't even peeked at the scans yet. Alert the OR team. I'll be there in 40 tops."

Rihaan could feel the adrenalin pumping in his veins as he jogged back. This was the reason why he loved his job so much. His skills could prevent someone from losing the use of his legs. In his mind, Rihaan could already visualize himself performing the delicate procedure. His hands never shook so nervousness wasn't a problem.

***

Success!

Releasing a prolonged sigh, Rihaan sunk back into his swivel chair at the Manhattan clinic of Central Neurosurgical Associates. Four long, bloody painstaking hours to extract the bullet, but he'd done it. The blood had been evacuated and the spinal cord saved. The boy would be able to walk again.

Grudgingly, he'd accepted the praise for accomplishing one of the toughest procedures that a neurosurgeon could undertake. But it was when the boy's father with tears in his eyes, had taken Rihaan's hands and reverently kissed them, he knew how valued his skills were. That was enough to validate all the years of toil and hard work he'd put himself through.

But his achievement failed to make the slightest dent in his mother's demands when he told her later that day. She screeched into the phone like a witch who'd discovered she'd slept through Halloween.

"Rihaan! Do you want me to kill myself? If so, prescribe me some poison!"

Damnit! Why can't I be left alone for even a moment! He closed his eyes, counted slowly to five and replied. "Okay Mother. I'll give the matter serious consideration."

"Wow, really?" She sounded excited, her voice raising an octave. He could imagine her eyes gleaming with delight. Indeed, she'd make an awesome witch. "Then shall I start discussions with the Sharmas for their daughter, Renu? She's supposed to be a really good cook. Or what about the Roshans? Their younger girl, Sush, is apparently very skilled in needlework."

"Ma...are you getting married or am I?" he barked into the phone.

"*Beta*, listen...I...just want to make it easy for you."

"I'm willing to listen," he retorted sternly, "but only on one condition. I'll choose my future wife entirely on my own."

The Girl

"**O**kay, my baby, whatever you wish Rihaan. Just be sure she can walk, and isn't a deaf mute. *Tumhara koi bharosa nahin.* (You cannot be trusted.) And *haan*, she should be Indian. Fine?"

"Mom, you are crazy!" Rihaan exclaimed, roaring with laughter before ending the call. At least she won't bother me for a while, he thought. He switched his attention over to his tablet to review the details of the next case, when it struck him.

"Oh damn! What have I done?" He'd just told his mother he was ready to get married. Was he insane? He staggered against his desk, sending the gadget along with several plastic models of the brain and vertebral column crashing to the floor.

"Dr. Mehta...anything the matter?" Anna, his secretary, popped her strawberry blonde head around the door of his office, followed by her baby pink-clad buxom figure.

"Uh...my mom...she..." He stopped short, his mind wandering as he looked at Anna. Rihaan had often wondered why his chief had opted for such a uniform. They ran a serious medical outfit, not a spa! Maybe it was to put their anxious clientele at ease. But was it working? Someone should do a survey.

"Your mother? Is she unwell?" Anna crept in to the room.

No! She's perfectly fine. It's I who's in urgent need of psychotherapy! Rihaan wanted to holler; instead he tried to train his lips into a placid smile. "Ah no... I just got off the phone with her and realized it's her birthday tomorrow. I haven't gotten her anything. Would you happen to have any suggestions?"

Anna smiled at him, sending an open invitation to sample her wares. "Of course, I'd be happy to."

Rihaan gave her an encouraging nod to continue, but Anna's brain ran a bit slow at times. He could have asked her to leave him alone, however that would hurt her feelings. Besides, he found her a good resource for a lot of things that a single guy like him knew nothing about, both at work and home.

She opened her dark pink mouth, her tongue lifting to her top lip for a moment before she spoke. "Your mother must have dropped some hints. They always do, mine certainly does. All you need is to give her what she wants."

Yeah, that's it! And die a premature death! *Kahaan aake phas gaya yaar! (What kind of terrible fix have I got myself in!)* He could picture his mother dialing up all her relatives at this very moment, telling them the good news that: *Mera* Rihaan finally *sudhar gaya! (My Rihaan is finally on the mend!)* He could also picture all of them fawning over him. The very idea made him break into a sweat.

Damn! I need to get myself together! And I need some advice! He looked amiably at Anna. "Awesome suggestion. I'll think on it."

She gave him a huge beatific smile. He knew he had made her day.

He stood up. "I'm going to take a shower, then I'll be gone for lunch for about an hour or so. Do you mind taking any non-urgent messages? And please, if my mother calls, tell her I'm busy in the clinic." When he saw her frown, he explained with a wink. "I want to keep her guessing."

Anna nodded and left the room, closing the door behind her.

Soon he was refreshed and dressed in fresh crisp garb, which included a jacket. Rihaan looked like the successful Wall Street Banker he wasn't. Still, he felt uneasy and awkward. He was more at home in his surgical scrubs dining in the hospital cafeteria, than in this fancy-schmancy restaurant with his childhood friend, who also happened to be his landlord—Rudra Jaiswal, or Rudy, as he preferred to be called.

Rudy was a stockbroker who worked in one of the big corporate banks and whose every minute was valued in the millions. But Rihaan needed advice, and who better to seek it from than Rudy, who had finally bowed down to pressure and got hooked himself.

They usually met every 3rd Thursday of the month to exchange notes and make small talk, but today Rihaan had called for an off-schedule meeting.

"No booze *dost?"* Rudy wiggled his eyebrows suggestively.

"Nope. Can't afford to slice the wrong piece of brain. I have a case at two."

"Oh yes. You neurosurgeons and your smart BS!" Rudy laughed, downing his scotch and soda in a gulp. Signaling for another, he ogled the big-chested waitress.

Rihaan chuckled. "Remember you are married."

His friend frowned, appearing to seriously ponder the statement. "I guess I am."

Rihaan was surprised. "I thought you were happy. Wasn't Shirin your girl?"

"Yes, she was, but now she's my wife. Huge difference!" Rudy said, leaning forward. "Let me tell you a secret. It wasn't my choice to marry. She got pregnant."

"Uh huh..." Rihaan mumbled. He was well-versed with his friend's escapades. It was bound to happen. "You did the honorable thing, then."

"Guess I did, but I wasn't prepared. Hell! Never before have I made so many excuses for not coming home on time like I do now," Rudy exclaimed with a wry laugh, then regarded his friend. "You're so lucky, dude! I envy your freedom."

Rihaan shook his head. "No more. Mom fooled me into giving her my word I'd marry, and soon."

"Really?" Rudy looked impressed. "Guess that's the price one pays for having parents. Congratulations!" He reached across the table to shake Rihaan's hand. "So, is it going to be that hot chick Renu who was all over you at my reception? I'd have fancied her myself if Shirin hadn't messed me up."

"Which Renu?"

Rudy burst into laughter. "You are blind. Truly blind, Rihaan. You missed a girl like that! She was Miss New Jersey or something, and man does she have curves!"

Rihaan gave a wry shrug.

"Okay, then let your mom choose your wife and live happily ever after with my blessings," Rudy said, grinning widely.

"No! Never! I can't!"

Rudy looked puzzled. "What do you mean?"

"I can't get married to someone she chooses. I'll be finished. All those obligations, parties, demanding wife and in-laws. No way, man, I'd rather kill myself."

"But that's what marriage is all about—compromise."

Rihaan nodded. "Exactly. That's why I've kept away from it this long. I don't want to compromise. I have no interest in assuming the role of a dutiful husband and son-in-law. What I want is somebody who will stay out of my way. Mind her own business while I mind mine."

"You don't need a wife. You need a servant."

"Don't get me wrong," Rihaan said. "I just want someone who will comprehend me and my work. I want to continue like I am now...without any distractions. She can do what she wants; kitty parties, *pujas,* whatever. Just don't expect me to be a part of it. We'll get a bigger place. She'll have all the luxuries she wants."

"If that is so, I agree. You won't find a girl like that here. Even if you do, her family won't leave you alone."

"Then what am I to do?" Rihaan asked, feeling desperate.

"Maybe you'll find someone suitable back home?"

"Really?" Rihaan was unconvinced. "Are girls less demanding there?"

"Well...that's for you to find out." Rudy shrugged. "Besides, a guy like you is a dream catch. Any father would give his right hand to get a son-in-law like you. Plus, the perk of coming here to the States. Anyhow, that seems to be the only reasonable option for you now."

"How am I supposed to find this mystery girl? Fly to India and search with a bloody microscope?"

Rudy shook his head in mock disbelief. "Pal, haven't you heard of the world wide web?"

***

Mulling over Rudy's advice filled Rihaan with skepticism. Was it ridiculous to assume a woman, especially someone who fit his requirements to a tee, could be found online. Perhaps Rudy was taking him for a fool just like his mother.

He seethed with indignation as he flagged down a yellow cab and slid in. *First I fall into my wily mother's trap and then my Casanova friend makes a mockery of me! What kind of idiot am I?* So deep was he in his thoughts, that the cabbie had driven several blocks in the wrong direction before Rihaan realized it and asked him to turn around and head back toward the clinic.

Rihaan tried to talk himself out of his quandary. "This won't do," he said aloud to himself. "I can't let petty things overtake me and curtail my life. My work comes first. I won't let my patients down."

Later that night, as he sat in his favorite spot on the balcony, holding a barely touched glass of red wine in his hand, Rihaan contemplated the island of peace (the park) in the middle of the concrete jungle, and let his mind drift. The two surgeries had gone well. He wondered what the biopsy on the mass in Mr. Hirsh's frontal lobe would show. The gross features had looked suspicious. He sighed. As a doctor he wasn't always a bearer of good news.

Not wanting to dwell on the morbid, he digressed toward something more cheerful. After finishing at the clinic that night he had walked back to the hospital to check on the young boy's condition. He had been pleased to find him chatting up a storm with his friends. The kid was eager to get back on his feet and to play league baseball. Rihaan, delighted at his enthusiasm, had assured his patient he'd get his wish soon. But just as he was about to leave, Rihaan was embarrassed with a bouquet of fresh blooms. He said a quick thanks and rushed to make his exit.

The ICU secretary had loved the flowers.

Rihaan smiled in the dark, closed his eyes, and awaited a wonderful restful sleep to overwhelm him. But he was betrayed just like yesterday.

Well aware of the cause, he flipped on to his side and broke out into song. The valiant effort didn't help much, rather scared a couple of roosting doves off their perch.

"God help me. Mom, how I wish I could strangle you," he cried, before slouching back into the darkness of his living room. "I guess you won't let me sleep until I do something about your bloody wishes!"

While he waited for the monitor of his PC to come alive, he thought; guess there's no harm in checking out Rudy's suggestion, even though what he says seems too fantastic to be true. Rihaan shrugged. No time like the present.

Typing 'India Matrimonial' into the search engine, he was struck by the numerous responses that popped up almost instantaneously.

His interest was piqued. Aside from a few, most results appeared to be fairly legitimate outfits. The usually traditional Indian wedding business had now turned commercial. All the marriage brokers and pundits who relied on matchmaking as their primary source of income would have to pack up their bags and move to the Himalayas, he thought chuckling.

He soon found himself engaged in the activity of browsing through the huge databanks of boys and girls seeking potential life partners. He was shocked at the variety he saw and equally surprised at the way they presented themselves, especially how particular they were about the kind of mate they wanted. It was just as Rudy had described—a huge marriage market.

Finally after having amused himself for a few hours, Rihaan fell asleep thinking there might just be a solution to all his problems.

***

Over the next few days, Rihaan got down to the serious business of finding a wife. And for once in his life, he knew exactly the kind of person he was looking for. And his requirements weren't many.

1. Mid-twenties (Not too young or flighty.)

2. College educated.

3. A fairly agreeable personality.

4. Not averse to moving to the States.

5. Did not have huge expectations from the marriage, and in particular from him. He didn't want to elevate hopes. He lay everything out in the open so the girl knew exactly what she was getting.

6. And the most important criteria of all—she should possess fairly ordinary looks; pretty enough to satisfy his mother, but not stunning. He had no desire to be overwhelmed by his future wife's beauty. That would be a distraction he wasn't prepared to deal with.

Soon he had narrowed his search down to ten girls. Then ultimately to one. She fit all the specs and also appeared empathetic with his views. In all, she seemed too good to be true but he pushed that uneasy notion aside.

Within the space of a week, the deal was almost sealed.

They chatted via Skype about the arrangements at two a.m. his time on a Sunday.

"Okay…so are we engaged?" she asked.

Engaged? Oh crap! Really? "I…guess we are unofficially," Rihaan replied.

"You can mail me the ring if you wish, but I really don't care about formalities," she assured him with a bright smile through the screen.

"That's cool," he said while thinking at the same time; these Indian girls are quite *tez*. Mom may be shocked!

"So when should we set the date?" Deepika said.

"Date? Ah..." The question threw him off. It was completely unexpected. In no hurry to tie the knot, Rihaan wanted to enjoy his bachelorhood a little longer. "Six months?" he suggested vaguely. That would give his mother enough time to make preparations to her heart's content.

"No, that's not soon enough." She shook her head. "Next month or the deal is off."

"What?" Rihaan sat up straighter on the couch in his living room. "I... That is not possible."

"Our family priest says that if I don't get married within a month, my father will die in a road accident," she said quite calmly.

"Is that right?" *Damnit!* His head had started to spin. He was losing control. It was unnerving, so he tried to stall. "Don't your parents wish to speak to mine?"

"They can do so when you and your parents come here for the wedding. My mom and dad have no objections. They love you already!" She smiled. "You *know* you are a dream catch!"

It was the second time he had heard the description and he didn't like it at all. He probed her eyes carefully on the monitor. She looked sincere enough. There appeared no reason to doubt her statement.

He shrugged it off his mind. He had to take chances in life, at some time or other.

"Don't worry. It'll all go without a hitch. My parents are pros at arranging weddings. You won't have to do a single thing."

He glanced at his schedule. "Uh, okay... I am long overdue for a vacation. I can try to make it there in a couple of weeks, or so." He stared back at her, hoping she would develop cold feet.

Not a chance. She agreed right away.

He could have said no and called the whole blasted thing off. But he didn't. Another girl like her would be hard to come by, and he was already feeling worn out by the entire process.

"So we have a...a date in two weeks or so. I'll see you soon. Till then, take care," he muttered with little enthusiasm before signing off.

It was odd, but he wasn't experiencing any of the excited anticipation that a new bridegroom is supposed to—at least that's what he'd heard—while he awaited D Day. Instead, Rihaan was filled with a strange dread.

Another thought spiraled in his mind—perhaps he deserved it.

He consoled himself with the good things he had learned about her. His future wife, Deepika, was realistic, mature, and a lot more experienced in these matters than he was. If she could handle the stress, so could he.

The Accidental Wife

The laws of attraction are too potent to be ignored.

Rihaan was a trustworthy man, though many might consider him cold and businesslike, he never went back on what he said. Well, almost never. Reliability and integrity came second nature to him. And this time was no different. Even though he wasn't certain of what the future held, he was bound by his word and planned to carry through no matter the consequences.

And since he'd made up his mind, he chose to reveal his intentions to his parents. Besides, he didn't want to delay the inevitable any longer. They needed time to absorb the shock.

So, on the day after his unofficial online 'betrothal' he made a surprise visit to the Mehta family residence. Without preamble he announced in a clear voice, "I'm getting married. Time to celebrate."

His mother, as he'd guessed she would, immediately dismissed him. "Rihaan, if that's supposed to be a joke then it is a very bad one."

"Maa… I'm telling the truth," Rihaan said. "I've found a suitable girl and the deal is set."

"Really? Is it someone I know?" she asked.

"No. I found her online. She lives in India and is a perfect match." He managed to speak with conviction even if he didn't feel it at all.

"Back home? Online? So soon? Are you *mad?*" Shobha looked crestfallen. Her desire of bringing her dear friend's daughter, Renu, home was clearly crushed. Apparently she had continued to hope, even though the day she had introduced the girl to him, he had failed to react. He hadn't even blinked, if he recalled correctly!

"No, I'm not mad," he replied, assisting her to a beautifully upholstered Victorian chair and handing her a glass of water.

He tried to dress his future wife up a bit. "This girl has all the qualities a good wife should possess. She's incredibly talented. She's a great cook (though he had no clue if Deepika could even turn the stove on), she paints, sews…everything." He stopped himself in time before getting carried away, or his mother would definitely become suspicious. "She's grounded and is pure *desi!* You'll adore her!"

Shashank suppressed a chuckle and said the only thing that seemed to concern him. "She certainly sounds like a rare gem, Rihaan. What about her family? We'd like to talk to her parents."

"You don't have to worry about them, Dad. I've checked them out already. They are great, just like their daughter," Rihaan confirmed quickly. He didn't want his father to launch into a prolonged investigation.

His mother having recovered a little, smiled fondly at Rihaan. At least he was getting married was probably what she was thinking. "Alright," she said. "But I wish to see her picture and, I'd also like to know her name."

"It's a surprise," Rihaan said mysteriously. "Just have a little patience and trust me. Next month you'll get your wish."

***

Two weeks later Rihaan couldn't fathom why people got married, least of all why they conducted these ridiculously-long ceremonies. He'd flown into New Delhi earlier than his parents to meet with Deepika before they met her.

What he discovered was that his wedding was utter chaos. It was a nightmarish ordeal which lasted over four days, or a few weeks if he took into account the day his mother had first dangled her sword over his head and coerced him to get married.

He'd hoped to keep matters quiet but that proved impossible. Shobha had made certain that everybody she knew (even the remotest acquaintance) was invited to come and give their blessings to her son and his bride.

Uncle Rajbir had been waiting for him at the airport and apparently had the next few days pretty well chalked out. Rihaan was allowed no say in any matter whatsoever and found himself subject to various rituals and customs that frightened him half to death, almost reducing him to tears.

All his relatives had a field day at his expense. His mother, who along with the rest of his family was caught in a snowstorm in Europe (she'd gone wedding shopping in Paris when every damn thing was available in NYC) seemed to be directing everything by remote control.

Fortunately, his future wife's family had come to his rescue. He was relieved when he learned they weren't much into tradition.

On the second day after he landed, Rihaan slipped the ring he'd bought in a hurry at Tiffany's on Deepika's finger and she had seemed pleased. In truth, she was more ordinary-looking than he had assumed (makeup can do wonders apparently and pictures can be doctored). Nevertheless, he was content when she assured him with a toothy smile that he'd get exactly what he'd bargained for.

On the third day, she signed her name alongside his in front of a registrar and the deal was official. On the fourth, the whole bloody thing was concluded with a wedding ceremony to please the hearts of all the traditionalists. Unfortunately or fortunately for him, his parents were still missing in action. But they'd watched everything live, thanks to the miracle of high tech and the internet.

And before he knew, it was all over. Rihaan had joined the ranks of hapless and bemused married men.

But somehow it all didn't quite gel for him. Something had gone wrong, yet he couldn't put his finger on it.

So when it came time for his wedding night, leaving his cousins and miscellaneous relatives behind to rejoice in drunken revelry, Rihaan headed to the room on the second floor of his uncle's house specially decorated for the purpose singularly determined to pull the veil off the disquieting mystery—his so-called wife.

He found her on the balcony. "Deepika?" he ventured tentatively.

She stepped out of the shadows.

But the girl who stood in front of him was certainly not the one he thought he'd married, *and* to make matters even worse, she was definitely *not* ordinary-looking.

She was stunning!

Just as his eyes affixed to her face, the wheels of his brain drew to an abrupt halt. What a face it was. That of an enchantress, no less.

Bathed in ethereal moonlight, with dark, wavy hair of shimmering black silk that flirted with her smooth and dewy complexion; regular, well-defined features; huge, luminous eyes that sparkled; lustrous lips, full and moist that curved into a mocking smile and...*brought him crashing back to earth!*

Goddamnit! This was exactly what he had been guarding himself against! This girl, this stranger, had already knocked him off his moorings when he was least prepared for it. Beautiful creatures like her should not be allowed to roam free on the streets, in particular creep unannounced into unsuspecting men's bedrooms! What was she doing here?

He wrenched himself out of the haze. There wasn't any way he could afford to be unsettled in his well-planned life. He cleared his throat twice before he found his voice. "You aren't Deepika. Where is she?"

"Yes, you guessed right," she spoke in a low soft tone. "I'm not Deepika. She's gone. I am Naina." She paused for effect. "Good bye, Rihaan. Nice to have made your acquaintance."

She turned to slip past him.

He stepped up to bar her way; his reflexes getting their act together before his brain did. "No...wait! How...how can you say she's gone? She's my wife for crying out loud!"

She cast a pitiful glance at him. *"Yes, she's gone.* And no, she's not your wife. I was the one sitting in the *mandap.* Don't tell me you didn't know that already."

Rihaan closed his eyes. He felt his heart take a free fall to his gut and continue to sink further. What he had fervently hoped to be a delusion of his conscience had turned out to be true. The worm of suspicion had begun to wiggle itself into his psyche as soon as he'd taken his seat beside his future wife on the marriage stage. But he'd ignored it. He realized now, for starters, she looked a lot slimmer than he remembered. He'd rejected the notion quickly, attributing it to some miracle diet drug.

What intrigued him even more was when he noticed her face shrouded in the *ghoonghat* throughout the ceremony. Surprisingly, she had suddenly turned very shy. But when it was time to tie the *mangalsutra* around her neck and place the vermilion streak on her forehead; he had caught a glimpse of her face and those strikingly luminous eyes, and all his misgivings were confirmed.

Rihaan teetered against the bedpost. He had been thoroughly duped, hoodwinked, ripped off, two-timed, etcetera.

"Are you okay?" Her hand gently gripped his arm, in concern he supposed but she appeared to be laughing silently at him.

"Hell!" He wrenched his arm away. "This isn't funny at all!"

She looked chagrined. "I'm sorry. I know you are badly shaken. But Deepika couldn't think of a better way out."

"Way out of what? Anyway, where is she now?"

"I told you. She's gone."

Yes, she was gone. But he had too many questions that needed to be answered. And now.

"All right, so she's gone. But what about her parents? They were there when Deepika and I signed the marriage certificate. Are they involved in this charade as well?"

"No they are not."

"Then…then why did they not come forward to identify you when they knew you weren't their daughter? Don't tell me you fooled them, too."

Naina offered a wry smile. "Perhaps they didn't recognize me, or more likely, they chose not to. Perhaps they didn't come forward because it would cause them dishonor and shame."

Rihaan could comprehend that. To declare that the bride was not their daughter could mean major loss of face for any parent.

"But why this big farce? Why did Deepika find me through a marriage portal, ask me to come here and sign on the marriage certificate, if all she intended to do was not get married at all! Why?"

The girl who called herself Naina (if that was really her name) looked exasperated. Two flattering spots of red surfaced on her cheeks. Digging into her purse, she pulled out a small notepad, briskly jotted something down and handed it to him. "Here, this is Deepika's cell. Call and ask her yourself. My job is done. I'm out of here."

"Job?" Overcome by an immense fury, he glowered at her. "What job? Do chicks get paid nowadays to do stand-ins at weddings?"

"No, and I don't do stand-ins!" She shot back with equal vehemence. "Deepika didn't pay me a dime! I was just trying to help my friend and I truly regret it. It seemed like a harmless prank. Now I know it was in very bad taste. I apologize sincerely, Rihaan. But really, I have to go now. It's getting late. Please call her. I'm sure she'll be expecting to hear from you." She made another bid for the door.

"Oh no, not so fast sweetheart!" he said, snatching her arm. "Deepika can go to hell as far as I'm concerned. I'll have nothing to do with spineless selfish cowards who don't think twice before hurting others. She has betrayed my trust…and *you…,*" he shoved her roughly onto the bed, *"…my* 'Accidental Wife' will supply me with the explanation I deserve."

For the very first time since they'd met those gorgeous eyes looked nervous. "It's a very long story…"

Rihaan pulled a chair in front of the door and settled himself comfortably in it. "I have all night to listen."

The Long & Short of It

Naina braced her arms on the edge of the rose petal strewn mattress of the antique four-poster bed and scrutinized the man sitting between her and freedom. He stared right back, his sturdy chin resting on tented fingers, his eyes filled with such intense anger and indignation it made her insides tremble with fear. But she didn't look away, she wasn't a coward.

Deepika had not only deceived this guy, she had pulled wool over her own friend's eyes. She had told her that Rihaan Mehta, doctor par excellence, was fat, short and ugly. While in fact he was just the opposite—tall, well-built, and incredibly good-looking—the kind that made one's throat run dry and pulse go pitter-patter. She'd also been told that he was 'a nose in the air SOB' who was too full of himself.

Naina wasn't exactly sure if that definition was true. So far his behavior seemed perfectly appropriate under the circumstances. He was angry as hell and truly justified to be so; after being cheated by the girl who had promised to become his wife.

Haaye is ladki ne mujhe kahaan phasa diya? (What kind of soup has this girl landed me in?) *Why didn't I consider everything before I agreed to take her place? He's not going to let me go anywhere.*

Her heart thudded wildly when her restless fingers came in contact with the silken petals. *Good Lord! What if?*

She glanced at him. W*hat if he's a rogue, a degenerate who preys on women? How could Deepika have taken the chance to place me, her friend, in such a situation? How could she do this to me?*

Naina tried hard to deduce his intentions. But Rihaan's expression had become inscrutable and she didn't like that at all. She hoped, as Deepika had told her, that he was a cold-blooded automaton, who was completely immune to the allures of the female sex. At least, she hoped he remained that way till she got herself out of here.

"I can't wait forever, woman. Get on with it!" Rihaan's voice rang out sharp like a bullet, startling Naina out of her musings.

"What do you want to know?" she asked.

"Everything from the beginning. For starters, where is Deepika?"

"She has run away, absconded. Eloped with her lover."

Rihaan looked perplexed. "Eloped? I don't understand. Why would she advertise in the matrimonial? Why did she insist on me coming here and signing on the marriage certificate? She could have as well completed the whole farce and then fled. Why the in-between?"

Naina interlaced her fingers under her thighs to keep them from trembling. She couldn't make sense of the situation herself, though she was trying her best. If she could paint a sympathetic picture of Deepika, perhaps then this man would feel kindly towards her and let her go?

"Deepika is...you know, a sentimental sort of girl. She didn't want to participate in the ceremonial wedding and take the *saat pheras* with you. It held a lot more significance to her than a piece of paper. Then she'd have felt 'really married' and it would have been harder for her to leave. So she asked me to take her place and I helped her out." She hoped he bought the ridiculous explanation.

***

"So in effect *you* are my wife and not her. It seems like she has done you in as well as me," Rihaan said feeling strangely amused. *What a bloody anticlimax!*

"Maybe, if you wish to say so," Naina retorted. "But I'm not planning to stay and carry it through. I was absolutely serious about not marrying anybody, and most definitely not you!"

She then had the grace to look embarrassed. "I'm sorry. I know this whole situation is very crazy and upsetting. You got the hard end of the bargain. You were the unlucky scapegoat."

*"What the F***!"* What? Me, a scapegoat? Rihaan Mehta, the brilliant sought-after neurosurgeon has been made a royal fool by a mere slip of a girl! How had he been so bloody naïve? "I can't believe this! You and your friend deliberately plotted to trap me in this mess!" Rihaan exclaimed, springing out of his chair and moving menacingly toward her.

She shrunk back, ducking away from his long reach. "Please calm down. It wasn't my idea. Really. It was Deepika's and you just happened to be available. You just wanted the label of a married man and didn't really want a wife. She didn't really want a husband."

Turning away from her, Rihaan leaned his forehead against the wall in an attempt to control his rage. He had to know the rest of the story, and that wouldn't happen if he got carried away by anger.

He swung back and saw her sitting on the bed, her sensible jean-clad legs crossed over feigning an appearance of nonchalance, though her frazzled nerves were betrayed by her pursed lips. Decidedly, she possessed much more courage than that rotten Deepika.

She cast a wary glance his way. "Deepika is really a very stupid girl. She made the mistake of falling in love."

"Oh...so falling in love makes someone stupid?"

"Yes. Especially if you fall for a man like she did. A loser! A spoiled, rich brat who thinks he's all that! Who drives around in flashy cars making girls like her swoon! He promises them the world, but in truth he can't earn even a decent day's living. I hate such men!" Her face was flushed and her eyes sparkled with fiery emotion.

Rihaan was glad that he didn't belong in that category; he'd definitely not want to be a victim of her spite. "So why didn't she marry him?"

"Because she couldn't. Her parents don't like losers. But she was in too deep and that creep was pressuring her; so were her parents. They were beginning to get suspicious. She had rejected several excellent matches, each one better than the previous and she knew she couldn't continue doing that forever. She was in a bind."

Naina fidgeted with the tassels of a heart-shaped cushion. Rihaan waited patiently.

"Then Deepika had a brilliant idea. She pretended to succumb to her parents' wishes but stipulated that she'd choose her own groom. She couldn't risk agreeing to one of the matches they'd chosen, 'cause if she had they'd be subjected to endless ridicule and ostracized by the entire community. Her parents agreed. She placed an ad online and found you."

Naina smiled at Rihaan. "You were heaven sent. Perfect credentials, stinking rich doctor, a neuro something or other, and best of all you lived outside the country."

"A neurosurgeon," he corrected, "and no, I'm not stinking rich. I work very hard for what I have." He was feeling worse than ever, wishing he had taken better precautions instead of acting so carelessly.

She shrugged her delicate shoulders. "That's beside the point. I wonder why Deeps preferred that fellow over you." Her gracefully arched eyebrows met together in a frown. "Perhaps that's why they say love is blind. I'll never let it happen to me though."

You can't predict the future, Ms. Naina, he smiled. She seemed to strike off on a tangent easily. "You were saying…?"

"So she found you, or you found each other. You didn't balk or ask questions when she asked you to come over here. Her parents didn't complain, rather they were delighted with her choice, and more so when they met you in person. She even applied to get the marriage certified and registered, thus assuring her parents she was indeed serious. So, to not find her sitting in the *mandap* must have come as a tremendous shock to them."

"Aren't they losing face now?" Rihaan asked.

"For all practical purposes, their daughter Deepika is married. I'm quite sure very few besides you and them noticed the switch. Therefore, if they keep it to themselves, everybody will think that their daughter left with her husband and is living happily abroad. She'll probably own up in good time."

It took several moments for Rihaan to absorb the information before he erupted. "Wow! Amazing, and as you said, brilliant. I'm stumped! Would have never come up with that myself. But what I want to know is, did she ever think about how *I* will feel after all this?"

Naina looked distinctly uncomfortable. "She didn't, at least I don't think she did. She…she called you a snooty bastard who really didn't want a wife. A maid or a robot would have served the purpose equally well. So I don't think she felt bad about it."

Rihaan was fighting hard, very hard, to keep his emotions in check. The gall of the girl to treat him so shoddily. After all he'd gone through for her. And *this* woman to be so casual about it all! She seemed as bad as her friend. Were all females this heartless?

"All right, Ms. Naina. You seem to have analyzed the situation to perfection. Your friend and her immature adolescent romantic illusions. Me, the handy dumb unsuspecting *snooty bastard* push-over, and even her parents with their hopes for a secure future for their daughter now permanently dashed. So tell me, how does an insightful, candid and intelligent girl like you allow yourself to be ensnared in this unholy mess?"

Naina chewed on her lower lip. "Uh… As you've seen for yourself, Deepika is very persuasive and an excellent actress. She told me her sob story laced with plenty of added *masala* and I felt sorry for her. I didn't know her that well, but I didn't have reason to doubt her. She was my roommate for a short time and I'd never seen her do anything so drastic before."

She looked up at him, meeting his eyes. "She also painted you in the most inglorious terms, saying you deserved to be taught a lesson in humility. So I went ahead, thinking I was doing my friend a favor. But now I know I was horribly wrong and I feel terrible about it." He saw her sling her bag over her right shoulder and begin inching toward the door again. "I hope you can get over this, move on, and find yourself a girl who is truly deserving of you Rihaan. Sorry…"

"*Sorry* isn't enough. I *demand* compensation!" Rihaan stood in her way again and brought his hands down hard on her arms.

"Compensation?" she squeaked.

"Of course. Compensation for my troubles…for the humiliation I've suffered at the hands of your friend, in which *you* had a major role. I want my marital rights and I'll extract them tonight with great pleasure from my beautiful wife," he said tersely dragging her to the bed, his usual restraint swamped by a state of extreme indignation. After all, he had married her observing all the traditional rituals and norms. And she was far more desirable than any girl he had ever met.

***

Terrified eyes took in the rose-strewn mattress. Her worst fears were about to be realized. "You want me to spend the night with you?"

"Yes I do. And perhaps many more to come. I'm sure I'll have no regrets!" Flinging her down on the bed, he began to fumble with the buttons of his *sherwani,* cursing aloud when they refused to cooperate.

"You've gone mad!" Naina screamed, managing to wiggle out from in between his knees. She rolled to the other side and jumped off.

But he proved equally nimble. Blinded by insane anger and an overwhelming desire to extract revenge, he yanked her into his arms and held her tight, seeming to derive wicked pleasure in seeing her squirm. He felt particular malice toward her, she knew that, but how could she calmly participate in this consummation?

***

Tears trickled down her cheeks but he didn't care. She deserved the pain. Knitting his fingers through her scalp to hold her head steady, he bent down, aiming for those lips that'd been bothering him for quite some time.

Then suddenly it struck him. Something was missing. "Where is your *sindoor* and the *mangalsutra* I tied around your neck?"

"I...discarded them."

"Why...why would you do that?"

"Because they hold no meaning. You...you thought you were placing them on Deepika; while I...I was just going through the motions. I believe marriage is a convergence of two hearts; a journey embarked on mutual understanding. I don't even know anything about you."

"Convergence of two hearts...puerile romantic crap!" He pushed her away. "Get out of my sight now!"

"I'm sorry..." Whimpering with relief, she ran to the door and struggled with the bolts.

"No, not that way!" He stopped her, realizing there were plenty of people still in the house and they were planning on staying up all night.

"Then which way?" she asked, before heading to his first floor balcony and peering down at the abandoned yard. She had swung her legs over before Rihaan caught her arm.

"It's at least ten or twelve feet down. Too dangerous. You may break your back or worse, split open your skull," he said, his medical instincts coming to the fore.

"I could do it if you give me a hand. Please?" She turned to look beseechingly at him.

He reluctantly nodded, finding no other practical solution.

Holding her firmly with both hands, he gingerly lowered her down so she could jump safely to the ground. He followed, scrambling after her as she raced to the back exit.

He took a quick glance around. The sky was inky black and the streets completely deserted. It was past one a.m. in the quiet, upscale South Delhi neighborhood. "I can drop you home..."

She wheeled a bright yellow Scooty out from behind a tree. "Don't worry, I came prepared. I'm used to taking care of myself."

Clipping a helmet around her head, she started the engine and smiled. "It was nice meeting you. I wish it had been under better circumstances, though. Good bye Rihaan." She raised a hand in a hesitant wave, then rode away.

He waved back and watched till she disappeared into the darkness. All of a sudden he was seized by a depressing loneliness.

Miscalculations

Rihaan lay back in his lonely bed and stared at the ceiling, contemplating life—what it had been and what had become of it.

The mission he'd embarked on to fulfill his mother's wishes and thereby get her off his back had culminated in a virtual catastrophe. He had ended up marrying not once but twice. Nothing could be more ironic—Rihaan Mehta, a man determined to stay unencumbered his entire life was now shackled to two different women!

A bubble of agitated laughter erupted in his chest causing him to double over. His stomach contracted with painful spasms.

"But for sure I'm at fault, too," he muttered after recovering. "If I had exhibited more caution, if I hadn't listened to Rudy's preposterous advice, if I had told my mother to go to hell! If... If... If!"

Yet there was something he couldn't understand. Why in the *mandap*, upon discovering that the girl sitting next to him was not Deepika, had he not stood up and called the whole shindig off in classic *filmi* style? Why hadn't he denounced her in front of everybody? *Why?*

Grabbing a handful of rose petals, he tossed them high in the air, then closed his eyes as they floated down enveloping him in a curtain of fragrant satin.

The only possible explanation was that he hadn't been himself. His body had been taken over by an alien force. Those magnificent eyes had mesmerized him and he had fallen hopelessly under their spell. They had defied him to stay seated and continue with the rituals, and he had accepted the challenge, proceeding to tie the sacred thread around her neck and apply the vermillion powder to her forehead. And it'd been under the influence of the same spell that he had almost bedded her last night. To do something like that would never have occurred to the real Rihaan Mehta—that girl Naina had bewitched him!

He sat up breathing hard. "Yes, that's it. She has magical powers! It's good she left or I'd have completely lost it. My perfectly ordered world would have come unhinged. She's way too dangerous. I'll be happy if I don't ever see her again," he announced aloud to the empty room, then collapsed back onto the bed feeling supremely relieved. Yet it was a very long time before he fell into a restless sleep.

***

Not unexpectedly, morning found him groggy and irritable. A loud, jarring, annoying clamor that grew steadily intense and more insistent, penetrating even through the thick pillow he had clamped over his head, had breached his slumber. He couldn't place the noise. The sound didn't resemble his pager nor his cell phone—his only two ever-faithful companions.

He lay on the bed for several moments trying to orient himself before realizing where he was and what he had been through in the past few days. It wasn't a nightmare. It had happened and now someone was knocking hard on the door.

"*Chachi? Aap?* Why...you needn't have taken the trouble," he blurted, discovering Uncle Rajbir's petite wife, Rashmi, standing outside his door. She was carrying a tray bearing two silver cups and a carafe.

"*Kya karein? (What can I do?)* I waited forever for *bahu* to come down to the kitchen. But when she didn't, I chose to take the initiative myself," she replied cheekily, while taking in his disheveled appearance. She ventured a peep into the darkened room but he blocked it with his broad torso. Her eyes chided him.

"You opened the door. Where is *bahu?*"

Rihaan inclined his head slightly toward his empty room and called out softly, "Sweetheart, look who's here."

Then smiling apologetically, he said to his puzzled aunt, "Seems like she's fast asleep. She's worn out."

"And you?" Rashmi asked observing his droopy eyelids.

"Yes, me too. We were up all night and we really need to get some rest. Sorry," he said stepping back, drawing the door close.

"Rihaan! *Besharmi ki bhi koi hadh hoti hai! (There's a limit to shamelessness!)*"

He stared at her, bewildered for a moment, before realizing what his words had implied. He colored, but didn't correct himself. *Let her think what she wants to. I'm not ready to reveal my folly yet.*

"All right, leave it." She smiled, round brown eyes fluttering mischievously. "But you surprise me, Rihaan Mehta. *Kahaan woh* bachelor *aur kahaan yeh* Romeo! (You've come a long way from sworn bachelor to Romeo!)* Perhaps *bahu* has cast some kind of spell over you!"

"No *chachi*...she hasn't! She..." He stopped when his aunt burst into a merry laugh.

"Don't worry *beta,* I was just teasing. But you both better wake up from your dreamland soon...*nahin toh toofan aa jayega!"(...or else prepare to face the storm!)*

"What kind of storm?" Rihaan muttered, utterly baffled. Had she already deciphered what he'd been so desperately trying to hide?

"*Bachu!*" she replied with an indulgent shake of her head. "It appears you have forgotten everything in your excitement. Your mom, dad, sister and her

33

husband are all going to be here in a short time. And Shobha is so worked up already for missing the wedding of her only son...guess what will happen to her if she doesn't get to see her *bahu* right away! She'll kill us all and both of you as well!"

Aunt Rashmi wasn't smiling anymore. She looked quite nervous herself. Placing the tea tray aside, she scooped up a large red and gold box from a table behind her and thrust it into his hands. "Here *Joru ke Ghulam!* Give this to your beautiful wife and ask her to get ready ASAP. You can spoil her rotten when you take her back with you, but please maintain some decorum while you are still here. *Accha impression banta hai (It makes a good impression)!*" She tempered her stern words with a smile and a fond tap on his cheek before hurrying down the stairs.

Rihaan tossed the box carelessly on the floor and began pacing the room. He was fraught with trepidation.

"Good Lord! *Chachi's* right. It completely slipped my mind!" He sunk into a chair, clutching his head in his hands. He could imagine his mother's reaction. She would be utterly devastated. But instead of pouring empathy on him she would launch into a tirade. He could see the entire scene play out in his mind.

"It was bound to happen," she'd begin, holding her tiny four-eight frame stiff and erect. Then, pausing briefly to glance around at her audience to assure their unequivocal attention, she'd continue. "My son is such a simpleton. He has a brilliant mind but that is only as far as his work goes, otherwise he's as unworldly as they come." Her ire would then turn onto his hapless dad and he'd be soundly censured for spoiling her son's ways. Then after his mother had calmed down some, instead of leaving him to his devices she would take it upon herself to find him a proper wife.

"No! That can never be!" Rihaan shuddered as he imagined himself being dragged around and exhibited like a dumb mannequin, and without his assent, betrothed to one of the girls of her choice; he would be relegated to a condition worse than Rudy's! At least Rudy liked women!

"God," he moaned. "What am I to do? If I can persuade Naina to act as my wife, maybe I can buy some time. Mom will be happy for a while and I can ponder over the next course of action."

But how would he find her now? Last night she had muddled him so much it hadn't even occurred to him to ask for her phone number.

Damnit! Damnit! Damnit! He started to pace again when his eyes suddenly fell on a tiny piece of paper lying beside the bed. He picked it up and saw Deepika's cell number, printed in Naina's crisp, clear hand.

He flung it away after tearing it into even tinier pieces. He didn't care to think of her name, let alone call her up.

There was only one option left.

In a few minutes he exchanged his deep red *sherwani* for street clothes. Bolting his door from the inside, he rushed to the balcony and jumped down. Then, after a cursory survey of the surroundings, he ran out onto the street.

He had to find his wife...and soon!

Laments

A nondescript 3rd floor apartment in the busy district of Karol Bagh, New Delhi

Rihaan rang the doorbell again, loud and urgent. He heard shuffling behind the door, then voices.

Mr. and Mrs. Kher exchanged nervous glances. "Whoever it is, we can't hide the truth anymore," Mrs. Kher lamented.

"I'll take care of them, Usha. You sit." Mr. Kher told his wife before opening the door.

After a few moments of stunned silence, Mr. Kher addressed Rihaan who he saw waiting impatiently outside. "*Damaadji*... You here? At this time?" Mr. Kher poked his head out of the doorway and inspected the passage. "And alone?"

"Please don't address me like that. Rihaan will do just fine. And yes, I've come alone. Nobody in my family knows anything as of yet." *But the situation may change very quickly if I don't find Naina soon,* he thought.

"Please come in, *damaad*... I mean Rihaan," Mrs. Kher said, hurrying to greet him. She led him to the only upholstered chair in the rather drab yet spic and span room.

Rihaan reluctantly accepted the seat of honor. Oddly, he was more agitated and fretful than furious. "I can't stay long," he said. "I... I need some information." He looked around the small living room where just three days ago he'd met for the first time the people he thought were his future in-laws to be. The place was unnaturally subdued now.

"*Zaroor!* Definitely." Both Khers said simultaneously in one voice, staring uneasily at him. Mr. Kher continued after a long pause. "There's really nothing more we can do or say to apologize for what our daughter has done. Except...maybe fall at your feet and beg your forgiveness."

"No, please!" Rihaan moved away just before Mrs. Kher could make a grab for his legs. "Don't embarrass me. As far as I know, you had no role to play in the entire gig."

"*You do?* Thank you, *beta*. May God bless you," Mr. Kher said looking much relieved. "But you see, kids these days are so mean and uncaring, except you...you are exceptionally *honhaar!"*

Yes, a honhaar idiot would be a more appropriate description, Rihaan thought dryly.

Mr. Kher continued ruefully. "Deepika had us both convinced she had broken up with that rogue, but see what happened? We were thoroughly deceived! *Kisiko muh dikhane layak nahin choda!" (We were made to hang our heads in shame!)*

"Saari beeradri mein naak kat gayi hamaari. (The entire community is looking down upon us.)" Mrs. Kher added with a loud sniff.

Rihaan couldn't do much except nod sympathetically. "I'm in kind of a hurry. If you can..."

"What a negligent host I am," Mrs. Kher exclaimed. "What will you have? *Kuch thanda ya garam?" (Something hot or cold?)*

"No, thanks. I..."

"It was a shock to us almost as much as it was to you, son. My wife... when she saw Naina, she nearly collapsed! I had to hold her up!" Mr Kher said.

Rihaan wondered how Mr. Kher had accomplished the feat. His wife was easily twice his size.

"Shock?! *Uncleji*...thank your lucky stars I haven't revealed my future wife's identity to anyone yet. I wanted to introduce her after the wedding so everybody would realize how competent I was and applaud me for it," Rihaan said, bursting into a wry laugh.

"You did a very smart thing, *beta.* Or both of us *miya biwi* would have died on the spot," Mr. Kher said.

"Have a samosa, Rihaan," Mrs. Kher suggested, directing his attention toward a plate heaped with the fried fritters before popping one into her own mouth.

"Samosa?" Rihaan asked.

"My wife eats when she gets stressed," Mr. Kher explained.

Rihaan couldn't help but stare in fascination at the munching Mrs. Kher. Deepika must have really stressed her mother out quite a bit.

"I want an annulment, of course," Rihaan said.

"Yes, *absolutely!* That's only fair. But do understand, we have severed all ties with our daughter. She's practically dead to us! *Kyon Deepika ki ma?" (What say Deepika's mother?)* Mr. Kher glanced at his wife.

He seems the kind of man who seeks his wife's approval on everything. Is that the secret to a happy marriage? Rihaan mused.

"Haan, Deepika ke papa." (Yes, Deepika's father.) Mrs. Kher nodded vigorously before reaching for another fritter.

Rihaan jerked his eyes away. He could feel bile rising to his throat.

"We hope you are happy with Naina, son," Mr. Kher said unenthusiastically. "Though she is a little *muh-phat* and bold at times..."

"And somewhat opinionated, assertive and disrespectful..." Mrs. Kher mumbled with her mouth full.

Wow! Naina has quite an awesome reputation!

"Yet overall, she's a much better match for you than our Deepika," Mr. Kher declared.

"Unfortunately I don't have the opportunity to find out because she has left me, too," Rihaan said.

"What?!" Both the Khers asked simultaneously.

"Yes, your precious daughter persuaded Naina to take her place just in order to teach me, who by the way she calls a haughty snob, a lesson! Naina told me so in not so many words before she jilted me last night."

"Oh you poor, poor boy!" Mrs. Kher wailed.

"And I, like the fool I am, let her go, without even considering the consequences. Such as, I'm not sure what will transpire when my parents arrive today and find that my bride has forsaken me. My mother is sure to raise hell and make everyone involved pay dearly! So please," Rihaan implored, "for your sake as well as mine, tell me where I can find Naina!"

Mr. and Mrs. Kher looked at each other again. It was clear they certainly didn't want to face the wrath of his mother, if they could help it.

"I can only supply you with her address. She and Deepika were roommates. We used to wonder why our daughter insisted on staying away from us despite living in the same city. Now we know." Mr. Kher got up and went to a side table and wrote something down on a piece of paper. His face was grim as he handed it over to Rihaan.

Glancing down at it, Rihann saw it was a location near the University Enclave.

"Naina is working on her Ph.D in English Literature at St. Stephens. She also works there as a teaching assistant. She is very…"

Rihaan bolted out of the door before Mr. Kher could complete his sentence.

The End or a New Beginning

So this is where she lives, Rihaan mused, as the taxi cab rolled to a halt in front of a series of quaint, old red brick buildings in a relatively quiet and secluded neighborhood just outside the Delhi University Enclave. The thick morning fog that cloaked the entire locale had just begun to lift bestowing an oddly surreal and mystical essence to the surroundings.

"Block D is right in front of you, *sahib,*" the cabbie remarked, pointing to the apartments at the very end of the street.

Instructing the man to wait, Rihaan sprinted in that direction.

The name board at the bottom of the stairs announced that Naina Rathod's apartment was located on the 4th floor. Deepika's name was not listed alongside hers.

Hope she's at home and in a receptive mood, he thought as he raced up the staircase.

"Ruko! Stop!"

Pausing mid-stride, Rihaan twisted around but didn't spot where the voice was coming from.

"Look down, mister!"

Rihaan craned his neck and detected a rail-thin, bespectacled boy barely over eight or nine years old scowling up at him.

"If you are heading for Naina *didi's* place, let me tell you she doesn't see anyone without an appointment. Do you have one?"

Rihaan cocked an amused eyebrow. "Uh…no, I don't. Perhaps she'll see me without one? By the way, who are you may I ask?"

Puffing up his frail chest, the boy declared with pride, "I'm her bodyguard and personal secretary. Anyway, you won't find her at home right now. She teaches tutorials every morning."

Rihaan took a quick peek at his watch. "I guess I'll have to wait then."

"Oh…you don't give up, do you? Are you one of her *aashiqs*? Haven't seen you around before," the boy asked suspiciously.

"Aashiqs? What *Aashiqs?"*

"One among her many students and colleagues who keep dropping by on some pretext or other, wanting to chat or take her out."

So she has bewitched quite a few other men as well! Poor rascals! Rihaan thought amused.

"Are you her boyfriend?"

"Boyfriend? Why do you ask?" Rihaan queried curiously.

"You are her type, I think. Serious, and…not really bad to look at," the boy admitted grudgingly. "If not, then I was going to ask her to wait a few more years till I'm all grown upwhen we can be together and…"

"Zip your mouth, *bachu*, cause I *am* her boyfriend," Rihaan erupted. *Gosh! Did I really say that? I must have gone mad!*

He cleared his throat. "We…had a slight tiff yesterday and I am here to apologize to Naina. So when you see her do not reveal that I'm here. I want it to be a surprise." He winked conspiratorially before continuing up.

After the passage of a harrowing ten minutes, when hope of her return had faded to a faint glimmer, he heard the boy shout excitedly down below.

"*Di*…you are back!"

Popping his head cautiously over the balustrade, Rihaan spotted the figure of a girl emerge from the fog, riding like the wind on a bicycle, hair flying loose and wild behind her.

His breath caught in his throat. *Why does she affect me like this?*

She jumped down, laughing and out of breath. "What's up, Saket? Didn't you go to school today?"

"No, *di*. I was practicing at being your bodyguard," the boy said glancing up pointedly.

Rihaan drew back in a hurry.

"Bodyguard? Why would I need one?"

"*Zamaana kharaab hai di, aap bahut bholi ho!*" (It's a bad world out there and you're very naïve.)

Rihaan heard the sounds of a scuffle, and then her crystal clear voice rang out, "First learn to defeat me in an arm wrestle, then think of becoming my bodyguard, Saket. Now get your butt to school and stop making lame excuses! *Chal phatt!*"

"Okay *di*," the boy sounded peeved. "But there's a surprise waiting for you upstairs!"

"Surprise? What surprise? Not one of your pranks, Saket!"

"Check it out for yourself, *di*."

Holding his breath, Rihaan pressed his back against the wall as her quick feet raced up the four flights of stairs and then came to an abrupt halt.

Don't look at her, Rihaan. Don't! But he had to. He was coerced by her beauty.

From the top of her lovely little head to the bottom of her scruffy keds, his gaze embraced her, drinking in her flushed cheeks, her soft lips parted in a surprised 'O', her lissome figure not disguised by the worn-out jeans, or the thick, beige turtleneck sweater or those beautiful, bright eyes…

Rihaan wrenched his mind back to sanity. "So…it appears I have to get an appointment to seek audience with my own wife?"

***

Meanwhile, Naina's brain had also taken a hike. *Oh God, no! It's him again!* Wonder what he wants from me now? I escaped narrowly last night. And worse, he looks even more hunky in those rumpled clothes and stubble, plus his red-rimmed eyes. *Bechara!*

"*Wife hogi meri jooti!*"*(Wife, my foot!)* she mumbled.

"What did you say?" he glowered.

Naina stepped back and would have taken a tumble down the stairs hadn't he caught her arm just in time.

"I...said that I'm not your wife."

"So the actuality of both of us prancing around the sacred flames not too long ago has already left your mind?"

"I... I just meant I'm not your wife in *that* sense." She snatched her arm away.

"Oh... I take it you mean like in the convergence of two hearts! You know very well I don't care for that sort of nonsense," he snapped.

She blushed crimson. "I don't either! Anyway, what brings you here? I thought we were over!"

"Darling..." He bent down, speaking in a loud whisper, his mouth close to her ear. "Don't you think it'd be better if we took our argument indoors? Looks like we may have an unwanted audience."

"What...?" Naina's voice shook as she glanced around and spied Saket ducking out of sight.

"Just get in, will you?" Rihaan grabbed the keys from her trembling hands and pushed the door open.

"I'm sorry." Naina was apologetic. "I...I have not been able to rest at all since yesterday. Deepika deceived both of us and many other things have been weighing on my mind, such as how am I going to afford the rent of this place anymore." She spread her arms in a helpless gesture.

Rihaan smiled. "It's okay. You don't have to apologize. By the way, you have a beautiful place here."

"It is small, but I try to keep it cheerful." She was inwardly pleased he liked it. The apartment was indeed quite pleasant, with simple wicker furniture tastefully decorated with cushions in bright pastels, large windows draped in sheer linen admitting lots of sun, and off-white walls displaying an array of art.

"They are gifts from a couple of students of mine," Naina said, when she saw Rihaan examine one of the pieces closely.

"Hmmm...that must mean you are a very good teacher."

"Nothing beyond the ordinary. Anyway, how did you find me and what do you want?" she asked, throwing her arms up and going into a lazy stretch.

Rihaan blinked, riveted again. She straightened up at once.

"I...got your address from Deepika's parents. I need a favor."

"You could have saved a lot of effort if you had just asked for my number last night," she retorted with a coy smile.

***

He felt something unfamiliar stir inside his chest. *I have only you to blame for my stupidity,* Rihaan thought, gazing silently at her.

"Oh My God! I suddenly remembered I am hungry! Have you had breakfast?" she asked, suddenly looking annoyed.

"Breakfast? No. But I don't have any time." He peeked at his watch again.

"Please!? Not a speck of grain has entered my stomach since yesterday morning. I will die of hunger, then I won't be of any use to you at all." She smiled again before heading toward what Rihaan assumed was the kitchen.

"I can make *phataphat upma* in just ten minutes!" she said peering at him through the open door frame. "Meanwhile you can relate your troubles to me. C'mon spill it. Don't be shy!"

Rihaan stepped into the tiny kitchen to find it dwarfed by his lanky frame. Folding wiry arms across his chest, he leaned gingerly against the wall and watched as she went about her task in a haphazard fashion. Her attempts at putting on a show of neatness and method were failing hopelessly.

"Go ahead, what are you waiting for?" she said with a virulent glare, incriminating him for her inefficiency.

"I want my rights."

"What?" She turned away from the refrigerator and gawked at him.

"My parents are flying in today and I want you to be there to greet them with me as my wife… I mean, play the role of my wife." *Hell! What am I saying? Asking? She* is *my wife!*

"Why would I want to do that? You know our marriage meant nothing to me!"

"Nor does it to me, but right now I'm in a major bind. If I don't produce a wife today, my mom is sure to kill me!" Rihaan said trying to assume his best beseeching expression. He hadn't found much use for it in recent years.

She regarded him silently. "You don't look that delicate to me. Why don't you just tell her the truth? She'll understand. She's your mother after all."

"If that was all it took I'd do so in a heartbeat. But my mother, she won't stop there. She will start by making a mockery of me in front of the entire family, then she will take it upon herself to save me by hooking me up with a girl of her choice back in the States. That's even worse than my current situation!"

"Really…is it?" Naina's eyes brightened with an eerie light. "Perhaps it's better for you to be a mama's boy and do as she says. Maybe the girl she finds would be exactly the one you need…beautiful, accomplished, competent, supportive…"

"And a nag! They have all been trained in the art…every single one!" he exclaimed vehemently. "I have personally witnessed the destruction of some of my friends' lives and I'd rather go to hell than join the ranks! Please don't say no. Naina, I…"

She put her hand up to stop him. "Okay…I need some time to think about it."

"But…they'll be here any moment now."

"Can't you wait a few minutes at least till the *upma* is done? Good heavens! You men are all the same. Want everything this very instant!" she said, hustling him out into the hallway. "Just go sit there and it'll be ready before you know it."

A few minutes later Naina walked into the living room with the food just as she had promised, and found him in deep perusal of a large album.

"This certainly doesn't look like the portfolio of an aspiring model," he remarked, scrutinizing the black and white photographs.

She placed a plate of the hot aromatic semolina dish on the table. Sniffing at the fragrance, he recalled that he too hadn't consumed much of anything even remotely nourishing since yesterday.

"Eat up first!" she said.

Placing a spoonful in his mouth, he chewed thoughtfully. "It's excellent."

"Thanks," she said with a happy smile before spooning some into her own mouth. "You are fibbing! I forgot to add salt!"

"I don't salt my food. It's bad for you. I like it this way."

"Well maybe. But I really think you said so just to please me."

"Can't I?"

She blushed, then quickly changed the topic and began speaking in earnest, pointing to various pictures in the album. They were of regular people; in particular children stricken by poverty—stark, bold and real.

Rihaan's brow furrowed in thought looking at the photos. "These are really good. Each and every one evokes deep contemplation. What's your connection?"

"I'm a freelance photojournalist," she explained simply. "And these are some of the scenes I've captured over the years. I strongly subscribe to the opinion that a single picture is worth a lot more than a thousand words."

"Really? This is amazing." He was in awe as he flipped through the remaining pages. "And what is this? I think I saw it in a magazine somewhere." He indicated a portrait of a terrified young boy clothed in rags fleeing from a mob of angry men, holding a piece of bread in his hand. "You took this, too?"

"Yes," she nodded. "It was for a feature on street children in *Landscape* magazine and this happened to be one among those chosen. I shot it in one of the slums of Mumbai. It's meant to illustrate that most juveniles steal out of necessity, not because they derive pleasure from committing an audacious crime. They are entitled to rehabilitation. Instead our society bundles them into prison where they are bred into hardened criminals. And *we* complain about sky rocketing crime rates!"

Rihaan observed quietly as she sat there stock still, staring intensely at the picture; fine eyes aflame, delicate nostrils flared, and generous lips pursed into a thin line. She looked different…driven.

"Hmm…very impressive and *interesting* at the same time."

"Why?"

"I thought you were just another good-for-nothing frivolous chick who gets her thrills by making fools of suckers like me."

"What? How dare you say such a thing?"

"Well, what did you expect me to think when you joined forces with your wonderful absconding friend!"

"I…I take offense to that." She shot up from her seat and glared at him. "You come to my place, asking for my help and then derogate me!"

"After all the lies both of us have heard, don't you think some honesty would be refreshing? I just stated what I felt when I saw you yesterday. I feel differently now. In fact, I'm having tremendous difficulty believing that you did what you did. You should have acted with more maturity!"

"Yes, I was immature and stupid. But how do you defend yourself—a brilliant doctor and that, too, of the brain no less?" Her eyes mocked him. "How could you have fallen so easily into a trap laid by a silly ordinary girl no less?!"

Rihaan's gaze shifted to the grey-brown mosaic floor. "I have no excuse. It was a moment of folly. I should have been more careful."

"Exactly! A moment of folly or weakness, or whatever you'd like to call it," Naina retorted passionately. "And besides, I was persuaded by someone whom I thought was in genuine need. I made the mistake of trusting blindly. The matter has been preying on my mind ever since I met you and I wanted to make amends. But not now…not after the way you told me off! Please leave," she said pointing to the door.

He got up and glowered at her for several moments, working hard to control his temper. The Khers had described her perfectly. Indeed, he could add a few more unflattering adjectives. "I've never come across a girl more defiantly impudent! Don't you feel in the least responsible for the state I am in right now?"

Naina's eyes blazed with indignant fury. Any lesser creature would have been incinerated on the spot. "I did, but I've changed my mind. Now I believe you need to suffer the consequences of your wrongdoing. Marriage is not something to be taken lightly. It's not a one night stand or a football game. It is a partnership, a beautiful journey through the ups and downs of life. And yes, it is also the convergence of two hearts! You can't find someone on a whim just to free yourself from the clutches of your controlling mother and then forget about her. Your wife is not a toy. She is a human being who has emotions and feelings just like you! Remember that for next time Dr. Rihaan Mehta! Now, will you please go!"

"I don't have any desire to stay here a minute longer!" Rihaan shouted, marching to the exit in long, looping strides. Then, pausing briefly, he looked back. "I hope I never see you again."

"Me, neither!" she echoed, turning away as he walked out, slamming the door shut behind him.

Captive

Rihaan applied an ear to his door. He faintly perceived the rumble of chatter from the crowd gathered below. Propping the door slightly open, he strained harder, but couldn't distinguish his mother's distinctive voice from the others. He knew that she, along with the rest of his small family, had arrived with much fanfare ten minutes ago when Uncle Rajbir's ancient *khattara* Mercedes had pulled up in the driveway. Had the main purpose of their visit bypassed their minds in the excitement of meeting the rest of the clan? He didn't think so.

What should I do? I can't just hide here in my room and wait for someone to break the door down! Naina is right. I have to face the music. And if my mother tries to twist my arm into getting hooked to her beloved Renu or somebody else, I will put my foot down and say I'll remain loyal to my wife as long as I live, even if she doesn't care for me!

The thought conjured up Naina's impassioned face, and with it came a sense of emptiness immediately supplanted by fury at himself. How could he waste time thinking about her? Certainly she had no place in his life. None whatsoever.

He was jolted out of his musings by a couple of piercing, loud whistles. He rushed out onto the balcony. There, he saw standing right below him a slim girl dressed all in white who was shielding her face with a thick *dupatta.* She was also waving wildly at him.

"Who in hell are you?" he shouted irritably, in no mood for congeniality, particularly with a female of the species.

"Hush, you idiot! *Tum toh bilkul gadhe nikle! (You've turned out to be a complete ass!)* It's me, Naina!" she said, lifting her veil while casting a wary glance around. "Who else do you think would try to attract your attention like this? So don't just stand there and stare. Give me a hand up!"

"What a weird woman you are," Rihaan observed with a perplexed smile, noting an immediate dissipation of his anxieties.

"Jaldi! Before I change my mind!"

Her words were enough to prompt him to propel his legs over the railing and jump down.

She inquired of him, "Don't you know of the blanket trick? *Picture nahin dekhte kya?"* *(Don't you watch movies?)*

"No. I think lifting you up would be quicker and far more efficient. You are such a tiny thing anyway," he said smiling at her. It had escaped him until now that she was indeed quite small and delicate. Her forceful personality made her appear larger than life.

She snorted and managed to look offended.

"C'mon, we have no time to waste!" he urged, cupping his hands together and going down on his haunches.

She looked unconvinced, but without saying another word removed her flip-flops and placed a dainty foot in his hands. Then using his shoulders as a step ladder, reached up for the iron railing and attempted to haul herself up.

Without a fraction's hesitation, Rihaan positioned both his hands on her backside and pushed hard, hoisting her upward. Then ignoring her appalled gasp, he followed immediately behind.

"How dare you handle me so intimately?" she exclaimed, her fair complexion hot and flushed.

"There is no place for modesty right now. Besides, feminine anatomy doesn't affect me," he retorted promptly, though he experienced quite the contrary.

But he wouldn't admit that to her, or even to himself. Instead he snapped brusquely, "Why did you come here? Did you suddenly take a liking to honesty?"

She burst into a loud laugh, not appearing in the least affronted. "I felt bad for you. At first I thought I would let your mother make a *bharta* of you, then…" She shrugged her shoulders. "…I felt remorseful and chose to come to your aid. Besides, I was curious to meet your tyrant mama." She smiled with a cheeky grin.

"I don't know what to say," Rihaan muttered. She had managed to upset his rhythm and it annoyed him.

"Don't say anything, then. Let's proceed," she smiled, as if well aware of the effect she was having on him and ambled over to the door.

"Hey, you can't go down like that!" Rihaan said, suddenly remembering the red box his aunt had given him. It was still lying on the floor at the exact spot where he'd flung it earlier that morning. He thrust it into her hands. "Wear whatever is in this and come down."

She took it reluctantly.

"Till then I will try to hold the fort. People might be getting restless," Rihaan said and turned toward the door.

And they were…

As he stood at the head of the stairs, Rihaan could sense a distinct undercurrent of unease. Anxiety was clearly written on many faces, while on others there was obvious bemusement. It was just a matter of time before all hell broke loose. He closed his eyes and sent up a fervent wish to be miraculously whisked away.

But his prayer remained unanswered.

"Rihaan!" a male voice called to him.

Schooling a pleasant smile on his face, Rihaan let himself be encased in a series of hugs.

"A married man at last!" his father exclaimed.

Rihaan couldn't believe it, either.

"My son!"

"Mom!" Grudgingly he accepted a loud smack on each cheek. His fingers rose automatically to erase the smudges left by the deep pink lipstick she wore.

"You look utterly nerve-wracked and upset! *Kya hua beta?"* (*What happened, son?*) Shobha asked, her discerning eyes sweeping over him.

"Ah…it's nothing, mom."

"Mama!" His sister, Rima, pitched in with a knowing wink, and in splendid time. "My diehard bachelor brother has just gotten married. He's still in a state of shock. What else did you expect?"

Rihaan smiled gratefully at her. Rima had always acted as his shield, protecting him from the brunt of his parents' wrath that he frequently appeared to kindle with his rebellious and unconventional attitude. It was fortunate for him the passage of years had watered it down into a grudging tolerance.

But Shobha wasn't convinced. Experience had fine-tuned her instincts to near perfection. She could smell a rat a mile away. "Where is my *bahu?* Or is she planning to remain incognito forever," she demanded, managing to shove her son aside despite her slight stature, and prepared to proceed up the stairs.

"Mom, please…she's getting ready."

"I don't care," Shobha said. "If I don't see her now, then I won't ever!"

At that moment a sudden hush descended over the entire room. Rihaan saw everybody's eyes, including those of his mother's, focus on the staircase behind him. He followed their gaze and identified the cause. An ethereal vision in jewel-encrusted gossamer was floating down to the accompaniment of the rhythmic tinkle of glass bangles, her identity concealed behind a veil of teal netting.

He wasn't sure if his heart stopped or his breath or both, but he was feeling oddly light-headed as she came to a standstill next to him.

A hard nudge in the ribs revived him, along with an urgent whisper, *"Ghoonghat!"*

"Wha…at…? Oh!" With rigid hands, he followed the implied instruction and stood gaping blankly, as apparently did everyone else. Even his toddler nephew's constant whimpering had died down.

Her glorious eyes bordered by shimmering lids stared meaningfully at him. He blinked.

His mother was the first to recover. "Rihaan, introduce us."

"Uh Mom, Dad…meet my wife, Naina…umm Rathod."

"No. Naina Rihaan Mehta. I wouldn't want to be addressed by any other name," Naina said demurely, her flamboyant eyelashes fluttering coyly downward.

"*Waah* Shobha *waah!* It appears that your *bahu* not only looks like an angel, but also knows how to ensnare your son's heart," roared Uncle Rajbir, breaking the silence and sending everybody into merry laughter.

Rihaan looked pleasantly confused, while Naina colored deeply as she was overcome with apparent shy pleasure.

"*Chalo,* take the blessings of your elders. Now that my little brother's beautiful mystery has been unveiled," Rima said, gazing with admiration at Naina, then enclosed her in a warm hug.

Rihaan stooped down, letting out an inward sigh of relief.

"No. First I have to satisfy myself that she is indeed worthy of being my daughter-in-law," Shobha said sternly.

"Aww, c'mon Mom! I took her as my wife in front of everyone!" Rihaan blurted out in an incensed tone, causing Naina to throw him a startled look. She gave him a reassuring smile before mutely allowing herself to be led away.

My wife?! What the hell did I just say? Rihaan thought, glaring at Naina's receding back. *She is certainly not my wife. At least not in the real sense. Or is she? Damnit!*

***

Oh God, now what does she expect of me? Naina mused fretfully as Shobha sat her down by her side on the settee and subjected her to a minute perusal. *Sasuma seems to have been watching a lot of TV soaps in anticipation of today.*

"Okay, my dear, let's have a look at you! You seem to like the natural look and that's good. I'm not fond of face paint. Makes girls look like *bhoots and daayans!*" Shobha said. "I also see that you can talk and talk well. But can you cook?"

Naina shook her head. "Not much…"

"Mom, your daughter-in-law's being modest," Rihaan volunteered. "She's actually a very good cook. She made superb *upma* today."

"What? When? In your dreams, Rihaan? As far as I'm aware, *bahu* hasn't stepped out of your room until just now!" his mother retorted aloud, prompting a general burst of merriment that made Naina turn and direct a withering glare at him.

"It was a good try to save your wife, but you failed, *beta,*" Shobha declared with a smug smile. Then she turned back to Naina, "It is a tradition in our family that every new bride has to make dessert for all of us without any assistance whatsoever!"

"But Mom! Naina…"

"Shut up, Rihaan! You've had your *manmaani*. Now it's my turn. What say, *bahu?*" Shobha said, inflicting Naina with her steely gaze. She received a dumb nod in reply.

"Good, then let's move on. Do you know any crafts?" Shobha said.

Naina shook her head again, thinking she was turning out to be a really lousy daughter-in-law.

***

"Mom, she's a photo journalist," Rihaan spoke up. "I've seen her work. It's fabulous!"

"Wow, seems like my bro is completely *lattu* over his wife. Nothing you do can change that, Ma. You lose!" Rima said with a giggle.

"As if I care! Get lost, Rihaan! You have no place among us women," Shobha said, banishing her son.

He left in a huff, leaving his wife looking utterly flustered. He took position in a secluded alcove, where he could monitor the goings on undisturbed. He watched silently as she was put through a thorough grilling.

"My parents? Uh...um I'm an orphan. I was brought up by my maternal uncle and his wife who were sort of obligated to adopt me. I've been on my own for the past four years. My *mami* hates me. She was happy to wash her hands of me. They were here for the wedding, and thereafter promptly departed for Malaysia which is where they reside now. If you contact them, you'll probably get a very poor report of me."

That came as news to Rihaan. But then he knew nothing about her at all. Naina was very much a mystery to him, and that included her odd behavior—one instant soft and genteel and in the next, aggressive and belligerent. He could tell she detested all the attention being heaped upon her, though she was trying very hard to appear cool. The fire in her eyes could burn the entire house down. Yet he felt no inkling of empathy. Rather, in his opinion, she deserved it. A sardonic grin flickered across his lips when her eyes flashed in his direction. She quickly looked away.

"Hey dude!" A familiar voice blared in his ear making Rihaan jump. "What's up? You can't take your eyes off her. They seem stuck as if by industrial quality duct tape!"

Rihaan was taken by surprise. "Rudy? You're here?"

"After I heard that you'd found someone, I couldn't control my curiosity. I had to see her," Rudy replied. "And let me tell you this. You've made an excellent choice. *Kya cheez hai yaar! (What a chick!)* If only I didn't have Shirin on my back..." He looked longingly at Naina.

"Watch it now," Rihaan spluttered with anger. "She's not like Renu, nor is she for sale. She's off bounds!"

His friend appraised him in wonder. "I'll be damned. You are smitten, absolutely besotted. Must say she is *some* eye candy. Girls like her can be really distracting. They aren't for the likes of you. Whatever made you choose her?"

"What the hell do you mean?" Rihaan countered. "She doesn't affect me at all. I...she just happened to fit my requirements to the T."

"If you say so," Rudy said, with a knowing smile in his hooded eyes. "But a girl like that needs attention. If you go about your business as usual, she may get bored and start looking elsewhere."

"Whatever she does, you have no business getting any ideas about her. She's my wife and I want to make sure you get that fact crystal clear!"

His friend grinned. "We shall see about that. No woman is immune to Rudy's charms."

"Rudy!" Rihaan blistered, his hands bunching into fists, ready to shatter his friend's impertinent jaw. But his honorable intentions were laid asunder by a small group of females who suddenly manifested in front of him.

His giggling sister pushed Naina to the fore. She was holding a small bowl with something in it. "Here!" Rima said. "Since you chose her, you get to be the guinea pig."

***

Naina's hands trembled as she held up a spoonful of *kheer. Please say it's okay. Please!* Her dark eyes implored silently.

Rihaan's face twisted into an expression of disgust. "You better taste your handiwork, too!" He reproved before placing a loaded spoon into her mouth.

Her eyes widened in surprise. "But it's fine!"

"Did I say it wasn't?" He grinned, teasing her.

"Wow! *Kya baat hai! Dulhe miyan bahut ishmart ho gaye hain! (It's awesome! The bridegroom has become very sly!)* Look how he makes our *bahu* blush!" Rashmi *chachi* laughed, as Naina's gaze sought the ground.

Shobha pulled her into a bear hug. *"Bahu,* I was just playing with you. I knew you were perfect for my Rihaan as soon as I laid eyes upon you. But what can I do, *aadat se majboor hoon!" (I'm a creature of habit!)* Then looking at her bewildered son, Shobha said, "Now what are you waiting for, won't you touch my feet?"

The rest of the evening went by in a rush—meeting and greeting relatives, receiving gifts and seeking innumerable blessings with Naina bearing the brunt of it all.

It was close to midnight when the last of the guests had finally taken their leave. Naina was ready to collapse under her own weight.

***

Rihaan relented. "My wife needs to sleep." He announced to no one in particular. *Poor girl, she has come to help me after all.*

There was an outburst of laughter. Everyone seemed to find them terribly amusing as a couple.

Naina glanced at him clearly confused, then her cheeks caught on fire. No one complained when they excused themselves and hurried upstairs.

***

"OMG… What a family you have!" Naina exclaimed as soon as he shut the door behind them and she began peeling off her sari.

He stared rapt.

"Turn around! This isn't a striptease," she said pushing him against the wall. "And no peeking!" she warned when she saw him glancing at the mirror.

He grinned, reluctantly obeying her instruction. "Yes, they are a bit crazy and overwhelming. My mother is the worst. Your pic must be all over the net by now."

"So you never shared Deepika's photograph with her?"

"No, I wanted to keep it a surprise." *Thank Heavens I did.*

"Here…take your *amanat,"* she said, handing him the jewelry she had discarded.

"Don't you want to keep any of these?" he asked separating the dainty anklets. Their tiny bells made a pleasant tinkling sound.

"Why? Do you think I'm doing this for some kind of payment?"

"No, I just felt…" He was chagrined.

"Keep your feelings to yourself. I don't want anything that wasn't meant for me. Maybe you'll find use for it in the future, when you consider having a relationship with someone other than your work." She headed over to the balcony.

"You are leaving?"

She looked back. "I'd better, I think. Before it is too late." Her eyes filled with a deep melancholy. But it seemed like a momentary illusion when she smiled brightly. "Besides I have a job and students who depend on me. I can't afford to go on a vacation."

He didn't hear a word she said. Her face absorbing all his attention. She looked like a dream. Perhaps that was exactly what she was—an impossible dream.

He followed her to the railing, automatically repeating the act of the night before. It was becoming a routine. "But what will I say when they ask me about your whereabouts in the morning?"

Rudy was right. A girl like Naina was not for the likes of him. But somehow the notion seemed to rile him.

***

She peered up at him. He was holding on tight to her arms and did not seem to want to let her go. A lump formed in her throat. She swallowed before replying, "Think of something. You're brainy enough, aren't you?"

He didn't respond to her question. "Please, Rihaan, let me go…"

His grip grew tighter as she began to struggle to free herself. He then let go, making sure she was safely on the ground, before briskly turning away and disappearing inside his room.

"Rihaan, please understand," Naina called after him, her eyes filling up

50

with involuntary moisture. But when he didn't respond, she steeled herself, and headed out onto the street where her scooter was parked. *It's better this way. We were never meant to be.*

At the gates, she looked back and waved to the empty balcony. "Good bye for the last time."

Not Just A Pretty Face

It was a miserable Naina who rode away into the darkness. Fortunate were those who had chosen to quit the streets and go home for this girl was on a rampage; she was fighting a losing battle with herself.

"Yes, I know. I'm being a regular bitch!" She iterated aloud as her scooter swerved dangerously toward the edge of the street. She recovered in the nick of time. Had she not, a few hundred famished sewer rats would have had the pleasure of a surprise feast.

"I'm a callous, insensitive, unyielding, merciless, pig-headed, vile bitch! A black spot on mankind!" she blistered. "Why didn't my heart melt at the sight of his dejected face? Why didn't I shed tears? Maybe that's going a little too far…but still!"

She breezed through a red light. "But there wasn't any other way. It had to be done. The thread of connection that had begun to take shape had to be snapped, however harsh it may seem."

But least was I prepared for the effect it would have on me, she mused, driving straight into a deep muddy puddle, effectively bringing the vehicle to a spluttering halt.

"Where the *hell* am I?" She muttered to herself, looking around apprehensively as an eerie silence enveloped her.

The street was deserted… Well, not really—if she took into account the numerous nondescript mounds of flesh splattering the sidewalk; those of innumerable homeless humans and their beasts who took their chances against the elements every day.

One of them stirred, appearing to find her of some interest, hence propelling her into instantaneous action. *Miserable wretches!* she thought.

The engine finally coughed, then engaged with a steady purr. She pushed ahead. Soon her desperate eyes lit on a familiar landmark—*Nirula's*. Home wasn't far.

She fell to brooding again, her mind still a quagmire of activity. The turn of events had left her completely rattled. She hadn't presumed Rihaan (being the MCP he was) would come pleading to her door, especially after becoming victim of such a humiliating farce. Nor had she expected him to be so beguilingly naïve in worldly matters. Deepika was simply the pits as far as she was concerned.

Yet Naina had chosen not to stay with him. The only reason for her appearance today was to buy him some time. A relationship like theirs was bound to fail. It was Deepika he had proposed to wed, not her. She had just been a stand-in, as he'd said. A role that could have been played equally well by any other girl. There was nothing special or unique about her.

A fresh wave of moisture adrift down her cheeks was disposed of with a swift rub from the back of her hand. *He'll be fine. He has a loving family and they'll find him a bride who suits him perfectly.*

With that notion, Naina made her way back to her lonesome abode.

But to dispatch Rihaan from her mind wasn't an easy task.

Pausing outside her apartment, she stared at the spot where she'd discovered him earlier that day trying to put on an act of nonchalance, and she couldn't prevent a smile. He'd reminded her of a puppy who had lost his master—hazel eyes forlorn yet full of hope.

"Stop perseverating, Naina!" she chided herself. "Rihaan isn't a puppy, nor are you his savior! He's a grown man highly capable of taking care of himself!"

But am I?

Refusing to pursue the thought, she threw open the door.

It was pitch black inside, but Naina didn't turn on the lights. Instead she chose to find her way about in the dark—an exercise she often indulged in when returning home late. An attempt to hone her instincts, to sharpen her brain...a vital skill for any woman, especially one who'd chosen to spend her life alone. *Alone! What a depressing thought!*

She walked into the bedroom and turned on the bedside lamp. Her head drooping like a wilted flower, she sunk down on the hand woven *dhurrie* on the side of the bed; a rare impetuous fling with luxury, but the bright splash of color failed to lift her spirits. The solitude of the apartment which in the past had afforded welcome solace from the hue and cry of her daily routine, now seemed to aggravate her sense of isolation and despair. What did the future hold? Would she ever find someone she'd want to share her life with every day? Or would she perish alone? Would she ever find love and have a family of her own? None of the omens appeared to portend such a likelihood.

This is terrible! I'm being made to pay dearly for my one impulsive error for which I've no one to blame but myself. And I'm calling the poor guy naïve? She rolled over in bed, in a desperate attempt to get comfortable...

This won't do! I need to get a grip, find my focus, get back to my life where there's no place for men or family! I'm a single woman and thus will I remain. "Yes!" she concluded, closing her eyes with a determined nod.

But sleep receded too far away from reach.

Family isn't really a bad idea, particularly one like Rihaan's, she mused. Even his mother, who resembles a consummate bully at the outset, seemed to harbor a softer side. *It'll be fun to parry wits with her for sure.* Naina smiled.

And then..., the very image she had been struggling so hard to fend away; that of the teasing gleam in Rihaan's eyes that made her heart skip a beat before leaping ahead into a mad dash. What did they mean to communicate? A mutually shared daring secret?

"No! Stop it, Naina! You can't go on like this! You just can't!" She sat up with a wretched cry, her body drenched in sticky sweat. Despite it being a muggy night, she had cocooned herself in oppressive folds of the cotton sheet—a flimsy defense against the hordes of voracious airborne parasites that migrated inside, who regardless of her dedicated and indefatigable application of much touted repellents she routinely squandered half her paltry income on, seemed to find her flesh particularly irresistible.

"Now who am I trying to fool?" she laughed wryly before getting out of bed and padding to the bathroom where she doused her face with cold water.

Oftentimes, the restless psyche is driven to find comfort in a favorite distraction and so was Naina's. But the consolation was tepid at best. She soon found that out while slowly flicking through the slides of the most recent photo essay she had done on the street children of Delhi, which she had submitted to *Landscape* a few weeks ago. She had yet to hear from them. It was the most ambitious and difficult venture she'd undertaken, and dangerous, too. Investigative journalism for a lone woman is not child's play, especially when she's trying to ferret out the merciless exploiters of innocence who operate in underground networks as convoluted and ruthless as any drug cartel. Fortunately she had the sense to reign in her enthusiasm in time or would have paid a dear price for her curiosity.

"It'd have been a different matter altogether if I was working with some kind of back up; I'd have dragged each and every one of those sniveling bastards to court and put them behind bars forever. *No!* Cowards like them don't deserve the dignity of a trial, they should be lynched in public, each one of them!" She said so with vehemence enough to upset her still full cup of cocoa all over the laptop keyboard.

With a horrified scream, she scrambled to salvage the precious device, when her eyes fell on the date on the desktop calendar.

A chilling dread settled into her bones. It was that time of year again.

She'd been trying to ignore it like she did every year, hoping if she did so long enough, it'd just recede and drop out of sight. But no, it always came back—all the pain and hurt she had worked so hard to erase—back in stark Technicolor and with uncanny precision.

Her gaze shifted to her reflection in the large poster frame that hung over her bed and she cursed the day she was born.

***

It was monsoon in the desert—a time to rejoice and celebrate. The local populace had been parched of good tidings however transient they may be. It was that time of the year when evanescent showers brought temporary relief from the hundred plus degrees of scorching heat. A time when Lord Shiva danced the *tandav* in the heavens and peacocks strutted proud and arrogant on the ground.

It was a time of hope—when the desiccated wells glistened with more than a hint of moisture, so the perennially suffering women of the villages could cut a mile or two off their daily treks for water.

And... It was also a time to rejoice twice over, because almost twenty-three years ago to this day, the Rathod household had welcomed their first and only girl child.

But the celebrations didn't last long.

Naina almost believed in the stories she concocted. They did vary from time to time, albeit slightly. Her most favored was the one she had narrated today—that she was an orphan and didn't really have much in the form of family. For her, the term felt alien. From what she had seen, family meant unconditional love, trust and support. No member would ever be considered an obligation nor would he or she ever be subject to intentional harm or used as a pawn on a chessboard for another's personal gains.

There was once a time when Naina felt she had a real family, when she had felt loved. That had been long ago when her mother was still alive. She passed when Naina was perhaps five or six, but she didn't recall the circumstances exactly. However, she did remember her mother—her beautiful, wonderful mother. Her revolutionary, trend-setting, modern woman mother. The one who had rebelled against the tradition of *parda* and refused to restrict herself to the *zanana* quarters. Indeed, after the death of her in-laws, she had taken it upon herself to abolish the practice altogether, even daring to converse freely with the male guests who visited the house. She was the mother whom Naina's father had fallen hopelessly in love with and who's only daughter's birth had been celebrated like royalty.

Though several of the memories were vague, Naina fiercely held on to them. She wove them together with whimsical threads of affection and kept them securely locked away within an area of her brain from where she could retrieve them at will. For they conveyed to her that her birth wasn't an accident, that somebody had wanted her and loved her; treasured her existence.

But just as the joy of the monsoon rains was fleeting, so were those moments of happiness.

Her mother succumbed to a sudden unknown illness right after she welcomed her eldest daughter-in-law home. And with her death, Naina's family fell apart. Her grief stricken father, blaming his only daughter for his loss (she being the natural target), banished her from his sight. Then a short while thereafter, having resorted to drown his sorrows in bottles of bourbon, he too perished.

Thus of her family, all that remained were those who considered her an unnecessary accessory, a mistake, and a weakling. Except perhaps her beloved brother, Yuvraj, (second out of a total of four) who had left home for the city to train to be a teacher, and then decided to stay there.

"Because city life agrees better with me," he told her.

But she had believed it to be otherwise—he wished to shield his young family from his prejudiced and overbearing clan who routinely sneered at his progressive ways. So, it came as no minor surprise when just before her thirteenth birthday, Naina found herself handed over to his care and dispatched to the city as well. Perhaps, her brothers thought it a better option than keeping her in a small town where her adolescent beauty and uncharacteristic streak of defiance made her a dangerous liability to have around.

As a consequence, she received an excellent education unlike the usual lot for most women in her community *and* she also grew independent, thereby essentially banning herself from the traditional marriage market.

Naina had just begun to believe the ties were permanently severed when a couple of years ago she received a summons to attend the anniversary of her mother's death. "Let us forgive and forget," she had been told and she had acquiesced gladly—after all, blood is thicker than water, isn't it?

Sadly it isn't, particularly if you are a lowly woman born in a misogynist society.

If mother was alive, she would never have allowed this to happen. But she isn't. I'm all alone.

Naina blinked away her tears. "But alone doesn't mean helpless, does it?" she said aloud to herself. *Think, Naina, think!*

There was only one way out; perhaps a desperate move—but she didn't see any other way.

***

The following morning, after whiling away as much time as he could in bed, Rihaan joined the rest of the brood at breakfast. It was probably best to face the situation head-on, as dodging it would only land him in a worse pickle than he was in.

He'd barely taken a seat at the table when the interrogation began—his mother had never suffered from jet lag. "Where is my *bahu*, Rihaan?"

"Still sleeping?" His Aunt Rashmi piped in with a knowing wink.

"No, she isn't," he said.

"Then perhaps she is getting ready; I can go and help," Rima suggested, starting up from her seat.

It seemed to Rihaan like she had adopted Naina as her younger sibling already. "You won't find her in the room, sis."

An immediate uproar of anxious and scandalous whispers along the dining table was heard among those gathered.

"Then where *is* she?" his mother asked.

Rihaan looked her straight in the eye; it was important he did. "She had to leave on an assignment."

"Assignment? What assignment? Isn't she supposed to be a teacher of some sort and shouldn't she be on vacation?"

"Naina also happens to be a much sought after photojournalist," Rihaan said, his brain racing as the falsehoods came pouring out. "She had signed up for a few projects a while ago that she's obligated to fulfill. The wedding was planned in haste." *That much he knew was true.* "She got a call last night. I wanted to go with her but..."

"What? Unplanned wedding? I don't believe it! What is going on, Rihaan?" Shobha said rising from her seat.

"Mom, listen..." he protested.

Then for the first time in his life, his phone rang and miraculously saved him from further discussion and embarrassing himself.

"It's her!" He shouted in genuine excitement. "She wants me to come right away. Got to go!" He was out the door in a flash.

Journeys

The few hours that followed had Rihaan seriously questioning his rationalizing skills. Truly he seemed to have taken leave of his senses. Feeling his skull gingerly with both hands, he sincerely prayed the wiring was still intact—his livelihood was at stake!

"Aww... Crap! What in hell was that?" The aggrieved frustration he'd been so stoutly keeping a muzzle on eventually found a release.

"A pothole," she said. "Don't you have potholes in America?" His beauteous companion replied with a sweet smile.

That maddened him even further. "You call that a pothole? It's more like a sinkhole! And no, we don't have potholes in America. And even if they do crop up now and then, they get fixed right away. We could've got killed back there! You should report it to the local authorities!"

"Really? You think that'd work?" she snickered, turning to look out of the window of the bus. "Dr. Mehta, what world are you living in? Even if they do take action, it'll be a patch up job, to be washed away with the next rains. Our society eats and breathes corruption; it's part of our lives. We'd be lost without it."

Then she burst into a hearty laugh at his astounded expression. "Don't worry. We made it this far, didn't we? It'll get better once we're on the highway."

Rihaan settled back, preparing to brace his frame against the worn out seat cushion. *Had they really made it?* He was having a rough time figuring out his wife—not in *'that'* sense as she seemed so often to admonish him. She had proved once again that she was a personality of extreme opposites—at times a silly school girl prankster who pitched in at a lark to help her 'friend' and at others, this compelling, brilliant young woman who spilled acidic *gyan* at the drop of a hat. Even a chameleon would be put to shame!

Why did he sense there was more to this beautiful disaster than she was willing to reveal? She sat by his side, unassuming and carefree like a village belle, swathed in pleats of gay silk, the edge wrapped tightly around her head like a makeshift shield against the gusty wind, with her pensive eyes trained into the distance. What did she see? The vast stretches of chaotic third world urban sprawl or something far different? What mysteries lay camouflaged inside those exquisite depths of her eyes? He urged to probe further, delve deeper, and have a conversation—an intellectual powwow with the brain behind that proud brow. It'd surely be well worth his while.

Just then, his body was clobbered by another bone crunching jolt.

Rihaan! What are you thinking? She's a female! And you want nothing to do with the likes of them, remember? Women, especially wily ones like her, can ruin your life! Just follow her advice, finish the task at hand and move on.

Yes, move on! Resolute, he shifted his attention in another direction and chanced upon a pretty young girl staring wide-eyed at him. He acknowledged her with a smile; she colored; her male escort sporting a particularly luxurious handlebar appendage bristled, and Naina giggled.

Rihaan balked. *Now what on earth coerced me to take this godforsaken journey?*

He didn't have to venture too far for the answer. *It's my brain,* he thought. *My wonderful eternally pragmatic intellect that of late has launched itself on an acid trip! What else can possibly explain the goings on?*

Earlier that day, just prior to receiving Naina's message, he'd almost been at the verge of wishing her to Timbuktu or another equally remote location for an indefinite period; notwithstanding whether his parents believed him or not. Perhaps he should have.

I need your help. Can you come to my place ASAP?

He had stared at his phone nonplussed. *What is with this girl?*

He didn't try to reason how she'd come by his number. It was glaringly obvious she was far sharper than he when it came to practical matters. Yet, he hadn't paused to deliberate. He had run like a lovelorn blockhead, leaving his bewildered family behind. His mother must have figured it out by now—he was insane.

"Sorry, I must have the wrong apartment," he blurted, stepping away when he saw a stranger open Naina's door.

"No, Rihaan, you are exactly where you're supposed to be. Thanks for coming so promptly."

The voice arrested him in his tracks. He swung around and gawked at the woman. Sure enough, it was her, but in an entirely new avatar. With her slim figure ensconced in a vibrant ethnic sari, a smattering of simple jewelry, and face bare of all makeup—not that she needed any—Naina presented the image of a chaste and comely *desi* bride. A sight beautiful enough to melt the most discerning of hearts.

He must have worn a profusely befuddled expression because she burst into a peal of laughter. He composed himself and mustered a straight face. It took some doing. "Care to clue me in?" He asked rather brusquely.

She sobered up. "Can you help me out? Accompany me to my hometown?"

His interest was piqued. "As what?"

"As my husband. To meet my family."

"But I thought you said you were…" He waited for her to stub her own toe.

She did so gallantly. "Yes. I *am* an orphan and…you'll know the rest soon. Are you coming? Yes or no?"

He scowled, bristling with indignation. *What does she take me for?*

She looked unruffled, prompting him to simmer down and nod without enthusiasm. After all one good turn did deserve another. And he was intrigued enough.

***

'You'll know the rest soon.' But how soon is that going to be? Rihaan thought passing a wary glance around the bus. Fortune had finally switched sides, or so it appeared for the time being. His arch nemesis, the swarthy owner of the gargantuan moustache, appeared dead to the world, snoring with his cave of a mouth wide open.

"Hungry?" Naina asked, attempting to deduce his sullen countenance. "Here, try these." Producing a plastic box from a large cloth bag she'd hauled from home, she snapped the lid open and waved it in front of his nose. It was full of what looked like fresh coconut cookies. "A few bad calories, doctor sahib?"

He shook his head, looking straight ahead, trying to ignore his hunger.

"I have plenty for both of us *and* they are homemade."

He hesitated for just a bare moment before digging in. They were scrumptious. "You knew I'd come?"

A smile danced across her lips. "I chanced a wild guess."

Wild guess? Like hell! Who was she kidding? She knew from the very moment she sent the message that I'd come. There wasn't any way I could refuse. Though I'm still at a loss as how she persuaded me to board this ramshackle cross-country bus.

***

Soon after he'd reluctantly agreed to her proposal, Naina had hurried him out of her apartment to a waiting taxi. The man took off before Rihaan could slam the door shut.

"Sorry you had to wait. My husband is a very hardworking doctor, sometimes he has trouble getting up in the mornings," Naina said to the cabbie while passing a contrite smile to Rihaan, but her eyes said otherwise.

He fumed, but kept his silence until they were deposited on the outskirts of what looked like a bustling fish market. It turned out to be a bus station. "Why are we here? What happened to the trains?"

She smiled, enunciating slowly as if talking to a small child, "I inquired. They are all overbooked."

Rihaan surveyed the surroundings. All his life, he'd harbored an extreme distaste for crowds, and the land he stood on now bragged a populace of greater than a million. He regarded with trepidation a vehicle, whose rooftop appeared entirely taken by some of his more agile cousins; the upcoming trek promised to supply the climax to his ongoing nightmare.

"How about hiring a cab?" he said, reaching into the back pocket of his denims. "I'm sure it'll get us to your place in half the time. Money isn't a problem. I think I should have enough."

"Are you out of your mind?" Naina had snatched his wallet and dumped it into her satchel before he could flip it open.

"Hey that's mine!"

"I know, and I'm trying to keep it safe." She regarded him as if he was some kind of halfwit. "Haven't you noticed something? Your *phirangi* accent and looks make you stand out like a sore thumb and now you wish to kiss all your worldly possessions goodbye? Besides, there's no way in hell I'll submit to being cooped up in a stuffy cab for any number of hours. I'd rather die instead. Now stop acting grumpy and be an obedient husband and get on the bus! I assure you it's going to be a lot of fun!"

***

That's how he'd landed on this hell on wheels, bulldozed and bullied by a wife with a fondness for hyperbole, so he could get his organs rearranged every few minutes. The heat and dust didn't even figure in the equation.

At least there's a constant supply of good nourishment, he thought, munching on savory fenugreek *rotis* that set his taste buds on fire—a source of considerable amusement to his wife. He glowered at her. She smiled serenely, and then to his surprise, doled out some tempering cucumber and mint yogurt dip. He was tempted to believe it was her way of showing concern for his delicate constitution, even though she pretended to act otherwise.

Mom is sure going to miss out on a lot, he thought. *And how about you, Rihaan,* sneaked in a faint but clear voice. He chose to ignore it because he was having the time of his life!

As she'd promised, the journey smoothed out. He began to unwind and relax, enjoy the moment, play a tourist in his own country. These were his people—a peculiar and fascinating collection of mankind he'd only heard mentioned in anecdotal references but never experienced firsthand until now (most of prior visits to the homeland having been expended in sterilized air conditioned environs). The thick rainbow turbans, the luxurious facial hair, the *beedis*, even a *fakir* with dreadlocks that his wannabe hippie buddies would kill for. All in all, a sight like no other.

His face must have shown it, because his companion asked with a perplexed frown, "You like it?"

"I love it! Its enthralling just like you."

She looked away, but not before he saw heat rise to her cheeks. He grinned. This jaunt was turning out way better than expected.

61

And then, just as the warm afternoon breeze mingled with the effects of a gratified stomach lulled Rihaan into a pleasant siesta, the bus came to a screeching halt causing him to lurch to the left, in the process pin his 'in-name-only-wife' under his weight.

It was a strikingly delightful experience; one which left him pleasantly benumbed. *Do all witches come loaded with such sultriness?* How was he to know, this being his first encounter. And she was positively steaming!

Sun-kissed cheeks stained a deep pink and those magnificent eyes widened some more, sucking him in, so he couldn't breathe... Dead, dead sea. "What's up?"

For chrissakes! "Ah... I'm sorry." He straightened himself while his eyes flitted around the small space. "Where the hell are we?"

The bus was leaning alarmingly on its side, on the unpaved shoulder of an abandoned stretch of highway. And he was treated to a sight that his untrained eye could only equate with a biblical exodus. "Are we under siege?" (*Bandit Queen* being his favorite childhood flick.) "Get down!" he warned, meanwhile attempting to manhandle his unwilling spouse under the seat.

"Stop fantasizing! It's a piss halt. To take a leak. Pee." She gesticulated with her little finger.

Gosh! He despised it when someone reminded him of his bladder.

She made it worse. "You may want to make use of the opportunity. And no, we don't have rest areas here."

"What if I get bitten by a cobra?" Rihaan asked.

"There are certain times in life when you have to take chances."

Was she laughing at him? He didn't pause to reflect, instead jumped out and after considerable exploration found relief within a grove of acacia trees.

As his fellow passengers were none too keen in resuming the journey, he chose the moment to stretch his legs and lungs and listen to the quiet—the crunch of dry leaves underfoot along with the plaintive song of the Koel and let his mind relax.

But it wouldn't. Bitter memories were ever on standby.

Memories like of his mother monitoring his bladder habits, to establish a routine. She had not only controlled his bladder, she had controlled everything—his clothes, what he ate, where he went, whom he played with—everything! His whole life had been planned out, developed and designed as per the dictates of Mrs. Shashank Mehta. And he would have continued in the role of a clueless campaigner, hadn't it been for that one fateful day, when as a freshman, he'd found her snooping in the school grounds—she being worried that her innocent son would fall for the wiles of some *chaloo* white girls. It was a miracle he hadn't made a break from home. It was then he'd pledged never to bow to the will of a woman ever again.

"Rihaanji!" Naina called. "You better hurry, unless you wish to spend the rest of the day sharpening your snake charming skills."

Women!

Discoveries

A gentle prod on the shoulder. "Time to deplane, sir."

Rihaan let out a muffled groan as he jerked awake and worked on uncrumpling his stiff frame. His body ached all over, his limbs were like dead stumps of wood and his gravelly tongue appeared stuck solid to his palate. Even his neck was horribly askew. Yet he didn't grumble. Instead, he hobbled to the exit and stumbled out only to be walloped by a blast of searing hot air.

With difficulty, he braced himself and ventured forward to peruse the vicinity. In a mere few hours, the entire landscape had undergone a drastic transition. Lush, verdant fields of maize, barley and *jowar* had given way to a brown arid expanse of scrub and brush. There were no tall dense groves of banyan and peepal to provide welcome shade; just an occasional thorny acacia trying to make its presence felt. Yet there was plenty of something else—dunes, loads and loads of them, rolling out in all directions as far as the eye could see. He had landed in the middle of a desert, hostile and downright deadly.

"Where in hell is this?" he seethed, seeking the slim figure of his reluctant spouse.

"We are in my hometown," she responded, suddenly popping into his line of vision. "Rathods—Rajasthan... Get it?" Her lips twisted into a smile.

"Doctor Sahib! This won't do at all! You look like a desiccated *vadi!*" She clucked in disapproval. "This place comes with a few but very basic rules." She thrust a bottle of water at him. "Hydrate *and* cover your cranium." Her tone rang with dry ridicule.

But before he could rally around and deliver a sound whack on her behind, she had disappeared leaving only the resonance of cheeky laughter in her wake. He felt like a henpecked husband already. *I can't tolerate this!*

"Get back here, right now! I command you!" he shouted.

But she didn't obey. His words were inaudible, lost in the parched realms of his throat. *Damn!*

Then all of a sudden, he became aware of a strange sensation. He was being watched. The locals were eyeing him with curiosity and of what could only be interpreted as amused sympathy—another *desi* kid straying off the beaten path in search of eternal *moksha*, instead discovering (too late) that he had seriously miscalculated his bearings.

I have to pull myself up and get my act together or I'm surely done for, Rihaan thought ruefully.

He emptied the bottle in one big gulp, feeling a sliver of revival rush through his core. Armed with a renewed sense of purpose, he embarked on the dusty road, steering toward a profusion of tiny shops, and stepped into what appeared to be the main bazaar. The partial shade provided by the gaily decorated awnings supplied instant succor. His eyes, so far narrowed down to tiny slits, snapped ajar. What he saw were narrow alleys of packed mud, crammed with vendors on either side, branching out in diverse directions—a situation he found most confounding. And as if that wasn't enough, he also had to endure a relentless wave of humans, seemingly bent on uprooting and evicting him from their midst. But tenacity was a trait he had been born with. He remained dogged in his quest. Fortunately it didn't last long—*pagris* were quite a popular commodity.

Toning down his accent the best he could, he haggled with a stone-faced stall owner and arrived at what he presumed to be a bargain—a bright orange and green turban for a mere 2500 rupees!

"1500! They cheat you mister!" a voice said beside him.

"Huh?"

He watched bemused as his unsolicited champion plunged into a heated exchange with the merchant. It ended just as abruptly, with him being presented with his purchase, at a paltry Rs.250 savings and much worse for wear. Gingerly Rihaan placed it on his head and assessed his reflection in a foggy mirror.

"Ahh! You look just like a Rajput prince! *Shandaar!* All you need is a mustache!"

Despite himself, Rihaan found it hard to suppress a smile. He turned to his rescuer and proffered a couple of 100 rupee notes. They were pocketed promptly.

"You need help? I speak English very good! You American? Me Rafiq." An eager hand was extended.

Though barely reaching above Rihaan's midriff, Rafiq was a grown man, somewhere in his mid-thirties. Dressed in clean yet threadbare clothing with worn out leather sandals on his feet, topped by a pair of cheap shades, he looked like what he was—a seasoned veteran of the hapless tourist trade.

"Me Rihaan, and yes, I'm from America." Rihaan solemnly shook the man's weathered hand. "And no, I don't need help."

But the hint was forsaken. The little man redoubled his pitch while trying to keep pace with the much taller Rihaan who took off down a thin lane in search of Naina.

"You need guide? Me very good guide. I show you lake, bird sanctuary, Rathod palace. Just $100.00. I have car, very nice and AC." He pointed to a beat up Ford that could have put many junkyard rejects to shame.

Rihaan regarded him warily. The fellow had probably a very good view of his bulging wallet—Naina's warning still lurked fresh in his mind. He patted his rear to assure himself of its presence and observed Rafiq's eyes following the movement. "No, thanks! I'm not a tourist." He muttered it dismissively while frantically scouring the vicinity for a particular bright green and blue sari. It was a tough task—the whole place was a virtual impressionist palette.

"There you are! Here's my *biwi*. My wife!" With a broad grin of discovery, he pulled the baffled Naina (whom he'd found at a stall struggling with some ridiculously tiny green bangles) firmly around by the shoulders and positioned her in front of Rafiq who, after surveying them both skeptically for several moments, reluctantly slinked away.

Sighing with relief, Rihaan turned to her. "Why did you disappear and leave me to fend for myself? In any case, why do you need these bangles?"

It took her but a few seconds to recover and disengage herself from his grip. Kohl-lined eyes with mile long lashes fluttered, quickly taking in his headgear. They appeared to approve which infused him with a sense of immense content for no apparent reason. "I can't go home without bangles on my arms. I wouldn't be considered married," she explained.

"Is sahib your *marad?*" Interjected the shopkeeper, claiming Rihaan's attention for the first time. The shopkeeper happened to be a pint-sized old woman with a lined, leathery face, bright beady eyes and a toothless smile.

"Yes, I am her *marad*. We just got married," he affirmed, nudging Naina who reluctantly dipped her head.

"Then he must make you wear these bangles, the smaller the better, so you'll have a wonderful honeymoon!" the crone cackled, her shriveled frame convulsing with delight.

"Might as well comply. I happen to be very superstitious in some ways," he muttered softly, proceeding to manipulate the baubles of colored plastic around Naina's dainty hand with distinct glee. Her features screwed up in distress but she didn't utter a whimper.

What the heck's gotten into me? He checked himself, tossing aside what he had and replaced them with a larger size. Then after arraying his new bride's arm with an abundance of color, he paid for the purchase, failing to notice the gleam of regard in her eyes. "Give us your blessings, they are worth a lot more than fake superstitions." He told the old woman who was clearly taken aback by his generous tip.

Then turning to Naina, he asked, "What now wife?"

She colored, appearing markedly disconcerted and made toward the auto-rickshaw stand.

He yanked her back. "No, that's not what I had in mind."

A few minutes later they were on their way.

"Are you sure you're okay?" Naina looked at Rihaan, concerned.

"I'm perfectly fine. Couldn't have asked for anything better." He let out a contented sigh, allowing his head to sink back into a pillow of fresh straw, and his worn out body to stretch along the length of the traditional *tanga*. With eyes closed, he inhaled deeply, filling his lungs with a mixture of the sweet hay and horse dung. The jerking rhythm, the clip clop of horse's hooves, punctuated by the shrill cries of the *tangawallah* as they made their way through the busy thoroughfare was strangely comforting.

***

"This is bliss, pure bliss," he said.

Naina smiled, shaking her head as she turned her attention to the outside. The streets of her hometown were still the same—little had changed in this relatively remote outreach of the Hindi heartland. True, technology hadn't spared anybody; even the lowly *chaiwallah* and the maid conducted their business on cell phones. Television had brought the world to every doorstep and the light bulb had swapped places with the customary lantern. Yet the attitudes of the populace remained constant; they continued to exist in perpetual darkness.

Her morose contemplation was abruptly interrupted when a young boy caught her eye. He stood in the middle of the street, waving to her vigorously while pointing upward, sporting a carefree grin on his nut brown face.

She followed the directive without much interest and found herself catching her breath. The cloudless blue sky had metamorphosed into a canvass of dazzling art. Myriad kites in all colors of the rainbow frolicked high above, tethered to invisible hands. They played an innocent game, vying for prominence in a battle of superiority and skill.

Craning her head, she watched a bright red and yellow kite climb higher and higher; it's progress seemingly unstoppable, when suddenly a roar erupted from the crowd—the kite had been snagged. She saw it drop like a wounded bird in mid-flight and gasped.

"What's up?" Rihaan asked. "Anything wrong?"

Naina started and glanced over her shoulder, not realizing that all along she'd been subject to his surreptitious perusal.

"No, it's nothing," she said, her voice short.

"Fine," Rihaan retorted. "You're welcome to your miseries. But please help me out of mine. I'm dying to meet my in-laws!"

The flash of anger in her eyes deepened his grin which infuriated her even more, but she chose to look away so he wouldn't see her expression.

"Hold on!" Their driver let out a shrill warning just as he took a sharp turn and began climbing a steep incline.

Rihaan reached over and made a grab for Naina's waist. She didn't struggle as she was too preoccupied with her own thoughts. Holding her close, he stared at her face while the rickety cart lumbered up the hillside.

The scenery was rustic and the situation tranquil, yet it couldn't belie the upheaval in both their hearts.

Relationships

Rihaan couldn't pass up an opportunity to tease Naina. He chided her, "You made a big mistake by not getting your family's blessings for our marriage. At the least they had a right to know."

"They wouldn't have agreed," she said, brusquely pulling away from his grasp.

"Then why tell them now and invoke their anger?"

"It has to be done. Or… I'll never be free."

"I don't understand," he said.

"You wouldn't."

His inclination to probe further was hampered; their journey had come to an abrupt end. The carriage had drawn to a halt just outside a tall arched entryway that led into a wide open courtyard overlaid with cobblestones and surrounded on all sides by low brick and stucco walls. But what struck him dumb was a stunning ancient edifice that towered five stories high; a structure of rare and exquisite craftsmanship who's red and pink limestone walls mirrored the brilliant colors of the sunset. He'd never seen the likes of it—except perhaps on the internet.

"The Rathod palace; my ancestral home," Naina explained simply, coming to stand beside him. "The only one that remains standing; a gift from a local Nawab in the 18th century. We come from a long line of well-known *zamindars* but there's apparently some royal blood running somewhere."

He dropped suddenly to his knees exclaiming, "I plead to you, princess! Punish me however you will for I've sinned, but please spare my head."

She stepped back and bellowed with wild laughter. Her face flushed a deep red and tears trickled down her cheeks. "Very funny. But I'm not a princess. Even if I was, I'd be a very unlucky one."

Thus, plunging him into a deeper mystery. She stalked on ahead and up a long, wide flight of flagstone stairs to the main entrance. On the way, they passed a small group of tourists who watched them go by with envy. *Curiouser!*

And as soon as the smartly turned out *Durban* laid eyes on Naina, he bowed low and threw open the heavy double doors.

Rihaan was impressed. "You must be bloody rich and *you* worry about paying rent!"

"My family's pride weighs heavily on my brother's shoulders," she said softly, eyeing the coat of arms above the entryway that displayed the rising sun. "Everything is mortgaged to the hilt."

"I don't believe it." He tilted his head up, taking in the magnificent domed foyer of the grand old *haveli.*

"The government takes care of most of the upkeep," she said glancing at him. "You saw the tourists outside. They also pay Shamsher Singh's salary. The family has been relegated to the old *zanana* quarters, including the men." She simpered. "My mother would've been tickled pink."

She moved on, not giving him any time to absorb the grandeur as he had to scramble to keep her in sight. He tracked her up a claustrophobic spiral staircase, then through a confusing network of corridors framed with decorative arches and lined with colorful miniature paintings as well as fine latticework *jharokhas* affording an unparalleled view of raspberry skies that one could enjoy from almost utter seclusion.

Though nothing seemed amiss on the surface, on closer inspection he could make out cracks in the plaster and peeling paint. "Then why continue to live here?" he asked, looking over her shoulder as she peered through a beehive window pane. A puff of breeze brought her veil skimming across his face, instantly transporting him to a tropical paradise replete with exotic fragrances and unlimited possibilities. He curbed his desires.

"My brother believes he's going to restore the Rathod name to its former glory and that I'm going to help him do it," she said, craning to look up at him.

Her complexion was awash with a patina of gold and unknown treasures lurked in the depths of her black irises. He had to focus to answer her. "Uh... how?"

Rose lips curved into a bleak smile, "You shall soon see."

***

Meanwhile at the local temple, Balraj Singh Rathod waited impatiently for the pundit to end his litany of complaints and petitions so he could take his leave. It was getting late and he was eager to get home. He, along with his wife, had just concluded the annual rite of distributing food and alms to the poor and needy; an event that over the years had lost its significance, and that seemed true for almost everything he did now. After making a cursory promise to take care of the repairs; one he had no intention of keeping, he beckoned irritably to his long suffering wife, before climbing into the chauffeured car he couldn't afford.

It's all a matter of keeping up appearances now, Srimati Rukmini Devi thought wistfully, studying her husband's proud profile as he gazed out of the window. His hawk-like features were unrevealing, but she knew he was much aggrieved; embroiled in deep financial and personal conflicts, most of his own making. She had seen it all coming. But her sincere attempts at caution had been thwarted with such harsh derision that she'd stopped trying.

There had been a time, long ago, when this same man had promised her the sun and the stars. But then calamity struck; many said brought on by the *Devi Ma* herself.

Beginning with the death of her mother-in-law and perpetuated by misfortune and greed, it pitched brother against brother, dispersing the family like leaves from a dying tree. Thereafter her husband, afflicted by the curse of gambling, managed to squander away most of their fortunes.

But two years ago when Balraj persuaded her young sister-in-law (who she loved like the daughter she never had) to come back home, Rukmini believed he had turned over a new leaf. But it was not to be. She had misread his intentions. And though she dearly wished to see Naina again, she prayed fervently she wouldn't return.

***

Rihaan saw Naina hesitate briefly in front of a heavy teak door before she pushed it open and ushered him inside. All at once he was besieged by an amazing solace as one does upon stepping into a temple. The reason was directly apparent.

In the center of the room, on a raised pedestal, amidst a cloud of incense smoke, stood the portrait of a woman of exceptional beauty and grace who bore striking resemblance to the girl who accompanied him. Mind racing with curiosity, he knelt on a floor cushion behind her, but chose to save his inquiries for later. He wanted her to have this private moment with her mother.

But the moment proved to be brief as the door snapped open once again and footsteps hurried in.

"Naina! You are back!" a woman called.

"Bhabhi!" Naina was on her feet in an instant, fondly embracing a pleasant-faced woman who seemed obviously pleased to see her.

"I can't believe you are here, especially after what happened last time," the lady said tenderly stroking Naina's cheek.

"And who is this?" she asked, turning to bestow a benevolent smile upon Rihaan.

"Yes, do enlighten us, dear sister. I'm curious, too," a commanding voice boomed from behind where they stood. "And pray, why are you dressed like a bride on our mother's death anniversary?"

A startled Rihaan swung around. His gaze alighted on a tall man of imperious carriage, clothed in pristine white, who had just stepped into the room.

Ignoring Rihaan, the man took his seat on a low divan and focused on his sister.

"The occasion called for it. Mother would have approved." Naina looked at Rihaan who smiled encouragingly at her.

"What occasion?" the man said. "Oh... I know!" His sober face lit up. "You, my beautiful little sister, has changed her mind. You have come back to honor your engagement and get married to my dear friend, Thakur Shekhawat's son."

"No, I haven't changed my mind." Her voice shook, but she continued bravely. "The engagement was nothing but a cruel deception so you could use me as a tool to remedy your errors and get back the property you squandered away. But I won't suffer for your sins. You can't intimidate me anymore. I'm married now and this is my husband, the love of my life." She came up to stand next to Rihaan who obliged by placing a secure arm about her shoulders.

This brought the man springing to his feet. Anger distorted his fine features as he fixed Rihaan with a glare sharp enough to slice him into pieces. "Absolutely impossible! You cannot marry outside our clan. He's not a Rajput. Look at him. He's not even a man!"

Rihaan fingered his clean shaven face. "Yes, that's true. I don't have a moustache, but I'm seriously considering growing one." He laughed. But no one appeared ready to share his amusement. He read the silent appeal in Naina's eyes.

He cleared his throat. "I'm not a Rajput nor could I ever pretend to be one. Naina and I met by chance when I was in New Delhi for a conference a few months ago." He looked down at her. "Something clicked. I went back home to New York, but couldn't stop thinking about her. Her eyes wouldn't let me sleep; they haunted me constantly." He was surprised at how easy it was to lie. "I proposed and fortune favored me. I came back and we got married."

They were all staring at him as though he'd lost his mind, including Naina. Maybe he had because he didn't sound like himself at all; more like a love-struck imbecile!

"I don't believe it," her brother said. "You're lying. She hired you. Go on, accept it!" He sneered.

There was no way Rihaan could let Naina down. All of a sudden he had a brainwave. He dug his phone out from his pocket. "You want proof? Here it is." Thank God for his snoopy mom who had shared the entire wedding on the internet.

A gamut of emotions flitted across Balraj Singh's face, ranging from stark disbelief to disgust, and then profound vexation as the video played out. But it wasn't enough.

"Naina, you can't do this to me, your own brother. Besides, I've given my word. We Rajputs never go back on what we say. You should know that!"

But she stood tall beside Rihaan. She was a Rajput, too. "Not at the price of my happiness. No, brother. And if you really do love me you'll forget your pride and let bygones be bygones."

"That'll never happen as long as I live!" he thundered and pointed to the door. "Leave before I do something I won't regret. Now!"

"As you wish." She took Rihaan's hand and together they left the room.

***

The shadows had begun to traverse up the far walls of the courtyard. The temperature had plummeted, setting the stage for a very pleasant evening. Rihaan sat on the low stone seat that circled a gigantic tree which he had been informed was a Jacaranda.

"It's fed by an underground spring that also supplies our well," Naina said.

He watched as she took a slow turn, pausing at frequent intervals as if to commit things to memory.

"It's odd, I've never missed this place as much as I'm going to now," she murmured staring up at the tree's dark canopy. "My mother used to thread the purple flowers into a tiara for me every spring." She sighed. Then seemed to snap out of it. "Let's go. If we hurry we should be able to catch the last bus for Delhi."

"Go? You must be kidding." With a short laugh, he leaned back crossing his arms behind his head. "I'm not going anywhere right now. Actually, I've begun to fall in love with this place and its people."

He snuck a sly glance at her. "Besides, I'm hungry enough to eat a camel!"

Aghast, Naina exclaimed, "Have you lost your mind? Didn't you hear what my brother said?"

He responded with a shrug of nonchalance. "He wouldn't hurt his own brother-in-law."

"Balraj Singh Rathod is not in the habit of doling out empty threats. At this very moment he's probably scheming to intercept us, abduct me and finish you off!"

"But what about the law?" Rihaan asked.

"He's a law unto himself." She grabbed his arm. "C'mon, hurry up. I don't want your death on my conscience."

Rihaan didn't want to believe her, but she looked damn serious. He stood up and tagged behind her as she skipped the main gate and ran toward the back.

"STOP!"

Turning as one, they saw someone hurrying towards them. The person's identity was masked by deep shadow.

"Keep moving!" his wife urged frantically at his side.

But before he could follow her down the narrow staircase, the voice rang out again, now a lot closer.

"Please stop, I beg you!" the woman called.

It was Naina's sister-in-law. The woman paused for breath. "I…can't let you…go like this and… I barely got to meet *damaadji."*

Naina smiled apologetically. "Sorry, *bhabhi.* You probably understand why. Rihaan, meet my eldest sister-in-law, Mrs. Rukmini Devi. And *bhabhi,* this is Dr. Rihaan Mehta, my husband."

Rihaan bowed gallantly.

Rukmini blushed. "I regret I couldn't welcome you properly."

He shrugged. "It happens. Family politics. I've seen plenty of it in mine. One of the reasons I'm here today."

Casting a doubtful smile at him, she grasped Naina's hands and threaded an ivory bangle on both her arms. "Your mother's gift to me; now they are yours."

"Oh *bhabhi,* I'll miss you so much!" Naina embraced her warmly. "Are you upset with me?"

"No. I'm proud of you and so would have been your mother. You've made the right choice." She eyed Rihaan with ill-concealed admiration, making him squirm in his shoes. "He seems wonderful—strong, clever and honorable. He'll take good care of you, I'm sure."

"We'd better go now," Naina said looking nervous again.

"Yes. But not without eating a decent dinner and some rest. Please go to Roshan *Bhai's,* our old *munimji.* I've called ahead. Shamsher Singh will take you to his house."

"But my brother?" Naina asked.

"Don't you worry. I'll handle him. You are his little sister after all."

***

A couple of hours later after indulging in a traditional Rajasthani *bhoj* fit for a king—he'd never eaten so much in his life—Rihaan relaxed on a *charpai* on the open terrace of a small cottage under a dense blanket of stars. He breathed in the crisp, desert air. It was the same universe he had observed at the other end of the earth. Yet this experience had never felt so raw, so real, that it almost seemed to find a home in his heart. All thanks to Naina.

He peeked at her as she lay on another cot nearby. This probably marked the end of their brief sojourn together as husband and wife; a very gloomy thought indeed. He really enjoyed her company.

He wondered what was playing in her mind. What was she mulling over? Was she pining for what she'd been forced to leave behind? He wished he could reach out, tell her she could depend on him, that he'd replace all she'd lost, be strong and dependable just as her sister-in-law had said. Yet he held back. Because that'd mean relinquishing control, not just the way he led his life but also at the cost of his independence—a thing he held most dear. *Or did he really?*

Why wasn't he sure anymore? Why were his own decisions leaving him so utterly dissatisfied and frustrated? He couldn't say. And that was annoying to say the least.

A Proposition

Rihaan slogged up the hill, pumping hard on his pedals. Upon reaching the top, he relaxed, letting gravity take over. His bike responded by surging forward, gaining momentum as it shot down the incline. Icy wind clawed at his face; the balaclava mask offering scant protection, yet he pushed on, pedaling faster through the unfamiliar territory. Not that he was worried of getting mugged. No honest goon would risk his fingers in this weather.

Besides the only thing of value he possessed was his bike and his vital organs, and they would have to kill him to get to either.

He laughed out loud heartily. Lately his brain had not been acting like itself, nor had his body. His short stint in India had not only turned his life on its head but also infused him with such a degree of unbridled excitement that he was having a tough time getting any sleep. Yet he wasn't the least unhappy about it.

He grinned. It had all begun a few days ago with four simple words…

***

New Delhi, Naina's apartment

"I have a proposition."

Rihaan sat forward in his chair but didn't dare to react any more than that. It was very probable he was hallucinating given the state he was in.

After being dragged out of his rustic bed in the wee hours of the morning, he'd been forced to participate in the Great Indian Railroad boot camp like any average commuter—*'My brother would never dare hijack a train.'* And he'd spent the entire journey either shielding his wife from unwanted male attention (a turn prompting no gratitude whatsoever) or struggling against being thrown off the train. It was a miracle he was still alive.

He stared skeptically at the plate of spicy *chaat* she'd ordered from the neighborhood *chaat* house after inviting him in for a cup of tea and a last goodbye. Then after a brief battle with his better judgment, he shoved a spoonful in his mouth. Surprisingly, it was delicious! Worth every trip to the toilet he may have to make.

Naina repeated her words, several decibels louder this time. "I said 'I have a proposition!'"

"Really? What kind? Aren't you satisfied enough with what you've done already?" he asked ruefully, examining his tattered collar.

She flushed. "I'm sorry. But this time I have a suggestion that could be mutually beneficial."

"Go on..." His interest was piqued.

A smile bright enough to lighten his troubles lit her face. She indicated the letter she held in her hand, "My dream has finally come true. *Landscape* magazine is going to feature my work on Delhi's street children as the lead story in their January issue."

"Congratulations, that sounds wonderful," he said, genuinely happy for her.

"...And they want me to come to New York City," she continued. "They want me to work for them, which would give me the opportunity to intern with some of their best journalists for a period of six months!"

"Does that mean that you can...?" Rihaan held his breath.

"Yes." She nodded. "I think I can, if you would help me with the visa and plane tickets. I can put this place up for rent," she said looking around her apartment, "and get my leave sanctioned. I've been preparing for a while for this eventuality." She smiled at him. "I hope it's not asking a lot of you. I promise to pay you back."

He laughed, jumping to his feet instantly. At last things were beginning to look up. "But of course! You can come back as my wife. As for accommodations, don't worry. You can stay with me."

"I...I don't want to impose. I'll move as soon as I find a place of my own."

"Don't even mention it," he said, impulsively grabbing her by the waist and swinging her high up in the air. "I'll do anything as long as you keep my mother off my back."

***

But obtaining a visa wasn't a cakewalk as Rihaan soon discovered. A marriage certificate was required for which he and Naina had to appear in front of the registrar, along with a couple of witnesses. Having heard rumors about the horrors of Indian bureaucracy, he chose to fess up to good old Uncle Rajbir, though not before swearing him to secrecy. To his surprise, he didn't react the way he thought he would. Instead Uncle Rajbir heard him out with a wide grin pasted on his good-natured face. He then patted Rihaan on his back, and agreed to assist after extracting a solemn promise from him to never let go of his wife. She was—according to him— *'laakhon mein ek.'(One in a million.)*

But the registrar Mr. Desai (a scrawny man with a mug wrapped tight in a woolen scarf) proved to be a different cookie altogether. Most of his statements were preambled with the words, *"Mein ek imaandaar aadmi hoon,"* (I am an honest man,) which was apparently more to reassure himself than his beleaguered clientele who happened to be quite a few. Rihaan and Naina were made to wait for more than three hours, despite having an appointment. And when they presented their request, he refused promptly. "No, impossible. Can't be done. It says here that you're already married to a...a Deepika. Where is she?"

"She...she absconded, jilted me. This is my real wife, Naina," Rihaan said, putting on his most sincere face.

Naina nodded, following suit.

Mr. Desai appeared to find it extremely hilarious. Hooting with laughter, he clapped his cluttered desk a few times. "*Yeh lo!* Absconded! Which *desi* girl in her right mind would give up a *crorepati* NRI and that too a *dimaag ka doctor?*"

Rihaan mumbled, correcting him. "I'm a neurosurgeon."

"Tell me a story I can believe in!" Mr. Desai demanded.

Rihaan stared helplessly at Uncle Rajbir who winked and said he'd take care of it. And he did. God bless him. A brief conversation held in a curtained alcove was enough to shake the man's integrity. Putting on a façade of serious reluctance, he carried out their bidding. His pockets had been lined well.

Everything else went without a hitch. Naina's leave was approved and her tickets were bought. Rihaan breathed a sigh of relief. When she came to bid him and his family farewell at the airport, promising to join them in a couple of weeks, he pulled her aside. He was having the jitters again.

Grasping her hands in his, he almost pleaded. "Promise me, you won't backtrack on your word."

She smiled, replying coyly, "I won't. Besides, in my husband's happiness lies mine."

Easier Said Than Done

"Sorry I'm late. Thought I'd left the clinic in good time but I forgot to account for the traffic," Rihaan blurted out in a rush when he came upon Naina sitting alone, looking exhausted and bleak in the near vacant arrivals lounge of La Guardia airport. "I hope you didn't think I had abandoned you."

He grinned when she didn't respond, but continued to stare blankly at him. He had forgotten how beautiful she was; more so now that she wasn't in her element. An aura of compelling vulnerability enveloped her.

She flushed. He'd read her mind. "I thought you wouldn't come."

"What? And let go of my ticket to freedom? Impossible!" he exclaimed, stooping down to gather her luggage. But when he looked up her lovely visage had turned pale. "I'm sorry. I didn't mean to sound like that at all. I..."

Her cheeks creased into a wan smile. "It's alright. I guess that's one way to look at it."

But it didn't stop him from kicking himself. The thrill of seeing her on his home turf had his brain unhinged. He was never one for social niceties but this faux pas was unpardonable. He almost wished he'd included his mother in the welcome crew. No, that'd be beyond cruel!

He sneaked a glimpse at her. She was looking morose again. *Damn!*

"Aren't we leaving?" she asked as he pulled her into a bustling airport café.

"Yes we are, but not before you get some java therapy," he said seating her at a table.

A few minutes later Rihaan found cause to alleviate some of his guilt.

"There! Just what I wanted to see." As if by magic, the tiredness had faded from her face after she took a couple of sips of the steaming brew. Giving himself a mental pat on the back, he squeezed in beside her onto the already cramped wall-to-wall settee. "I hope you had a decent journey."

***

"Yes, I practically slept through it," she said a little too quickly, squeezing her thighs together to avoid any kind of contact with him. The impact of his overwhelming charisma was disconcerting enough. Actually, she hadn't slept a wink. The entire fifteen some hours had been spent chastising herself. What had come over her to make such a rash decision? What whim had urged her to pack her bags, abandon her steady stable life and move to the United States? Did she feel obligated because she was wedded to him? No. In her book, he still belonged to Deepika.

'Belonged to Deepika.' Naina's heart sank, but it was followed by immediate self-reproach. Unwittingly, she'd allowed herself to be drawn toward this attractive man who at this very moment was perusing her while wearing his disarmingly-lopsided smile. That wouldn't do. It certainly didn't belong in the book of Naina Rathod or for that matter Rihaan Mehta.

"Let's go," she said jumping to her feet like a coiled spring.

***

"Don't you want to finish your coffee?" Rihaan asked surprised at this sudden display of energy.

"No, I've had enough. Thank you," she replied tersely, hurrying to the exit.

Rihaan capitulated reluctantly. He should have known; she was as volatile as quicksilver.

They walked out smack into a wall of dense arctic air. Rihaan flicked up his collar and watched with amusement as Naina stoically battled the subzero temperatures as they stood in line for the taxicab.

"Welcome to New York," he said offering his coat.

She refused it, instead wrapping her arms tighter around herself.

"Suit yourself." He shrugged and stuck a forefinger in the air. "Feels like snow."

"How can you say that? Are you the…weatherman?" she scoffed in a halting stutter.

"No." He said before shoving her roughly into a car. Her chattering teeth had begun to sound like a concrete drill on meth.

As luck would have it, the cabbie turned out to be one of the ubiquitous South East Asians who owned the NYC cab service *and* who liked to keep his temperature up by carrying on a nonstop conversation, either with his cell phone or his passengers whether they liked it or not. And when he discovered it was Naina's first visit, he treated them to an impromptu joyride around town. She emboldened him by rolling down the window and sticking her face out to gawk wonderstruck at the skyscrapers.

"Do you want your head chopped off?" Rihaan barked, yanking her back inside while the Bangladeshi cabbie chattered up a storm, much to Rihaan's considerable annoyance. But he kept his cool for Naina's sake when he saw her visibly relax; perhaps finding for the first time someone she could relate to since her arrival.

She was smiling and almost back to her usual self when they finally disembarked outside his old brownstone. Rihaan nodded a greeting to the janitor, who informed him cheerfully that the elevator had broken down again.

"She's having one of her temper tantrums," the man called after them, poking his head over the balustrade as they trudged up the stairs; his rheumy eyes affixed on Naina.

But Rihaan carried on up the steps, not yet ready to put the lonely old soul's speculations to rest; he could do with some excitement.

Yet, when Rihaan turned to Naina to gauge her opinion, he found her engaged in curiosities of her own; having opened the door to his apartment she was rapt in the scrutiny of his living room. Seeing her this way, he took the opportunity to step back and appraise it himself. He concluded that it represented a perfectly respectable bachelor's pad though with nothing much to write home about. The furnishings were nominal but sturdy, and utilitarian, and the decor with its muted colors and heavy drapes bordered on the gloomy side. The only indulgence he'd allowed himself was a large, misshapen, overstuffed recliner that frequently served as his resting place and invariably gave his mother a headache—thus effectively banishing her from his lair but not his hair.

The person who was now going to accomplish that tough task was standing in the center of the room looking expectantly at him.

"You're wondering where everyone else is?" he said hitting the nail on the head.

"Yes."

"You'll see them tomorrow," he told her in his most reassuring tone. "They live in Queens, in an independent house, so my mom can grow her own vegetables. This place just happens to be my very own little one bedroom pad."

"I… I can't stay here," she said, quickly turning apprehensive. "A motel, perhaps?"

He grinned. "I anticipated you'd say that. Not to worry. You can take the bed and I'll sleep on the couch."

"No, I'll sleep on the couch," she retorted, though doubt still lurked in her eyes.

"Nope. Not this time. You are my guest. Besides, I'm called in on emergencies. I wouldn't want to disturb you."

"But…"

He raised his hand. "I'll hear no more on the subject. Tomorrow is going to be a long day and you'll need all your strength. Why don't you take a nice warm shower while I put together something to eat?" He carried her brand new scuffed up suitcases into the bedroom, and then hurried out, leaving her alone.

After shoving the frozen *paneer masala* into the microwave and pouring out tomato bisque soup into two large bowls, Rihaan placed a skillet on the stove and turned the heat on low. He then ripped open a brand new pack of Mission tortillas and reached into the shelf to pull out a couple of dinner plates. Everything was store bought, nothing prepared from scratch. It was unfortunate, but that was the life he led. He had never felt the need nor the inclination to cook. Most of his meals were taken in the hospital cafeteria, except on some rare weekends that he spent at the Mehta villa. His diet and palate for the most part remained unchallenged.

Having set the table to his satisfaction, he looked up at the clock and decided that forty-five minutes was time enough for any girl to get ready for dinner. But when repeated raps on the bedroom door incurred no response, he tried the door. Finding it unlocked, he stepped inside.

The room was icy cold despite a healthy fire burning in the fireplace. Puzzled, his attention shifted to the sliding glass doors that led to the small balcony. Sure enough it was ajar.

Cursing under his breath, he rushed over to pull the doors closed when he was struck by a singular sight. His companion of a few hours was standing outside barefoot, clothed in a mere bath towel with her tongue stuck straight out, aiming to catch the first snow flurries of the season.

He didn't hesitate a fraction.

"Have you lost your freaking mind?" he thundered. Then forcibly picking her up, he tossed her over his shoulder and carried her back inside like a sack of potatoes.

"You were right," she cried, unfazed and breathless as he unceremoniously deposited her on the floor near the fireplace. "It did snow and it tastes delicious."

"You are nothing but an imbecile! You'd have frozen to death!" he snapped with barely controlled fury. Then without warning, he jerked her towel off in one movement, paying no heed to her gasp of alarm. And while she scrambled helplessly for cover, he calmly yanked off the bedding and wound the sheets snugly around her, adding his own sturdy arms to the mix.

As he rubbed her back with rough, broad strokes, he felt her shivers gradually subside. But that didn't cause him to let go. He was invariably trapped.

Tugging at the wrap that covered her hair, he watched the damp ringlets tumble around her delicately-boned face that shimmered like gold satin. The large eyes that stared back at him no longer looked terrified. He found himself drawn irresistibly to her generous mouth, wanting to cocoon those ashen lips with his own, thereby restoring them to their natural luster.

Rihaan! A tiny voice cautioned. And it was enough. He thrust her away with a violence that surprised him.

"Get dressed and let's eat," he said, and walked away.

79

A Tough Dilemma

"So what's your opinion? Did your daughter-in-law make the cut?" Shashank asked his wife as she walked into his home office grinning like a Cheshire cat. Having spent thirty odd years of his life in her company and after much trial and error, he could now claim to quite easily guess her moods by her expressions. And this one indicated either that she had struck a very good bargain, or had got hold of some juicy gossip.

Shobha sat down and waited impatiently for him to shift his attention from the vagaries of the stock market to her. "I don't have any complaints; at least not yet," she admitted somewhat grudgingly.

Her *bahu* Naina, whose behavior to begin with had seemed quite unorthodox, even dubious to a certain extent, appeared to have come around. Despite obvious fatigue from the transcontinental voyage, she had complied with all her dictates without a murmur. She had dipped her palms in red vermilion and imprinted them on the side of the house (which was certain to launch a new art deco craze) and then replicated the same with her pretty feet all along the marble entryway much to the delight of her American guests. "I must admit, she has exceeded my expectations," Shobha concluded.

Shashank grinned. Rihaan's wife had accomplished a rare feat. She had stumped his mother. Which meant that she was either a simpleton or an uncommonly shrewd young woman. By establishing an early rapport with her mother-in-law she aimed to free herself and her husband from future conflicts and intrusions, which every Indian daughter-in-law buys into. His son had made a sound choice, which came as a surprise. He'd have expected him to be a lot more naïve.

"Do you think I should ask them to come and stay with us?" His wife piped in, interrupting his reverie.

"Absolutely not. Rihaan moved away to be closer to work and I believe it to be the same for Naina as well. Indeed even on a day like today he had to leave right after he brought her here. I don't want us to make life difficult for them. They need their space," he retorted in a tone sterner than he intended.

"Naina doesn't have to work," Shobha persisted. "Rihaan earns more than enough for the both of them."

Shashank sighed. "I believe she wishes to work not out of necessity, but for her own sense of self-worth. It's a different thing. Being a woman you should understand. Your son has done his duty. He has granted you your wish. Cut him some slack," he said, turning the TV back on thus signaling an end to the discussion.

***

"Do you ever file your nails?"

"No, I don't," Naina replied to the manicurist wondering if she was guilty of an irreparable crime. The woman eased her mind, assuring her it was no big deal and asked her to relax and enjoy the pampering organized courtesy of Mrs. Shashank Mehta.

Naina smiled doubtfully before easing herself back in the lounge chair. Her mother-in-law had meant well. She had arranged an evening gala during which she proposed to introduce Naina to the world at-large. Therefore not without reason, she wanted her to look her best. Hence Shobha had taken the liberty to convert an entire guest room into a virtual spa, complete with well-qualified professionals. All Naina had to do was submit quietly.

She winced as the masseuse worked on relieving the tension in her neck. For a while Naina had been trying to let the various exotic aromatic oils and liniments tranquilize her and put her to sleep, but it was proving to be a vain exercise. If her mind would just stop thinking!

There it goes again!

Last night a near disaster had been averted. Not by her surprisingly, but by him. Why? How? Was it her tired mind or the consequence of his appalling stunt that had rendered her stupid and incapacitated? Or was it just him—his quiet strength, natural poise and his wicked intelligence? Whatever it had been, she had craved his touch with an intensity that scared her. The virtual wall of defense that had served her so well in the past had become practically ineffectual—and would have crumbled hadn't he withdrawn in time.

She shuddered to think what'd have occurred if he hadn't. She couldn't allow such a situation to develop again. *No way!*

Her eyes finally drooped shut. Blessed sleep.

***

Naina tugged at the pearl-encrusted veil of her cleverly disguised sari dress in an effort to camouflage the ample curves she didn't know she possessed. Her hand was arrested and she was soundly scolded. "Stop! You'll ruin it!"

"But I feel so exposed. This is so not me!" Naina protested, staring in horror at her reflection. The dress was so delicate and wispy it may very well have not been there. Spun from the finest of silks, it swirled in virtual folds of blue, green, red and silver around her statuesque figure and revealed her body unabashedly to its full glory. It was enough to suffuse her complexion with a deep shade of red.

Rima, her sister-in-law, burst into a peal of teasing laughter. "You look absolutely adorable. And this happens to be the newest trend." (She'd know as she owned the boutique it came from Naina had learned.) "What's more, Rihaan will be stunned senseless!"

Maybe that wouldn't be such a bad thing, Naina thought with a secret smile. She'd give anything to upset the good Doc's excellent reflexes.

But alas, he was nowhere to be seen. His tall, striking figure was conspicuous by its absence.

"*Kuch urgent aa gaya hoga. (Something urgent must have come up.)* You know how it is with these doctors. Their schedules are so unpredictable," Shobha said as she produced the standard excuse that probably came second nature to her.

But it didn't pacify Naina, rather it infuriated her. It appeared he'd chosen to flee the coup, leaving her to face the music on her own.

"Is something wrong? Don't worry. My little brother will be here soon," Rima consoled her with a sly wink before leaving to tend to her year old son who was tormenting his father—a shy, soft-spoken engineer.

Naina concentrated on training an attentive smile on her face and dispatching, at least temporarily, the frustration from her system, as her mother-in-law proudly paraded her around, moving from group to group. She needn't have tried, because most of the female guests seemed intent on comparing her looks and dress with some Bollywood actress or the other. They didn't appear keen on getting to know her better. It felt as if she had taken on several different identities and lost her own. And that suited her perfectly well. She was least eager to gain more notoriety than she no doubt already possessed.

But there were a few who wished to probe further. The reason was obvious, as she had removed one of the most eligible bachelors from the market. One whom any mother would have loved to snare for her own offspring. How had she gone about it? Or had his heart melted for a stray? The inquiries were direct and brazen and Naina fielded them in a casual spirit. Indeed, she found the exercise quite amusing as it gave her access to a juicy lowdown on her husband that he was least likely to volunteer himself.

And just as she was really beginning to enjoy herself, she was introduced to Mrs. Sharma and her daughter, Renu. They both looked peeved and didn't bother to hide their resentment.

"I hear you are a teacher," Mrs. Sharma sneered.

Naina felt affronted but kept her cool, aware that Shobha was watching her closely. "Yes, I'm an assistant professor of English."

"How awfully boring," Renu pouted her Angelina Jolie lips and reached forward to finger the string of exquisite pearls around Naina's neck. "Wonder how much these cost."

"I wouldn't know. Anyway I couldn't afford them," Naina laughed.

"Of course you can!" Renu insisted.

"No I can't. Not on my salary."

Mrs. Sharma's derisive cackle rang out like a whip effectively silencing the rest of the crowd. "Oh lord! Your husband, Rihaan, is swimming in money. This won't even make a dent in his paycheck."

"I don't believe in spending just for the heck of it, especially on something superfluous. And my husband's money is his alone," Naina said quietly.

"Why not spend his money? It's any husband's duty to attend to his wife's whims and fancies," Renu declared.

"Then you want a lap dog, not a husband." Naina's blunt retort left no scope for any further dialogue. Even Shobha took off leaving her to her own devices. Was she upset? It was hard to gauge her feelings, but Naina was too weary to care.

A female voice spoke beside her. "Hi! I'm Shirin, Rudy's wife. You must be Naina. Gosh! I must say you are beautiful!"

Naina looked up and smiled at a very pretty girl of mixed heritage who plunked down beside her on the loveseat where she'd been trying to make herself unobtrusive.

"Rudy's wife?" Naina repeated.

"I don't think we've been formally introduced." A sleek young man with a flashy smile said, bowing low from the waist. "I'm Rudy. Rihaan's friend, confidant and advisor. We met very briefly in New Delhi. And yes, my wife's right. You *are* indeed gorgeous."

Naina stood up in a rush and flung her veil across her shoulders. Rudy's frank appraisal was making her feel uncomfortable.

But Shirin appeared oblivious to her husband's antics. She chirped on, while sipping her drink. "You are just the girl I imagined Rihaan would fall for. How did it happen? Where did you meet? Tell me everything!"

"Rihaan and I…" Naina hesitated.

"They met through a marriage portal. Nothing even vaguely romantic. The bastard just got lucky," Rudy smirked.

"No," a deep voice droned behind her. At the same instant a large hand sprung out of nowhere and clamped down on Naina's bare waist. She jumped nearly out of her skin. Her missing spouse had finally chosen to show up.

"We…met through a mutual acquaintance," he said enclosing her in a warning glance. "A chance occurrence that blossomed into something very deep and meaningful. Like the meeting of two lonely hearts—wouldn't you agree, sweetheart?"

She shivered, wondering what had gotten into him. Why was he mocking her? He'd always been so affable and courteous until now.

He didn't leave her side thereafter, appearing in a jocular mood; laughing, performing the role of an attentive lover to the hilt; at times appearing so sincere that it even confused her. And his hand continued to linger on her waist.

At times she even found herself leaning against his muscular frame, causing her heart to flutter with apprehension. He was toying with her, keen on extracting his pound of flesh. And if he sensed her discomfort, he didn't show it. Rather it appeared to please him.

The DJ offered some distraction by kicking up the music several notches.

But it did nothing for her spouse's mood. Unable to handle it any more, she accepted Rudy's offer to dance—something she'd have otherwise loathed to do. But she was desperate. Anything to get away from Rihaan.

And then when she saw his seething face, she couldn't resist to say, "Don't you know how to shake a leg, Mr. Rihaan Mehta?"

She had gone too far.

Rihaan pulled her onto the gaslit open terrace. The snow had stopped falling but it was still very cold, making her helplessly cling to him, which she suspected was exactly what he desired. He drew his arms tight around her. There were no thick blankets today to separate them; only the flimsy see-through fabric that served as her only covering and his sleek form-fitting jacket.

She knew he could feel every curve of her body, just as she could sense his every sinew, enough to cause a surge of red heat rush through her. But she didn't break away. She couldn't. He drew her in with an animalistic intensity that she found dangerous yet strangely comforting.

He swung her in a slow circle to the tune of a soft romantic ballad that only they could hear. He was playing to the gallery. People were watching from behind the French doors; gawking at them, conversing in excited whispers.

"What do you think you are doing?" he growled in her ear.

She sensed the antagonism in his voice. He was pissed. She stoked the fire some more. "Having fun. How else does a poor woman entertain herself when all she has is a husband who is forever somber and serious?"

His hand slipped below her hip and squeezed.

She stiffened, gasping at his audacity. But he stayed put. She began trembling again, this time with fear. "You're behaving shamelessly! Get your hands off me!"

"Two things," he hissed ignoring her demand. "A warning… Stop leading bastards like Rudy on. *And* a reminder; the reason why you are here. I don't want anyone to have any doubts about our relationship. You are my wife, whether you like it or not!"

He grasped her face between his hands and then in an apparent surge of passion, bent down and brushed her lips with his own.

If anyone had any doubts, they were dispelled by her red cheeks.

No one, not even his mother raised any objections when they left soon after.

Cold Snow, Warm Honey

Ten a.m. on a Sunday morning and no sign of my alleged husband. And here I am, his alleged wife making myself sick on a bag of peanuts. Naina's hands automatically reloaded her mouth as her brain raced aimlessly helter-skelter only to come up against dead ends as to where he would be.

Not that I miss him, not at all. She sulked, tucking herself deeper into the confines of his warm recliner and stared out at the ice crusted shingles across the street. *Actually, I couldn't be happier.*

He'd snuck out sometime around four in the morning. 'Snuck' was too nice a word—he had blasted out, blundering and bullying his way around in the dark. Might as well have turned on the light for all the din he'd made.

Not a word had passed between them since their public display of affection last evening. Nothing was left to be said. He had exerted his will; pummeled and bludgeoned her into obedience. The truth had been revealed. The cloak of innocence, at times beguiling candor had been shed. He was nothing but a self-centered creep, drunk with his own importance. Not unlike her brother and most other men she'd had the misfortune to meet.

Since they'd crossed paths, her life had been reduced to a guessing game. But his antics last night were the last straw.

Uncoiling her legs from beneath her, Naina jumped onto the hardwood floor and walked over to the window. *If he thinks he can control and intimidate me into doing his bidding, he is sadly mistaken.*

Her face broke into a smile. Things appeared to be looking up.

She had watched the snow fall all morning from a sky as pale as watered down milk. Snow as soft as cotton candy—softer—covered the city. Wiping clean the film of moisture condensed on the glass, she peered outside. The sun had come out at last and what a difference it made. The uniformly dismal grey terrain had transformed into a dazzling bed of white diamonds. Winter birds cavorted among trees whose naked branches brandished a new coat of white icing. Smoke spiraled lazily out of chimneys. People were on the move again, diligently shoveling the snow from their doorsteps and sidewalks. She could hear the gentle *swoosh swoosh* as the piles of powder grew taller, as well as the harsh grate of metal rasping against concrete; and also the shrieks of happy children—reassuring sounds, everyday sounds.

Jittery with excitement, Naina rushed into the bedroom, grabbed her camera, and rushed back to the window. It did wonders for her mood to imagine the photos she'd take. The viewfinder was her writing pad—a canvas where she composed her essays and wrote her stories. She could alter the picture by tweaking the perspective a tiny smidge—a side street could become a boulevard, a giant tree turn into a sapling, or an ant mutate into a fearsome monster.

Just as she was warming up, who would come careening out of the street corner on his bike with a blue winter scarf knotted around his neck but the very person she was trying to put out of her mind? Her arch nemesis—her husband.

Her psyche admonished yet her fingers continued on, defiant. The man was so irresistibly snap worthy!

Click, click, click—her lens—an extension of herself—zoomed in on his long lean length. It lovingly caressed the angles of his face, weaved fingers through the shock of luxurious blue black hair flopping boyishly over an erudite forehead, peeked inside those beautiful brooding eyes, slid across the unconsciously arrogant tilt of his jaw that had scraped her skin and then smooched those warm sensuous lips. Her breath caught in her throat. He was doing it to her again.

She closed her eyes briefly but when she opened them again, he was gone. She heard a door bang loudly somewhere down below. Riddled with panic, she almost dropped the camera on the floor. Frozen, several agonizing seconds passed as she waited for the key to turn in the lock.

Had she been daydreaming? Or was he playing a vicious game? Whatever it was, she couldn't allow him to daunt her any more.

Shrouding herself in a thick parka from the coat closet; not shirking away even though it reeked of him, Naina stepped out of the apartment, then down the stairs and through the front door into the crisp winter sun.

The nameless janitor she'd met on her arrival, tipped his cap. "Careful on 'em steps, Miss. Them are icy."

The advice was timely, preventing an ungainly tumble and perhaps a few cracked bones. She rewarded him with a grateful smile and stood on the sidewalk watching a huge snow plow lumber through the street and a couple of carefree children assemble a crooked snowman.

I can do it, too! she thought, gravitating toward a small white hill when suddenly she was swept off her feet, by a large lump of snow. She came up gasping for air, only to see a supreme specimen of manhood looming over her, armed with that familiar sly twinkle, and extending a not so subtle challenge.

She responded with a bull's eye smack in the center of his chest which prompted a look of surprise and an immediate retaliation. Then as if on cue, the children from across the street joined in, along with a parent or two and there ensued a neighborhood snow brawl with fewer hits than misses but plenty of slides, shrieks and collisions.

Somewhere in the middle of it all, he caught her staring petrified at her blue hands. "I can't feel a thing," she said.

Propelling her back indoors, he hurried her into the kitchen. He turned on the tap and plunged her hands into the sink, firing a barrage of questions at her while she tried her best not to scream as circulation returned to her fingers.

"Go ahead, answer me!" he demanded.

"Answer what? I didn't understand a single word you said," she muttered examining her hands. To her surprise they looked and felt normal.

Staggering back against the counter, he dissolved into spasms of laughter. "God, how senseless you are! What am I going to do with you?"

She glared at him, tears of frustration threatening to spill over. "Yes it's all my fault that I volunteered to come and stay with you all alone in this horrible place! Only to be pushed around, manhandled and abused!"

He stopped laughing. A familiar smile tugged at the corner of his mouth and his honey eyes softened with a tenderness she hadn't seen before. Her heart did a little rumba inside her chest.

"I'm sorry. Sometimes I forget that I'm not at the hospital. But you could have lost your fingers," he said scooping her hands in his. "I'm just kidding." He smiled at the terrified look on her face. "But you do need to keep warm."

She snatched her hands away, they were shaking badly.

"I promise to behave from now on," he said solemnly. "How about we do some shopping and go out for lunch."

She was pacified only a little by his suggestion. She needed to stay on her guard.

Walking on Eggshells

The tiny indistinguishable Greek eatery was bursting at the seams, yet Rihaan managed to secure a couple of seats near a large picture window. He deposited Naina there before making his way through the crowd to join the hungry line at the counter.

She put her head down on the table, thankful for the temporary respite. She was weary, confused and unable to pin him down. Who was Rihaan Mehta really?

Before coming here to the restaurant, he had taken her to a trendy sports store where she was outfitted in lavish winter gear including buying her a couple of jackets (light and heavy), scarves, gloves, hats and boots. When she protested, he'd said, "Would you rather be holed up indoors twenty four-seven throughout the winter?"

He also insisted on getting her a 'reliable' bike, smoothly dismissing her outcry at the price-tag. "I doubt you want to get fat. Besides, it'll get you to work in fifteen minutes flat which is a lot thriftier than a cab." Thereby effectively rendering her speechless on the topic.

Naina's eyes drifted to the window. Just outside a young couple stood in an intimate embrace, oblivious to the world around them. Embarrassed, Naina tried to look away but couldn't. They were kissing with passion, their limbs glued together in a conspicuous sexual pose, yet not for a moment did the act appear vulgar.

"Looks good, doesn't it?"

Naina turned to her side sharply. Rihaan had the habit of sneaking up behind her and catching her unawares, that too at her vulnerable worst. She chose to take him head-on. "Yes," she said, "a beautiful picture of love."

To her surprise, he broke into a wild cynical laugh and almost choked on his monumental gyro sandwich. She glowered at him, her arms folded tightly across her chest.

"That, my dear," he said finally, "is basic biology, as primitive as it gets. For god's sake don't dress it up. Be practical. The guy wants something from the girl and so does she. Am I right?" His eyes locked her in.

She flushed, but had to agree.

"Everybody in this world has a selfish agenda," he continued wryly. "Nothing comes for free. It's give and take. As long as we get that we'll be fine."

She nodded, staying silent. So that's what life was all about. 'Give and take'. It was nice of him to remind her. She had begun to let emotions cloud her perspective. But now it was clear. As clear as cold glass. They were both here for a purpose; to exchange favors and honor debts. End of story. She left the restaurant with a different outlook.

The small incident seemed to resolve the virtual impasse between them. As they were both supposed to be operating on the same side, it was imperative to remain civil.

Things began falling in line. For all purposes, Rihaan and Naina gave the appearance of being in a congenial relationship. To his family they presented the image of a modern young couple in love, but not excessively so. That'd be unrealistic, both agreed. Whereas to the rest of the world they looked like two particularly friendly roommates (they never volunteered the actual nature of their relationship).

She got up with him in the morning and fell into the routine of breaking fast at the corner bagel shop, listening in as he exchanged notes with young Gil behind the counter. His acquaintances became hers and there weren't many. Central park evolved into a favorite hangout. "Its beauty in winter is only surpassed by spring," Rihaan informed her as they strolled through the grounds. They jogged along the idyllic bow bridge, soaked up the spirit of the Imagine Mosaic while a random fan strummed a much-loved Beatle tune. They observed novices and pros as they lurched, wobbled and glided across the ice rink while skyscrapers stood sentinel above the low-lying fog.

They walked and biked the streets, traversing every inch of the city's gigantic subterranean web. They talked, though not much—finding plenty of distractions elsewhere—he with his sharp nose often buried deep in a book and she ever on the lookout for new prospects to ensnare within her camera's lens. Indeed, they became fairly affable outdoor enthusiasts.

Naina held her own in front of *sasuma*, making inroads into her heart by playing the devoted wife who catered to all her husband's whims and desires, *and* by assuming the role of the ideal daughter-in-law with incredible poise and grace. She was pleased that Shobha didn't demand too much of her time—a working woman needed her space—except for the occasional shopping trips and phone conversations during which she coached Naina on the art of keeping Rihaan's attention engaged and his mind kosher: *"Mera Rihu bahut bhola hai."* (*My Rihaan is very naïve.*)

Naina wanted to yell back—*then you don't really know your son!* But she kept her thoughts to herself, instead conjuring up ways of steering the conversation to things far less personal. After unearthing Shobha's singular interest in all things edible, she became quite adept at concocting elaborate menus that became a focus of heated discussion with her poor husband the much touted but fictitious guinea pig.

Naina accomplished what Rihaan wanted her to; shielding him without appearing to do so. Shobha wasn't dumb to not know what she was up to, but instead of being outraged she was pleased—a daughter-in-law who knew how to keep both sides happy.

But when participating in clan gatherings became obligatory, the sharp young pair came up with a cunning, crafted smokescreen. It wasn't uncommon for friends or family to stumble upon the couple cozying up in semi-secluded spots or observe them exchanging secret smiles and furtive glances. Hence when permission for an early withdrawal was sought, it was rarely denied—their recent exploits fresh in everybody's mind.

Yet when it came to spending time alone, it was a different ball game altogether. Rihaan and Naina went to extremes to avoid one another. Conversations were stilted at best, and silences so loud they were deafening. They were making a conscious attempt to safeguard themselves and each other from a force so tangible it threatened to shatter the basis of their existence.

Thankfully for Naina, work brought a welcome diversion. Everything was so exciting and disorganized. They weren't really expecting her—her boss' secretary who doubled as the human resource manager was off on maternity leave—yet she was welcomed like a long, lost friend. It wasn't easy to get familiar with the work culture (there seemed none) or her coworkers (an eclectic collection of oddballs from all over the planet that it felt like she was entering the Tower of Babel every day). Yet when it was time to return home, she cringed. She couldn't handle the strain of having him around, in the same space, breathing the same air and act as if he wasn't around.

Apparently Rihaan felt the same way, too. Because one night he came forward with his hand outstretched. "I'm Rihaan Mehta and who the hell are you stranger?"

Naina gawked at him. The guy was so weirdly charming that she wanted to fling her arms around his neck and hug him tight. But she restrained herself. She couldn't afford to give herself away. She managed a smile. "Just hand me a gun and I'll shoot you."

He keeled over and pretended to play dead and she collapsed on the floor laughing.

It was a rare moment for them to laugh together.

On one unusually warm December night, they decided to have a late dinner on the balcony. She had cooked his favorite *upma* on special request and he had helped by making sure it was spiced right.

"Any thoughts about the future? Or do you just want to keep saving lives and be a hero?" she asked breaking the silence. It was getting easier to do so now.

He grinned. "You got it right. I don't think I have space for a wife and kids in my life. Not that I hate women..." *Especially if they are like you.* "But..."

"You don't have to elaborate. I understand," she said rather bluntly and stood up.

"What about you?" he asked casually, though he was eager as hell to find out.

"I'm not sure. Maybe if I find the right guy..." She leaned against the railing. "But there aren't many around I'm sad to say." She returned abruptly to her chair. His perusal was giving her goosebumps.

"The right guy… And who may that be?" he persisted.

"Someone who understands, loves and respects me. Cares for how I feel. Treats me like a person. There are times when I want a child I can hold and love unconditionally. But I can adopt one, can't I? What's all the fuss about?"

"Yes, what's the bloody fuss about?" he agreed.

They had a wonderful laugh and then got drunk on root beer.

King of Pain

Dr. Rihaan Mehta was taking advantage of an unusual break in his routine. The OR had been taken over by a spate of urgent orthopedic cases, brought on by a sudden bump in the temperatures, which had emboldened the little old ladies to come out of their nests and shatter their fragile bones on the ice.

Stretching his long legs along the length of his office table, he tried to conjure up a power nap. But unlike several of his colleagues who could dictate their circadian rhythms at will, he fell miserably short in the department.

Sighing aloud, he opened his eyes and scanned the decorative cornice that wrapped around the ceiling—a design which always reminded him of the narrow undulations of the cerebral cortex—not unlike the fluctuations of her voice, the rhythmic cadence of her laughter or the vivacious dance of curls about her heart-shaped visage...

"For God's sake, gimme a break Naina! I've got work to do!" he exploded in frustration, then burst out laughing.

Yesterday had been wonderful. Perhaps the most fun he'd had with anyone in a long time. They had wandered over to the Library for the Performing Arts to check out what was on in the Silent Movie Clown series. To their pleasant surprise, they were playing Buster 'Stone face' Keaton's 'Sherlock Jr', which happened to be Naina's personal favorite—one she'd watched several times over and never grown weary off. As a consequence, to Rihaan's delight, she supplemented the soundtrack with her own insane dialogues, throwing him into splits and consequently leading to an embarrassing eviction from the theater.

He admitted grudgingly that Naina wasn't what he expected all girls to be. She wasn't a nag. She understood and appreciated his space and seemed to have a tremendous instinct for his moods and feelings. She knew when to start a conversation and when to leave him alone. She never inquired on his whereabouts. It was very odd to him indeed for a new wife to trust her husband so implicitly.

New wife? Husband? What is making me think like that? In such a domestic fashion? Damnit!

Rihaan stood up suddenly sending his chair crashing to the floor.

"Are you okay?" Anna inquired when she saw him standing in front of the window, a tense set to his broad shoulders.

He swung around and stared vacantly at her for several seconds. "Yes I'm fine. Anything you need?"

"Not really. The phones haven't been ringing off the hook as usual," she said, coming to stand in the middle of the room. "It gets kind of boring when you're not busy."

"Yes, it does but don't jinx it. Enjoy it while you can. I'm sure there's other work to keep you busy," he said with a dismissive smile, not really enjoying her keen scrutiny. Was it because he hadn't bothered to change out of his dull grey surgical scrubs, or that his beard was over two days long?

"Do you have a girlfriend, Dr. Mehta?"

"No. I don't. Anna, I really have to go over this case for tomorrow. It's rather involved." He turned toward his computer.

"Then you must be gay."

His mouth dropped open. *The gall of the girl! She's asking to be fired! But then, where will I find a secretary as good as her?* "Of course not! Whatever gave you the idea?"

"Well…" She shrugged her shoulders innocently. "A handsome man like yourself who doesn't have a steady girlfriend is either a sociopath or gay. Most of the best-looking men out there are and that's such a waste." She eyed him deliberately before leaving the room.

Rihaan was perturbed. He wondered what else was floating around in the grapevine about him. He'd hoped to keep his work free from his personal life. It appeared he had no choice but to expand the web of deceit. *So be it.*

***

It's such a small world, thought Naina, observing her table mates. No matter who we are or where we come from, our problems unite us.

Naina had been getting a late snack at the Soup Spot, located on the first floor of her workplace—a 1920s neo Gothic skyscraper right in the center of downtown Manhattan—when she was joined by two women who proclaimed to be her greatest fans. They introduced themselves to her as her colleagues: Maria, a six foot tall Swede, silver-maned, basketball player who spent her time deep sea diving off the coast of Queensland, Australia trying to deduce what ailed the Great Barrier Reef; and Adamma, a ravishing French Nigerian, whose life's sole mission was to bring the ruthless ivory poachers of South Africa to book. Overawed and flattered, Naina could only listen in wondrous silence as they extolled her achievements as if she was the Jane Goodall of street children.

Naina finally broke out laughing. "I'm sorry but you are mistaken. I've done nothing of the sort. They are just photographs I took to raise awareness. Though I wish I could do more."

"You can and you will," Maria said. "Everyone who comes to *Landscape* does. For instance, take your absent mentor, Farzad Abadi. At one time he used to be a boring professor of anthropology. Now he's among the few

93

brave enough to be reporting from the dead center of the Syrian civil war! Talk about Indiana Jones in real life!" She laughed, seeing Naina's face turn apprehensive. "There's no pressure to emulate him. It's just his way of keeping himself from missing his wife."

At this Adamma let out a sigh of languish. "Don't remind me. Men!"

And then the discussion turned to the usual—boyfriends, spouses and beleaguered sex lives.

Maria's dull face lit up abruptly. "Now that's someone I'd love to share my bed with anytime! And am I lucky or what? He's coming this way!"

Naina looked up and spotted none other than Rihaan striding toward their table with his hazel eyes fixed intently on her. She swallowed hard, trying to look composed as her spoon slipped out of her hand and fell to the floor with a loud clatter.

"I need you to come with me right now," he said grabbing her arm. "Sorry ladies, she'll be back before long." He winked at her agog colleagues and led her out the door without further preamble.

"What do you want me to do?" Naina asked nervously as they rode the elevator to his fifth floor office suite.

"Be my wife as always." He gave her an enigmatic smile before waving her ahead through the automatic glass doors.

She was at once impressed by the aesthetically designed interiors intended to put the anxious mind at ease or at least try to. She saw a couple of patients in the waiting area, one of whom came hurrying forward to shake Rihaan's hand the moment she saw him. Seeing the respect and gratitude in her eyes, Naina's heart swelled with pride.

"Come with me." He grasped Naina's hand and led her through a side door into the back area where offices and exam rooms lined the hallway on either side; then through another door into what looked like a lounge, where a few women in scrubs sat around chatting. They all looked up curiously at the both of them.

"Here's my surprise," he announced, "my lovely wife, Naina."

There was a moment of bewildered silence, and then a bustle of activity all at the same time.

"Oh no!"

"Are you sure?"

"Yes! I knew it! The wily rascal!"

"Awww...she's adorable! You truly deserve her, doc!"

These were followed by a volley of indignant, but good-natured questions which Rihaan fended off as best as he could, while Naina, keeping a bright smile on her face, tried to unobtrusively extricate herself from his solid hold.

Rihaan introduced the curvaceous, young blonde as Anna, his medical assistant. "She keeps my life running like a well-oiled machine, while my beautiful wife happily reduces it to shambles. I couldn't do without either!" He laughed as if at a fantastic joke.

Naina saw Anna's face crumble. Rihaan must be blind, but to her it was as clear as if Anna had written it in bold letters on her forehead— "I'M CRAZY FOR MY BOSS!" Truthfully, Naina mused, Anna could have been the ideal companion Rihaan sought. She was familiar with all his needs and would have adjusted perfectly to his schedule. But would she have been able to handle his aloofness and cold rationality? Would she be able to check her emotions?

Anna will recover, Naina thought. She's young and pretty and probably has many suitors. *But what about me? How will I heal my heart?* She stared accusingly into Rihaan's eyes before walking out.

Something's Gotta Give

The weak afternoon sun wasn't very successful in burning off the thick fog that surrounded the boat. It looked as if they were in a funeral procession rather than a sightseeing jaunt. But the captain was in a great mood.

"The met had forecast a frozen harbor today," his gruff voice boomed over the loudspeaker echoing eerily throughout the dual decker ferry. "You guys lucked out."

Naina caught Rima's accusing glare and she mouthed a fervent apology. How could she have known? Having never ridden the Liberty Island ferry in the dead of winter before? Why hadn't anyone warned her when Shobha had proposed the trip and Naina had raised her hand, virtually compelling everyone else to join in, reluctant or otherwise.

As the boat sped into the open waters, icy wind gusts soon dispersed the gloomy shroud giving way to murky grey skies, though it didn't provide much solace. Naina withdrew her arms inside her jacket leaving the sleeves hanging loose and tried to rub some heat into her chilled bones.

She looked across at Shirin with concern. Her complexion had turned pasty grey. The poor girl was pregnant and sick and the rough weather wasn't helping at all. Abruptly she stood up and lurched toward the restroom. Naina rushed before her, opening the door for Shirin.

After violently regurgitating her entire lunch, Shirin clung gratefully to Naina while she mopped her perspiring brow with a damp paper towel.

"Did you see Rudy anywhere? Where is he?" she demanded, aggrieved frustration clear on her little pixie face. "I know he doesn't like me when I'm in this mood, but he contributed to it! He put me here! I can't go on without his support. He's my husband, isn't he? Rihaan would never do it to you Naina." Then she dry-heaved into the sink.

"He wouldn't, believe me." She repeated earnestly when she saw doubt in Naina's eyes. "I know him well. He's a reluctant husband, yes, but he'll never abandon you when you need him the most. Trust me."

Naina kept her silence. She wasn't so sure about that.

Entrusting Shirin into Shobha's motherly embrace, she hurried away, up the stairs toward the open deck, blinking away the tears that had pooled in her eyes. *Reluctant husband.* She couldn't have come up with a better description. Shirin was wonderfully intuitive. *It was odd what fate dealt out to various people*, she thought, standing aside to give way to those climbing down.

"It doesn't hurt to have another warm body in climes like these." A plump middle-aged woman exclaimed cheerily, hanging tight to her burly companion. "I'm so glad to have mine."

Naina's lips contorted into the semblance of a smile before she continued upstairs. Outside, it was certainly brighter though not by much. Icy cold water sprayed the deck as the boat bucked and rolled on choppy waters. Finding a relatively sheltered spot, she let her vision pan around and found some consolation in that they weren't alone. There were other foolish wretches out there, wandering like outlawed ghouls in a spooky cemetery.

Shaking the doldrums out of her head, Naina instead tried to concentrate on the view—the city skyline, even more magnificent from the bay. And out in the distance, growing more imposing as they approached closer was the Lady of Liberty, a symbol of eternal freedom; of dignity and independence that inspired millions all over the world. *But freedom is such a lonely word.*

The boat hit a large swell making it totter to one side and Naina slid back on the deck. She grabbed for the railing, then smiled when a pair of strong arms wrapped around and held her up. Yes, this was exactly what she needed. Tenderness and support. The notion made her relax. As Shirin had said, she could trust him. She could trust *her Rihaan.*

The grip got uncomfortably tighter. She wiggled, laughing. "Stop it, Rihaan. I'm fine. Anyway, no one's around that needs to see us!"

Then a sudden fear gripped her chest. *No! What has got into me? It can't be him! He is in Miami presenting a paper on some brand new surgical technique. He just left yesterday, beside himself with excitement!*

Terrified, she clawed at the hands as they reached inside her coat, her nails digging into the flesh. The man let out a loud oath before releasing her. Wrenching around, she stared aghast at Rudy, Shirin's errant husband.

"How…dare…you? What do you think you're doing?"

"Sorry," he muttered, not appearing so at all. "I thought you were Shirin." He then stepped back and ambled away.

Naina remained rooted to the spot. She knew he was lying. Shirin was wearing a white jacket while Naina's was charcoal grey. It was a deliberate act of vile mischief. But why?

She'd never felt this vulnerable before.

Rihaan, how I wish you were here.

***

It was 5 p.m. on New Year's Eve. Rihaan, done for the day, walked out of his office and was surprised to find Anna still there. But she wasn't in her standard pink scrubs. Instead she wore a little black dress that accentuated her substantial curves, and she was busy texting on her phone.

He paused by her desk. "Expecting someone? By the way, you look stunning."

She blushed, scrambling quickly to her feet. "Thank you. Yes, I'm waiting for my boyfriend."

"Boyfriend? I didn't know you had one."

"I haven't for a while, but I couldn't go on living with a broken heart, could I?" she asked seriously. But when she saw his eyebrows scrunch together, she said, "Let's just forget I said that. What plans do you have?"

"The usual. Drink a toast to the television and fall asleep well before midnight. I'm a pretty boring guy. Anyway, have a great night and watch out for the crazies." He turned to walk away.

"Gosh doc! Flip out of it! You aren't single anymore. You have a wife; a beautiful, loving wife. Take her out to dinner. Tell her how much you love her. Make it special."

He gave her an odd look. "I'll try Anna. Thanks for the idea."

Later he stood at the bus stop (having opted for a different mode of transport that day) and hesitated.

Celebrations were already underway. Groups of revelers were cruising around, bright-eyed on dope and alcohol, and well underway to getting plastered. He spotted a couple of youngsters with pupils as wide as saucers. They'd be visiting the emergency room tonight and would play a deaf ear to all the advice because it was the New Year. It was another chapter in their lives with hope for change and happiness.

Anna was right. This year was different for him. He had a companion to share it with—his wife, Naina. She deserved a good time for all she had done for him. He observed the streams of customers drifting in and out of the gaily lit Amish Grocery store across the street. It was open late tonight.

The past few weeks in his life had gone rather smoothly. So smooth that it stunk! And it was all wrong, and so messed up!

He could see the change in Naina. Ever since he had returned from the conference she had been ignoring him. It was evident right away. She looked lost, absent in some other space. He missed her laugh, her smile, her witty repartees. Had it been something his mother had said, because when he'd inquired about the family jaunt, Naina had clammed up at once. He had picked up the phone intent on calling his ma and asking her to leave his wife alone. But on second thought, hadn't. The move was bound to backfire. Naina would be condemned for something she hadn't done.

The strain had begun to show, of living with a man like him who was so used to his own company. There'd been a few times he'd caught her looking at him with disappointment in her eyes.

And he felt it, too. The strain of spending each and every day with a beautiful and highly desirable woman in his house. He had consciously adopted a zero alcohol policy, for fear of losing control. But he was by no means an ascetic and the effort was draining.

One night, he thought he heard muffled sobs coming from the bedroom. He should have, like any normal husband, gone to her, consoled her, asked her what was wrong. But he hadn't, afraid of what she might say—that he was the source of her troubles. That he was the problem.

No, he thought. *Naina doesn't deserve a man like me nor a life like this. She deserves a lot more. Much, much more.*

***

Naina didn't return into the building. She preferred to wait on the sidewalk, even though she couldn't keep her extremities from going painfully numb, despite rubbing and fidgeting with her gloved hands and warm boot-clad feet. She was excited. On edge. Rihaan had asked her out on a date tonight. Well, not really. Yet he'd sort of made it appear so in his text:

> **Naina, let's celebrate the first 6 weeks of our 'marriage' with dinner and talk about the future. Later perhaps welcome the New Year on Times Square?**

It'd be the first time they would meet by design and in the absence of his family. Maybe it'd all come to nothing. Still, it was a beginning.

Or had he conned her? She had been waiting fifteen minutes already...

Suddenly he was there, the handsome bastard, terrifying her out of her wits, holding a large bouquet of red carnations in his hand and saying, "Here, take these. The flowers are for you."

"Oh." She was stumped for words.

"Don't you like them?" he asked, narrowing his eyes.

"Of course I do! They are gorgeous! Thank you."

"Well, it wasn't any effort. I got them at a grocery store right across from work."

She regarded him indulgently. Just like him to make it sound inconsequential. "But the idea was yours, wasn't it?"

He shrugged and grinned boyishly. "Guess it was." Then taking her arm, he steered her toward the crosswalk. "C'mon girl, let's not waste any more time. I'm crazy hungry!"

But they were forced to step back when a long black limo drew to a halt right in front of them. A man in a black dinner jacket jumped out causing Rihaan to let out a loud curse. "I'm sorry, Naina, I've nothing to do with this." He looked at her. "This man thrust himself on me."

"Playing hooky with the very person who gave you a ride. Talk about gratitude!" The man in the dinner jacket swaggered over to them.

"Shut up, Rudy. Go and take care of your wife. Naina and I plan to have a cozy dinner together. It's been awhile."

"Has it? How terrible. Hey Naina. You look ill. Has our dear Rihaan been ignoring you?" Rudy sneered.

"Naina?" Rihaan examined her. Indeed, she had turned pale as a sheet.

Shirin emerged from the car pulling her stole tightly around her shoulders. "Rudy, do as Rihaan says. Leave them alone."

99

"Hmm... Shirin don't be cruel," Rudy said, but his eyes were focused on Naina. "Rihaan's poor wife is sick. Perhaps we can drop them somewhere?"

They got inside the limo but it was a quiet ride. Unfortunately, Rihaan's tardy attempts in securing a table for two proved disastrous causing Rudy to magnanimously offer to share his own. Shirin squeezed Naina's hand as she gazed morosely out of the window. They were dropped off at an exclusive Japanese restaurant.

"I feel horribly out of place, Rudy," Rihaan said as he took in the elegantly turned out clientele. "Please do excuse us. Naina and I prefer something slightly more modest."

"Oh you aren't cramping my style at all. In fact, your beautiful wife is enhancing it considerably," Rudy retorted, plucking Naina from Rihaan's side much to his chagrin.

They all sat uncomfortably at a table while Rudy carried on a pompous monologue.

"How was your sightseeing tour, Shirin?" Rihaan asked her with a smile. She looked miserable.

"It was horrible! I hated it!" she cried.

"It was wonderful," Rudy interjected with a broad grin. "And I can assure you bud, your wife had the time of her life. She didn't miss you at all."

Rihaan felt as if he'd been punched in the chest. He looked sharply at Naina, but found her staring steadfast at the sushi chef who stood near their table accomplishing the impossible—juggling an egg yolk.

The broad steel spatula flew high in the air. Shirin jumped and ran screaming out toward the door.

Rudy stood up and went after her. Rihaan and Naina followed. "Now what?" Rudy snapped when she refused to go back in.

"How could you, Rudy?" Shirin screamed. "When you know I am allergic to the very smell of the sea. And I bet you hired the man to murder me. Look at me while I'm speaking."

"You aren't worth looking at!"

"Really?" Shirin scowled at him. "What's your problem?"

"My problem is that I married a girl who is pregnant. I can't recognize her. She looks like a disgruntled hippo. And I don't even know if it's my child!"

"Rudy! How can you think that? You know very well I was an innocent when I met you!"

He rolled his eyes. "Sorry. A pregnant wife is overwhelming. I need to get drunk."

Shirin suddenly clutched her belly and collapsed to the ground. "I think I need to go to the hospital!"

"For heaven's sake! Give me a break!" Rudy yelled at her.

"I think this could be serious. She may be having contractions," Naina said anxiously to Rihaan when she saw Shirin double up.

And even though Rihaan thought the contractions were false he wasted no time in summoning a cab and packing both husband and wife to the closest

ER, which he alerted by calling ahead.

Naina looked on curiously as Rihaan chatted with the ER doc.

"Hi, Ben. How's business?" Rihaan asked. "Not much going on? Don't give up hope. The night's still young... Listen old chap, I'd like you to do me a favor. I'm sending over my friend's wife. She's about six months or so pregnant and is having pains. They started tonight when we were at a restaurant having dinner together... No, she hadn't had anything to eat yet... My gut tells me they aren't real but a little reassurance goes a long way especially if it comes from someone like you." He grinned. "Thanks for taking a look at her. Her names's Shirin and she's got her husband with her. He could do with some psychotherapy too..."

Later, when they were alone again, Naina asked, "So you think she'll be fine?"

"Yes. I believe so. Shirin will be A-okay!" He smiled. "The little drama queen wanted to teach her wayward husband a lesson. Besides, how could I ignore *my* wife's opinion?"

"You're so bloody confident about it all, aren't you?" Naina shot back.

He burst out laughing. "Sorry. I didn't mean to sound like that. It's habit. I'll try hard to curb my instincts in the future, if you wish."

"No. Don't. I like it," she said and blushed. "Anyhow, at least this way we get some peace and quiet."

And sure enough, despite the merrymaking all around them, the environment seemed tranquil as they strolled companionably through the streets, window shopping and getting blinded by the dazzling colors of the night. They satisfied their hunger at an all-night deli before steering toward the overcrowded Times Square.

"Wait!" Rihaan suddenly exclaimed before running inside a small trinket store.

He emerged a few minutes later with a Wonder Woman pin that he fastened to her coat.

"For me?" she exclaimed, nonplussed.

"Yes for you," he replied softly. "For being so good to me. I hope I can repay you for it all someday. Until then, keep this as a reminder."

There were several street vendors doing brisk business. Rihaan grabbed a large hot chocolate for himself. "We need something to toast with. What would you prefer?"

"I'm not thirsty," Naina politely refused.

***

As soon as they entered the famed square, she was overcome by a pulse of excitement that seemed to throb through the entire gathering. She knew Rihaan felt it too, even though he didn't mention it. She glanced up and saw him looking at her and not at the stage where Bruce Springsteen was belting out "Born in the USA." Rihaan's eyes were unusually bright.

She shivered. "You said you wanted to talk?"

"Not now, later," he said loudly before folding her tight against his chest. "So you don't get lost."

She didn't care if he was lying or telling the truth. It was the best prescription he could have made out for her. She rested her head on the soft wool of his coat and closed her eyes, abruptly seized by an overwhelming urge to peel away the layers and connect with his bare flesh. She grew warm at the thought.

A sudden hush descended on the crowd and the countdown began. She watched with baited breath at the glittering crystal ball as it dropped, but her vision was obscured when a pair of sensuous lips came down hard upon hers.

Hot chocolate never tasted so good.

Sweet Love, Harsh Words

Late one evening Rihaan returned to the apartment and immediately stepped back to check the number. He wasn't hallucinating, it was undoubtedly his. The reason for his ambiguity was legitimate: the usually quiet and peaceful place was abuzz with activity, and the ambience that greeted him was most decidedly *desi*—the man of the house; in this case his father, lounged in front of the living room television, sipping fresh *kadak chai*, while the females (his mother and wife he presumed) generated domestic fervor in the kitchen.

His eyes automatically sought the couch and were relieved to see no traces of his bedtime accoutrements.

"My son! Welcome home. Long day at work?" Shashank exclaimed, half rising from his seat.

"Why are you here?" Rihaan retorted, not particularly elated.

"Oh c'mon *beta!*" Shobha cajoled, smiling cheerfully, as she emerged bustling from the kitchen. "Give your parents some leeway. We were in the neighborhood and decided to surprise *bahu* at work and she graciously invited us home. Right, Shashank?" She glanced pointedly at her spouse who concurred.

"Naina is a very smart girl. She understands that I want to indulge in my mother-in-law instincts which you've so efficiently managed to curb. But more than that, I wanted to see my son and his wife playing house for real. *Ghee seedhi ungli se na nikle, toh ungli tedhi karni padti hai.*" (If we don't find a way, we have to make one.) She gave a wistful sigh before heading back.

He followed, intent on making it clear, that just because he'd taken a wife, by no means did it give her, his mother, free reign over his life. But what he saw there brought an immediate diversion to his purpose—the image of his beautiful wife wrapped in a traditional sari. It was a simple yet clever garment worn with a dual purpose in mind—to please her in-laws by presenting them a vision of ideal domestic harmony, while simultaneously promising her husband never-ending conjugal bliss. The lure of the unstitched garment was such that it transformed his already lovely wife into a beguiling *apsara* causing his nerve endings to go on edge thus making him lose control over all his senses.

"The *paneer* is burning," Shobha said, gently removing the spatula from

103

her daughter-in-law's hand. "Rihaan! Stop making your *biwi* nervous." She popped a couple of savory *pakoras* into his startled mouth. "Now leave us women to our work and take your Dad outdoors. I want to air the apartment. The smoke tends to irritate his lungs."

Shobha unceremoniously hustled both father and son out and began throwing open the windows.

But as soon as they were on the street Shashank dug into the inner realms of his overcoat and produced a cigarette. He then proceeded to light it.

"Dad!" Rihaan exclaimed. "I thought you said you had quit."

"I have," his father replied after taking a long drag. "But sometimes I like to smoke because it helps me think."

"Think?" Rihaan broke into a short laugh. "It only helps you die a nasty death."

"You're being exceptionally blunt today, son."

"Yes, but sometimes 'blunt' is what works," Rihaan replied unfazed.

"Alright, then I'll be forthright with you too," his father said looking him straight in the eye. "Something wrong between you and Naina?"

"No, absolutely not. Whatever gave you the idea? Anyhow, I don't appreciate you poking your nose into my personal business. Mom has done enough damage as is." Rihaan looked down, embarrassed, his eyes fixed on his shoes.

"It *is* my business," Shashank remained steadfast. "You are and so is your wife. She's now my daughter and her happiness is my concern. I understand in a new relationship there can be some rough spots, but *you* chose her and it is obvious she chose you. Perhaps you both rushed into it, but it's been awhile now and she's a gem. It's hard for me to believe that you don't get along. I'd love to help if I could."

"You can't, because nothing's wrong. Not a damn thing!" Rihaan said, leaning back against the iron fence, his lips pursed into a thin line.

"You were a wonderful boy who has grown into a wonderful man and I'd also like to say a loving husband. But I'm concerned you're not happy."

"Don't think too much, Dad. It's bad for your health," Rihaan said grinning suddenly. He walked up to Shashank and put an arm around his shoulder. "It's time to savor the toxic waste our dear wives have together concocted for us, don't you think?"

An hour or so later, Rihaan paced back and forth across the living room floor. His father yawned, not the least under the influence of the high carb Indian meal he'd just overindulged in. "Relax, and sit down for god's sake."

"You aren't leaving?" Rihaan asked.

"Well...we are as soon as..." Shashank started.

"No, we are not," his mother said, emerging from the bedroom after a prolonged tete-a-tete with her daughter-in-law. She shook her head. "Rihu, my baby, I can always trust you to be polite. But your wife, she wants us to stay as it's late. And I'm tired and so is your dad."

"She would never..." Rihaan began then stopped short. He closed his eyes and took a deep breath. "Okay. But you both have to make do with just one narrow bed."

"Oh no. We are sleeping here in your living room!" she replied beaming. "I've always wanted to sleep on a couch and your dad has fallen in love with your recliner. And we'll be out of here at the crack of dawn. You won't even know we've left."

Rihaan didn't argue any more but walked into the bedroom and closed the door softly behind him. Going up to the window, he held the curtain aside and waited. Sure enough, about five minutes later, a cab drew up in front of the building, uploaded his parents, and drove away.

Yet he didn't leave the room. Something was holding him back.

On the bed he could make out his wife's slight form even in the faint light. She was sleeping peacefully...or was she?

Not pausing another moment, he slid in beside her. Laying his head down on the velvet blanket of her hair, he spooned himself alongside her back, torso to torso, hip to hip, leg to leg.

He willed himself to hush his heart that all of a sudden had embarked on a mad joyride. Something vibrated annoyingly at his belt. His fingers reached automatically to silence it. Yet the turbulence didn't seem to disturb her at all. She lay still apparently at peace.

He traced the side of her body with the tips of his fingers and sensed her stiffen, then relax again, as he continued undeterred. It was like gently stroking the strings of a guitar, the pleasure defying definition. Feeling more reckless, he fondled the contour of her hip, easing over to the flat plain of her midriff, before mapping the satin of her shoulder with his lips. Desire reared its head like a beast roused from slumber. He wanted her more than anything. He nuzzled into the soft warmth of her neck.

Turn over my lovely lady, turn over please? Let me take you to a place you've never been to.

A loud jarring clamor jolted him nearly out of his skin.

He stared dumbly at the source—his cell phone that lay discarded on the nightstand. *What in hell was going on?*

He grabbed it and rushed into the living room, shaking with irritation, angry at himself for having succumbed to his preoccupation.

"What is it?" he snapped, then listened with mounting incredulity to the voice on the other end as it delivered an urgent message from the hospital.

***

Naina lay on the bed, staring at the same spot on the ceiling, for a long time after she heard the front door close trying to overcome an acute sense of disappointment. She had so wanted him to hold her close and make love to her. And why not? They were both lonely and frustrated. After the kiss on New Year's Eve; that spontaneous, spur of the moment, Happy New Year kiss which had lingered a lot longer than it should have, leaving her breathless and aching for more. Ever since, their conversations had become stilted, consisting of monosyllables and prolonged awkward pauses; looks and heartbeats conveying a lot more than words. While striving to keep each other at arm's length, they'd also found excuses to bump into each other and savor the sensations of *if only...*

Her train of thought was suddenly disrupted by a shrill siren wail which didn't die down but echoed over and over again, steadily increasing in volume. Clamping her hands over her ears, she ran to the window and was witness to a scene like none she'd ever seen. The entire city's emergency resources had been summoned and they were choking the streets in droves, advancing like a raucous, unruly army headed off to war.

What was happening?

***

"I'm sorry, ma'am, but I cannot let you in. We are in a lockdown," the burly cop, standing guard outside one of New York's busiest hospitals, reiterated sternly to Naina, who to him probably just looked like an agitated young Indian woman. Still, she didn't budge.

"But I'm Dr. Mehta's wife. I know he's here. I need to see him," she said peering over his shoulder. Then as soon as she saw the doors slide open, she dodged around the man and barged into the ER.

The place resembled a mini war zone.

"Dr. Rihaan Mehta?" Naina asked a passing attendant.

With a flick of his head, he gestured to the double doors behind him.

"Ma'am, you aren't allowed here!" The tough cop had followed her in.

Just then, she spotted a familiar tall figure emerge from one of the rooms and tear off his bloodied surgical shield mask in an expression of exasperation.

"Rihaan!" she cried.

He looked flabbergasted. "Naina! Who let you in?" He glared at the cop.

"Sorry, doc. We couldn't stop the lady. She insists that she's your wife," the cop said.

"So she is..." Rihaan's gaze shifted to Naina, most likely taking in her disheveled appearance. And she could see it did nothing to ease his temper. "How did you find me?"

She drew the edges of her robe tightly around herself. "Your answering service. They told me. Are you all right? I heard in the news about the massive subway accident and a possible terror threat. I got worried."

"Of course I'm fine. As for this..." he said, indicating to his blood spattered surgical gown "...it belongs to the poor wretch who bled out on the table."

The sliding doors slammed open and a group of emergency personnel escorting a gurney barreled toward them. Rihaan pushed Naina against a wall but wasn't quick enough to get out of the way himself.

She held his arm as his jaw clenched in pain. "Rihaan, sit down. Can we please get some help here?" she called out.

He shrugged her off. "I don't need any help. I can take care of myself. This little mishap wouldn't have occurred, had it not been for you, distracting me like always and getting in my way."

Naina stepped back, clearly bewildered.

"Officer! Kindly have my wife escorted back home. We are done here." Rihaan instructed the cop as to the address and walked away without another glance in her direction.

"This way, ma'am."

Naina gave the cop a blank stare, then quietly followed him outside.

'Freedom'

Rihaan was running on adrenalin, doing procedures back-to-back, until one of his colleagues forced him to go home.

When he arrived, he found Naina packing. "Are you going on a trip somewhere?" he asked curiously. She seemed agitated which he thought was unusual for her.

"No. I'm leaving, as in moving out," she said, continuing to cram clothes into a large suitcase.

"Why, if I may ask?"

She glanced at him, and it only served to agitate her further. "I've overstayed my welcome," she snapped.

"If it's because of what I said last night, then I'm sorry. Don't take it personally. I was just..."

"...venting in a stressful situation?" she retorted.

"Yes," he said, unable to conjure up anything better.

She smiled, but the expression didn't meet her eyes. "You weren't. You meant every word you said. And by doing so you woke me up from a deep sleep. Thank you."

"I don't understand. I *woke* you up?"

"Yes, woke me up, and at the right time too. You'd made it quite clear in the beginning that we were in a sort of business relationship. It was just me, foolish me, who began to read more into it. I shouldn't have. This arrangement won't work anymore," she said looking cool and serene.

"Tell me why not?" he demanded, not thrilled at the image she painted of him.

***

"Because I don't want to get attached to something that doesn't belong to me. Got it?" she said, her voice trembling, as she fought to keep her tears in check. She succeeded narrowly.

He didn't respond.

Naina could see that her words had thrown him off completely, as if he'd had no hint whatsoever. How dumb could he be? She nearly felt sorry for him. He had the same 'lost puppy' look in his beautiful eyes, the one that had proven to be her undoing, landing her in this painful situation in the first place. No, she wouldn't, *couldn't* allow herself to be hurt again. Regarding him calmly, she said, "If you're concerned about your family finding out, don't worry. Your mother has my number and she knows to call me first for anything and everything. It'll be just like before and no one need be the wiser. But we can't continue living together here."

"But where will you stay? You can't afford a place of your own," he interjected.

"Someone at work has offered to share their pad with me…it's not here, maybe an hour or so away. But it'll do fine, I think."

"Then please let me help. I can ask around," he said, not giving up. "I'm sure we can find you someplace more convenient."

"No. I will not accept any more of your help. I don't want to impose on you any more than I have already." She dismissed his offer with a firmness he couldn't contest. "Au revoir Rihaan."

***

Hands thrust deep in his pockets, he looked on as she struggled with her bags, politely refusing any help. She was right. It was a perfect arrangement. She had provided him with an easy way out—a godsend, no less! But why wasn't he elated?

He watched her leave in a cab from the window, just as he had his parents the night before. He snapped the curtains closed in a gesture of finality, then marching into the bedroom, dove straight into bed and closed his eyes.

I'm free. Yes, I'm finally free!

Always on my Mind

B ut freedom can be a mean bitch and Rihaan discovered it the hard way. The evening after Naina left he found himself on the phone, calling the apartment and letting it ring till his own voice informed him curtly that no one was home. Yet the reason why this futile exercise was repeated the following evening and the evening after that, he was at a loss to answer. Maybe it was his subconscious wanting to hear her voice, having not yet reconciled to her absence? He pressed his temples hard with his fingertips. Psychology had never been his forte.

But that was just the start. His subconscious proved obstinately tenacious. Mornings and weekends had him retracing the routes they'd taken together— the neighborhood shortcuts, the surreal vistas of Central Park, the idle rambles through city streets and mellow sips amidst imposing corridors of power—nothing felt the same.

He stopped for lunch at one of the street vendors and ordered what Naina usually did, not realizing he'd done so until he bit into the wrap and was overwhelmed by a burst of delicious flavors. So this is what made them different—his drab, cold winter to her bright, warm spring. He quit the routine altogether.

He tried making *upma*—a way of showing how self-sufficient and capable he was. But the whole thing came out a soggy mess.

Upon returning to the apartment one day, he found a bag on the coffee table with a large box inside, along with a note from her. It said she'd been out shopping with his mother who had presented her with the gift:

She meant it for her daughter-in-law.

There's no way I could accept it.

He opened the box and removed from it an exquisite Banaras silk sari. Naina was being callous. She was reminding him of the folly he had knowingly committed. Reminding him of the day they had first met, when she had sat beside him during the wedding ceremony. When he had lifted her veil, and discovered the betrayal, and she had confronted him with an open face, without an iota of treachery in her large eyes. She had given him every opportunity to walk away. But he had spurned it, instead had gone ahead and tied the knot. That one telling moment had sealed his fate forever. He had willingly admitted her as a permanent part of his life, doing so with all his faculties intact, and then intently had chosen to blame her for it all. He'd been a coward and a rat. The disquiet and confusion he'd been experiencing all along was due to him working hard at refuting the very same fact. *Accept it, Rihaan, accept it! You are as bad as she is...worse!*

He laid down on the bed and pulled the sheet over his head, ashamed. There was no sleep for him that night.

And if that wasn't bad enough, Anna added insult to the injury, when she chanced upon him finishing a hasty lunch in the hospital cafeteria. She held him by the arm as he made his way toward the stairwell.

"Dr Mehta, you look a fright! You need a holiday bad. A nice little vacation with your wife, somewhere far away and warm like the Caribbean or maybe even Costa Rica should do you some good. What do you think?"

He swung around and fixed her with a glare so ferocious that she stepped back. "Don't talk to me about her. You can do whatever you wish with your life but please spare me unsolicited advice."

He plunged headlong into his work and transformed into someone cold, robotic and distant. The kind, caring doc had vanished replaced by a man who was stripped of all emotion.

But he was unable to sustain himself as before. Naina was plaguing his thoughts constantly. He offered to take extra calls, so to spend all day at work and avoid going home. He survived by chugging down boatloads of caffeine and sucking on ice. He drove himself to exhaustion, yet averted sleep at all costs, because when he did lie down, he dreamed of her.

This went on, he had no idea how long, until one day he was summoned by the department head, Dr. Esmeralda Rivers. He approached her office with trepidation, wondering what was in store for him. Dr. Rivers was a woman who had shown her mettle by holding her own in a mostly male-dominated discipline for over twenty-five odd years. Her slight figure and unassuming ways belied nerves of steel and a fiery temper. She had been known to make not only her residents but also her colleagues squirm in their seats. Therefore, when she spoke, you listened.

But the tone of voice with which she addressed Rihaan was decidedly maternal. She took a slow turn around her peaceful oasis decorated in traditional zen style, while he fought to keep his eyes open. "I love coming by reports of doctors who are devoted to their profession, but not to such an extent that they are found nodding off in the elevator! Really is it that bad, Dr. Mehta? I didn't think so," she said turning toward him. She didn't look amused. "By your actions, you're not only endangering yourself but also your patients."

Her grey eyes softened. "Life isn't easy, then why do we try to make it even harder? Ask me. After three bitter divorces I should know. It's an achievement I'm not proud of."

Rihaan looked down at his hands, feeling restless and uncomfortable.

She patted him on the shoulder. "The mantra for success and happiness does not reside within these four walls. I think you know what I mean." Rihaan glanced up and was surprised to see her smiling. "C'mon son, bite the bullet and mend your fences. You won't regret it."

Won't I?

Shrugging the doubt away, he exited Dr. Rivera's office and made a beeline for home, where, after a quick shower, he changed into clean street clothes, and took the cab to Naina's place of work. He had to see her. He was tottering on the edge of a nervous breakdown and she was the only one who could prevent it. All he needed was a glimpse. Maybe that'd be enough to tell him what he needed to know and release him from this insane obsession that he finally admitted he had. Even though it happened to be in direct contradiction to all his goals and beliefs.

Yet once he reached his destination, he found his enthusiasm faltering. He couldn't muster the courage to confront her. What could he say? How was he going to apologize for his abominable behavior?

As he stood debating his next move in front of a large bank of elevators, he felt someone jog his arm.

"Hello there, we meet again!"

He turned to see a tall, blonde, amazon-like woman who looked vaguely familiar. "I'm sorry, but I can't place you."

She didn't appear to take offense. "Yes. We weren't introduced, as you were in such a hurry when you came and took Naina away. We met right here, in this very building at the Soup Spot. I'm Maria, her colleague." She grinned broadly and extended her hand. "And who are you? I've tried asking Naina, but she's always putting me off with some excuse or other. Are you a relative, a brother perhaps?" Her grey-blue eyes were bright with expectation.

So Naina wants nothing to do with me. Can't blame her, thought Rihaan, as he returned Maria's greeting. "No, I'm Rihaan Mehta, her husband."

The woman's face fell. "Oh... I'm so sorry, but Naina has never let on that she was attached in any way. For that matter, she doesn't speak much about things other than work." She broke into a friendly smile, "Do you want to see her? I can call to see if she's around. She's been so busy lately, volunteering for all kinds of assignments, coming in early and leaving late so she can turn them in on time. But you should know that."

"No, I didn't know that," he said. And when he saw her baffled expression, he tried to come up with an explanation that didn't sound ludicrous. "We fought over something petty. She moved out without leaving a forwarding address. The fault was entirely mine and I want to apologize."

She clasped both her hands in delight. "How sweet! I will ask her to come down and you can surprise her."

"No, that won't work." He turned to look outside through the glass walls, at the clouds of steam escaping from the manholes obscuring the Charles

Schwab sign across the street. He didn't want to sound casual, nor was he prepared to reveal the truth. "I fear she hasn't gotten over it yet. I'd rather pay her a visit and do it properly. Give her a chance to scream at me, you know." He winked at Maria and she agreed with a discerning nod. "Do you think you could get me her address?"

"Why yes, of course!" she said and disappeared into an elevator.

It was just a few minutes before she was back, with a slip of paper in her hand. He perused it with a smile. He knew exactly where the place was located. It was close to where his father had bought his first house. "Thanks. And if you can tell me please, what time does Naina get here in the morning?"

"Mmm... Around 7:30, quarter to. I think she takes the subway."

"Thanks!" Rihaan grinned, feeling much better as a plan began to formulate in his head. "You are a savior, Maria." He placed a miniscule peck on her cheek. "I should get going."

She had turned pink with pleasure. "Anytime."

And then she called after him, as he hurried toward the exit. "Good luck! Take a box of Belgian chocolates with you. Maybe then she won't scream as much."

"Maybe." But he wasn't so sure.

Can't Stop Falling

Rihaan wasn't concerned about Naina's screams, not at all. Rather he'd welcome them. What he was afraid of was that she might turn a blind eye and ignore him completely. What would he do then? If she didn't seem to care for him at all? The possibility shot his nerves to pieces.

Toying with the idea of absolute rejection, he lingered at the 86th Street subway station, the one from which he was certain Naina would board the train to work. He stood anxiously, scanning the faces of his fellow commuters. He hadn't dared to go by her apartment and knock on her door because he wanted to first have the opportunity to observe her on the sly, get a feel for how she was doing on her own, without him. Yes he was being a coward, no doubt, but this was the only chance he had and he didn't want to screw it up.

He began to grow restless. Three days in a row and he was yet to spot her. Had Maria given him the wrong address? Had she warned Naina about his intentions?

The platform shook underfoot as the train rumbled through the tunnel. His eyes swung along with the rest of the commuters, as they all watched it approach, and he began to fear the worst. What if Naina had taken ill and she was all by herself, helpless? If something happened to her, he'd never be able to forgive himself.

The doors opened with a loud whoosh. The impatient crowd shifted and surged forward as one, yet instead of joining them Rihaan turned and made a beeline for the stairs.

Just then something caught his eye. It made his heart leap and his legs go weak. He had been a fool to think a mere glimpse of her would satisfy.

***

Naina made her way slowly down the crowded aisle. When she saw all the available seats occupied, she sighed and found a pole to lean on. She braced herself the best she could, resolving to be more aggressive in the future and not while away time in wasteful preoccupation. She tucked her hands deeper inside the pockets of her coat and tried to rub some feeling into them. Her fingers continued to be cold despite being encased in the extra warm gloves that Rihaan had bought her.

And just as one thing leads to another, her mind invariably swung to another cold snowy day in the not-so-distant past, when her so-called husband had dragged her inside the apartment and forcibly dunked her hands into the kitchen sink after filling it with warm water. Then he had put her through the third degree, coming down hard upon her for not taking better care of herself. A film of wistful moisture clouded her vision which in turn gave rise to a vehement self-accusatory rant. Those actions of his that she'd found sweet and endearing were just that. He had been playing the role of a caring doc. A cold-hearted but caring doc.

Naina sniffed hard. *I can't afford to go on like this. I have to, no, I need to stop thinking about him. But the only way to go about that is to systematically get rid of all the things that remind me of him.* She then made up her mind to go shopping for new winter gear come lunch break.

The train took a sharp turn. She lurched forward and would have hit the floor hadn't a couple of strong arms materialized out of nowhere to prop her back up. And there they remained, enveloping her in a secure, warm cocoon.

"Thank you," she murmured with a grateful smile and caught herself gazing into a pair of honey-glazed eyes.

"Don't mention it," he said, his voice reverberating through the tangy mint-tinted air.

With a shudder, Naina looked away to conceal the excitement on her face as a wave of wild frenzy took over her entire being. She closed her eyes a moment and inhaled deeply. *Calm down!*

"Naina," Rihaan asked as she pulled away. "Are you all right?"

"I'm fine!" She retorted too quickly, maddened at her reaction. "What are you doing here?"

He smiled, appearing to waver. "I…"

Gosh that smile. Oh, how much I have missed it. "Yes..?" She prompted, a little too eagerly.

***

Damn!

Rihaan's mind raced. Naina as always had managed to stump him and put him on the defensive. What should I say? *I'm here because I'm sorry.* Sorry for what? For being an insensitive jerk? For ticking her off in public? For projecting on her my own frustrations? Instead he managed a lackluster excuse. "I've some patients I had to see."

"I didn't know you worked around here."

He made a big deal of clearing his throat. "I don't, usually. I'm just covering for a colleague who's down with the flu. You know, doctors fall sick, too." *Just like I am now. Sick as a dog!*

But she continued to look skeptical.

Therefore, in order to prove his point, even though it made him miserable, he got off the train at the next stop. "This is where I say goodbye. Call me if you need anything, day or night."

***

Naina watched ruefully as he waved from the subway station. So it was a mere coincidence. Of course it was. Why would she expect otherwise?

The following day she got up earlier than usual after having tossed and turned in bed all night. She was excited at the prospect of seeing him again. There was absolutely no way she could deny it. Meeting him by chance had helped rekindle the dormant flames of hope, so she took extra care with her dress. Not excessively, *just a tad*, she thought as she propped a bright red beanie on her head. It was her way of demonstrating that she was doing perfectly well without him.

***

Rihaan smiled as he wound through the cars toward her, noticing the added piece of bright color, but also that her lips remained pale and bare. *All the better, so I can taste her without having to pry through artificial barriers.*

Yes, he thought. I want to kiss her and I want to kiss her bad. I want to punish her for breaking my resolve, for making me feel so inadequate that I hate myself, even though I adore her more than ever for doing so.

She wants children, doesn't she? She can have as many as she desires, to chase all over the place and cuddle. As long as she'll let me make love to her not once but a few hundred million times.

She noticed him and was giving him that weird look again.

He groaned. *Damn this life!* He couldn't afford to scandalize her, a hot-blooded Rajput princess, and run the risk of being thrown off a moving commuter train.

So he made do with insipid conversation. He talked about his patients and their problems and what he was doing to solve the cases. In the least, it gave him a chance to study her without appearing to do so.

She listened keenly, impressing him with her astute observations, and appearing impressed in turn. It was indeed quite bizarre that they shared the same wavelength, yet were deeply embroiled in an obscure and irrational conflict...all of his own making, of course!

"How long?" Naina asked.

"How long what?"

"How long can I expect to see you on this train?"

As long as you'll let me. "A week. Till Sunday when I discharge my last patient."

The week passed. He couldn't come up with any more excuses to meet her. She seemed to be doing fine without him, though she did look unduly stressed and fatigued at times. But he wasn't. The self-reliant, almost rigidly individualistic Dr. Rihaan Mehta was no longer the same. For a while he'd been having trouble reconciling with his changing outlook, but now he was sure. The goal post had shifted. He needed Naina, his wife, by his side. He was worried she didn't reciprocate his feelings though, and that made him feel particularly insecure.

He hunted for and bought all the current and past issues of Naina's company's magazine *Landscape* and pored through each one of them, cover to cover, looking for her name, for an article or a photograph. And when he did, he was elated.

He examined the pictures and tried to see her in them, imagine her somber face as it peeked through the camera lens. The exercise only served to renew his agitation. He needed to see her again.

He waylaid her one dreary, icy wet afternoon as she waited to cross the street and yanked her beneath the green awning of a restaurant.

"What are you doing out in this nasty weather?" he scolded.

She laughed, after overcoming her initial surprise and pointed to her umbrella.

Is my desperation that obvious? he thought.

"It's you who has ice crystals in his hair," she said raising a concerned hand.

He mumbled, shrugging off her worrying fingers. "I know you've just had lunch, but sit with me. You can watch me eat. I'm famished."

"Did your mother want to see me? I haven't heard from her in a while," she asked, looking on as he made an utter mess of a blueberry scone.

"Yes." He nodded then immediately shook his head. "No. I just wanted to check on you."

"Why? Are you concerned that I may have a boyfriend on the side?" She smiled coyly.

He stared at her. *A boyfriend? A man...another man? Would she? What's stopping her?* He pretended to appear unaffected though the anxiety of not knowing was making his hands shake.

He discarded the cold scone and looked her directly in the eye. "Are you seeing somebody?"

"So...did you save any patients lately?" she said in a rush, ignoring his question.

He was breathing hard now. He couldn't help himself. "No. I killed one... pronounced him dead on the table."

She drew in a sharp breath. "Who was it? A son, a father?"

"No, a husband at death's door, with a young wife who was not ready to give up, even though I painted the worst possible picture. She'd rather take care of a vegetable. I didn't think she understood what that portends."

"Perhaps it's you who doesn't understand. Maybe you would if you had a similar experience."

"Naina?"

"Yes?" She surprised him by meeting his eyes.

"Are you really seeing someone?"

***

She didn't reply immediately but took some time to scrutinize him closely. He seemed absolutely sincere.

He isn't just a moron, he is also blind as a bat, she thought. *How could he think that anyone could ever replace him in her life?* Even if he had utterly and unabashedly rejected her. Even though he'd never really been hers?

He stood up abruptly. "You don't have to tell me. I don't want to know. See you around."

"Rihaan!" She called out.

But he was gone.

Love, etc.

Naina got up from her seat and ran out onto the street, wanting to hail Rihaan back, tell him that his suspicions were baseless, that she was only taunting him.

But then she stopped herself. No Naina, he can't have his way all the time. He isn't a child. Don't feed his ego. He's not entitled to treat you like a plaything. He has hurt you and you shouldn't forgive him easily, even though you'd like to do nothing better. Let him doubt and suffer; he needs to be brought down a few notches. He hasn't even apologized for his behavior. I can't expect the high and mighty Rihaan Mehta to say he's sorry, but at least he can express it. Or even simply say he needs me.

But he'd never do that. Not Rihaan...

Thus composing herself, Naina headed back to work. She powered up her desktop and opened the article that was to be a part of a feature on the homeless in New York. It was supposed to show her perspective as a foreigner, particularly one who hailed from an abundantly less privileged society.

She tried to concentrate on it, but instead could only think of losing herself in Rihaan's arms.

It was Friday, exactly two weeks since she had marched out on him. Two weeks of chaos, of coming together with a new way of life that had completely occupied her energies so she could strive for a new even keel.

Or so she had thought. At least until Rihaan had shown up and shattered that illusion.

She felt a hand drop on her shoulder and looked up. "Oh hi, Maria."

"What's up, girl? You don't seem to find time to mingle anymore. Whenever I see you, you are busy, busy, busy, constantly on the run. I'm not even able to get a word in edgewise."

"I'm sorry, Maria. Farzad really needs this by evening," Naina said quickly. She was in no mood for small talk. Besides, Maria had grown very inquisitive of late.

But her new friend remained there, parking her substantial behind on the edge of Naina's desk. She picked up an issue of The Economist from the horde of books and magazines Naina had gathered for research and pretended to leaf through it. "Why do I get the feeling that you are agitated for some reason, as if you are trying to escape from something?"

Naina squirmed in her seat, wondering where this was leading to.

Her colleague bent forward and peered curiously at her. "Besides, you've been looking kind of peppy lately."

Shrugging, Naina said, "I just happen to love my job."

"No. Not that kind of peppy, dearie," Maria laughed. "I meant the kind that comes with a new man. Who is he?"

Naina flushed. "I don't have a new man. I don't have any man!"

"Don't play with me," Maria said, arching a dark brown penciled eyebrow. "How about the gorgeous hunk Adamma and I saw you with the other day, the one you were so rude not to introduce."

"Oh, you mean Rihaan."

"Ahh Reehaaan…" Maria closed her eyes and blissfully rolled the name around her mouth as if it was some immoral decadent confection. "What does he do?" she asked dreamily.

Naina told her, fighting to keep her voice even. She found herself growing more and more indignant.

"Wow! A hot nerd!" her so-called friend cried out while fanning herself with a hand. "I find nothing more arousing in a man. Just like Ira Glass. No, even better. He can mess with my neurons anytime. Can you get me hooked up with him? Arrange a blind date or something? My schedule is very flexible."

"No I can't, *I won't,* set you up!" Naina retorted, abruptly getting out of her chair.

"Why not? Not like he's your boyfriend, or is he seeing somebody else? He's free, is he not?"

"He's not my boyfriend. Nor is he free. He's my husband!" Naina said, before turning on her heels and marching away.

***

Naina is fibbing, she has to be. She can't be seeing anybody. She's just saying so to keep me on edge, thought a stricken Rihaan as he struggled to calm himself. But he couldn't bear the suspense any longer. He had to know.

He found his feet spontaneously veering in the direction of her address after work or whenever he could make the time. It didn't matter how weary he was. He would walk by her place, looking for the light in the window of her 4th floor apartment. His heart would gladden when he saw her shadow and he would imagine her going through her usual routine—shower as soon as she got in from work and relax in front of the TV while sipping a cup of hot chai. Then after scrambling together a late dinner, she'd begin working again until around one or two in the morning, when he'd hear her whisper goodnight to him and close the bedroom door softly behind her. He missed their silent rapport.

He wanted her. He wanted to inhale the fragrance of her skin and seek refuge in her softness. He wanted to forget his life, his ambitions and goals, lose himself in the moment, relax and let go. Nothing could be more wonderful, more profound, or more worthwhile than being with her.

***

Late one night, after returning from a hurried trip to the grocery store, Naina found herself struggling to find her keys. The contents of her bags spilled on the floor of the hallway. She heard someone as they dashed up the stairs to lend a hand.

"You?" she asked.

"Yes me. Hi. You are hauling quite a load there. If you aren't careful you might break your back," Rihaan said with a bashful laugh.

"Seems like you've lost your way," she remarked, not looking very astonished.

When she didn't hear a reply, she said sharply, "Did you need me for anything?"

"Ah...no." He stared straight ahead.

"Are you stalking me, Rihaan?"

"No...I'm not. As I happened to be in the neighborhood, I thought I'd stop by."

She smiled archly. "Don't hedge Rihaan. You *are* stalking me. I've seen you pass by a few times and look up at my balcony. And last Sunday when I stepped out to jog, I saw you duck into the café across the street. Then you followed me until I managed to lose you. But when I returned, I saw you sitting in the restaurant again. You can't fool me. I'm a woman of the world."

"All right," Rihaan submitted. "But my intent is honorable. I wanted to make sure you're fine. I feel responsible for you."

"I'm *fine*, and I don't need you to hold yourself accountable. I'm a grown woman and I can take care of myself. I've been doing so for most of my life. I'll give you a call if I need your help," she stated with an assertive tilt of her chin.

He hesitated at the top of the stairs.

After a short while she said, "Do you want to come in? It'd be rude of me not to ask you."

His face brightened. "I'd love to cool my heels for a few minutes, if you don't mind."

She unlocked the door and they walked into her tiny studio apartment. It was somewhat cluttered but neat and cozy, a throwback to when he had accosted her at her place in Delhi—but the situation now was much direr.

Naina went into the galley kitchen and pulled something out of the fridge, then proceeded to heat it up. He stood there, awkward, in the middle of her domain until she invited him to sit down.

"Sorry, but this is all I could pull together," she said, handing him a plate of steaming hot lasagna.

"It's fine. Better than any Italian restaurant." He grinned, tucking in eagerly.

She laughed. "It's store bought and ready to eat. Maybe you're just hungry."

"Maybe I am," he said, carefully probing her face. "You seem to be settling down well."

"Yes, there were a few hiccups as expected but overall I like it. People are nice here and helpful. And I am gradually mapping the neighborhood." She smiled, the expression reaching her eyes.

"I hope you are not out late by yourself too often."

"I'm not. And even if I am, I know the places to avoid. I'm not a child for god sakes!"

An awkward pause ensued as Rihaan gathered his thoughts.

"Naina, can we be friends?" he asked.

"No, I don't think we can," she said, looking stern.

"Naina, please... I..." he pleaded, but didn't finish his sentence.

***

She relented with a smile, she'd kept the poor man guessing long enough. "How about discussing it over dinner on Friday? I promise to put together something far more appetizing."

"Sure. It's a date."

Yes it is a date, she thought, standing in her balcony, waving goodbye to a person whom she'd never seen look so tremendously joyful. She wondered how he'd have reacted if she'd invited him to stay the night.

***

Rihaan could barely contain his excitement as he approached Naina's apartment on Friday evening. This was going to be the night, the moment that would change his entire life. He could feel it in his bones. Even from a block away he could recognize her slim elegant figure as she stood on the sidewalk, waiting impatiently, eager to see him just as he was to see her.

He regarded the dozen long-stem red roses and the box of fine Belgian chocolates he'd bought for the occasion. They were meant to give her an intimation of his intent, one which he planned to build on.

Giving his tie a final tug and his unruly mop a conclusive run-through, he quickened his pace.

He was just a few yards away, when he saw a cab pull in front of the building and a strange man step out. Rihaan proceeded, thinking nothing of it.

But then he heard Naina's distinctive voice raise in excitement. She was talking to the man, and obviously knew him quite well. And then he saw the stranger put his arm around her shoulder and they walked into the building together.

122

The box of chocolates slipped from his hand and fell to the ground with a thud. At once Rihaan was seized by a singular jealousy and mind-boggling dejection. She had implied at the truth, while he had gone on believing in a dream.

Surrender

After pounding the pavement outside Naina's apartment for nearly three quarters of an hour, Rihaan returned home. Imagining another man in his stead had knocked down his self-confidence, leaving him feeling broken and listless. He had wrestled with the idea of banging on her door and demanding an explanation, but then dropped it, not knowing what he'd do if the guy turned out to be who he feared. Rihaan was quite sure he'd react violently and then run the risk of being banished forever from Naina's life—something he simply couldn't imagine doing.

What right do I have to interfere, he asked himself, staring down at the dark alley that ran alongside his apartment. When I've never really claimed any ownership on her, or on our relationship for that matter. I've never treated it beyond a mere contractual obligation, one that we've both mutually agreed upon—though it has grown to mean far more to me. *But has it for her?* There've been some indications, but she has declared nothing with clarity. To be fair, how can I expect any expression of commitment from her when I've never asserted myself?

Though I did mean to do so tonight if it weren't for that…*that pretentious son-of-a-bitch!* He kicked blindly at the low patio table, then cursed aloud as a shock of pain shot down his shin.

Morning didn't bring any solutions to his predicament as he'd hoped. Instead it made it even more warped and twisted. And though he tried really hard, Rihaan couldn't bring himself to be charitable. It was just not within him. When he, as Naina's lawful husband hadn't been given a fighting chance, how could any other man?

Rihaan called the clinic and asked Anna to cancel all his appointments. There was no way he could bring himself to do any decent work that day, given his current state of mind. He was thankful he wasn't scheduled in the OR, as the only thing he was in the mood for was hacking a certain man into tiny little pieces, not performing delicate surgery.

He examined his face in the bathroom mirror. It'd been a while since he'd paid anything beyond cursory attention to it. The striking, handsome features, the shock of thick wavy hair, his broad shoulders and lean yet well-muscled, athletic physique scored a pass. But his imaginary rival scored even less. With his ridiculous bow tie, goatee and beady eyes (even if it was purely imaginary) he looked like a sly fox and as slimy and repulsive as a pickled eel. If Naina would just open her eyes!

He grimaced. One never knew with women; they'd been known to romanticize toads and other miscellaneous creatures of questionable repute.

Could it be a platonic relationship? No, not with Naina. That notion was dismissed immediately. Naina's beauty was such it would tempt even the most pious cleric to abandon his calling.

She was committing an error, a grave error.

***

Rihaan sat at the glittering café bar, nursed his dirty martini and wondered for the hundredth time what he was doing there. He'd been summoned here, to this swanky jazz club in the heart of midtown by Anna— "It is a matter of great urgency, Dr. Mehta," at a time when he could've been knocking on Naina's door, confronting her along with her lover, maybe even challenging the bastard to a duel of some kind.

He wondered if the blackguard had stayed overnight, and if he had, had she let him share her bed. *How in hell could she?! That spot belongs to me, goddammit!*

Slapping a twenty dollar bill on the bar, he scrambled to his feet.

"Hi!" Trilled a familiar voice, followed by a hug that reeked of Chanel no: 5. He turned around irritably.

It was Anna, in hot pink with a neckline that plunged almost to her navel.

"Sorry, am a bit late. Thanks for waiting and making it at such short notice. And I must say you look hot!" she gushed.

He brushed her aside with a wry twist of his mouth. Though he was grateful for having the presence of mind to pull on a wrinkle free shirt and custom tailored jacket that he kept in the office for emergencies, especially as the club's clientele appeared uniformly hip and well-heeled. But he didn't get one thing. He looked at Anna. "Can you tell me why everybody is wearing red or pink? Is there some kind of dress code you didn't tell me about?"

"It's Valentine's day, silly." She laughed giving his shoulder a playful shove.

"Is it?" he muttered under his breath.

"Oh, I'm so sorry! You should be with your wife. It completely slipped my mind!"

His lips drew into a thin line. "Never mind that. Get to the point. Why did you call me here?"

She hesitated, taking a sip of his unfinished drink. "The idea is to make my boyfriend shit in his pants with jealousy. He's been taking me way too much for granted."

"Hmm..." Rihaan looked at her, as if seeing her for the first time.

"Will that bother...uh...your wife?" she asked.

"My wife? No, absolutely not. She's generous to a fault when it comes to matters of philanthropy."

And while Anna wrinkled her forehead over his statement, he mused; *Wonder how it'll affect Naina if she sees me with Anna right now?*

"Dr. Mehta…" Anna began.

"Call me Rihaan." He grinned. "We've certainly been working together long enough for us to be casual with names. So, what did you tell your boyfriend?"

"I told him I was going out with my boss who's a regular dish. He's seen you so he knows I'm not lying." She giggled. "I also texted him this club's address."

"You did. And what does he do, this gentleman friend of yours?"

"He's an amateur boxer and a pretty good one at that."

Rihaan wondered what mess he'd got himself in.

Right then he heard something which consigned everything else to oblivion. Her voice—Naina's—as radiant and light as a summer breeze, that his ears were tuned to detect even in the noisiest of clubs. He swung around on his barstool.

Yes, there she was, looking unbelievably fetching in a crochet blush pink shift that admirably complemented her flawless complexion, and with her silky hair knotted casually at the base of her neck. She was sitting at a table, with a few other companions, but his eyes focused on only one, the villain of the piece, her lover, the buffoon who looked even more despicable at close quarters.

"Let's dance," Rihaan said, standing up abruptly and forcibly pulling Anna by the arm to the clearing in front of the small stage where the saxophonist had gone into a prolonged, flamboyant solo, egged on by a cheering crowd.

Keeping his mouth close to his partner's ear, as if carrying on an intimate conversation, he swung deliberately close to where his wife was seated so Anna would brush against her arm. Naina glanced up, and her eyes widened with the shock of recognition. Then, as he looked on, her lovely face flushed red with indignation, including the tip of her pretty little nose. Rihaan felt a wonderful sense of achievement. He inclined his head slightly to acknowledge her presence before swinging away.

But the very next moment he saw her get up and walk away. He gave chase, after hurriedly transferring Anna over to a stocky young man, who'd been glowering silently at them for some time, and whom she nervously addressed as Ricky.

"Why did you leave?" he asked his wife, spotting her on the sidewalk. She looked frantic.

"I was just bored. And tired. It's been a long day. So now if you'll excuse me." She stepped off the curb and waved at a taxi. It whizzed by.

"You left because you saw me dancing with Anna," he snorted.

She pretended not to hear him and took off down a side street at a brisk pace.

He was equally quick to pursue. "You just couldn't stomach it. You were hopping mad. Isn't that right?"

"Why? Why should I feel anything?" she retorted over her shoulder. "You are *free* to do what you want...dance with whom you like...whenever you want."

"Am I? But I'm sorry you are not!" he exclaimed, grabbing her arm and holding her back before she could cross the road. "That man...that buffoon whom I saw you invite into your apartment? Who's he and what's he doing with you?"

She seemed nonplussed for a moment. "What...? Oh...so that's why you didn't show up that night. I'd been wondering. By the way, his name is Farzad and he's not a buffoon. He's my mentor at work. A very nice and kind man who happened to let me rent his place for practically nothing, because he rarely gets to use it. He was there to pick up some stuff before leaving on his next tour, and he was so excited since he'd get to see his wife, who is in Cairo. But anyhow, I don't think I owe you an explanation." She glared fiercely at him. "When I know that you don't care about what I do with my life or who I choose to spend it with."

"I do care." He gripped both her arms, compelling her to look into his eyes that burned with a flame she'd never encountered before. "I care because you're my wife and you belong to no one else but me." He jerked her closer. "Only me."

And then his lips found hers.

She struggled, but when he didn't let go, she gave up. Letting out a long relaxed sigh, she wrapped her arms around his neck. Naina leaned into him, keeping her body flush against his. He supported her weight, holding her in a snug embrace, as they continued to kiss while Anita Baker crooned out of hidden speakers on the sidewalk.

Their coming together seemed inevitable.

He whispered into her ear, "We are just two blocks from my place."

She couldn't tell how, but in a matter of moments they were at his door.

He discarded his jacket onto the floor, undid his belt and flung it across the hall, then proceeded to fumble with the buttons of her overcoat. She came willingly to his aid. His ardent kisses were all the encouragement she needed.

Soon she was lying on his cramped bed. He turned on the bedside lamp, then holding her face between his hands, probed deep into her eyes. Her thoughts seemed to match his.

He rolled his thumb over her mouth. Her lips parted, and without wasting a moment he dived in and lost himself. He kissed her neck and her throat. He felt her body through her clothes, and then without the garments.

He didn't want to stop. He couldn't.

He wanted to pull her inside, absorb her, make her an inseparable part of him. No need of his had ever been more urgent.

Though medical school had taught him all he needed to know about female anatomy, he'd had no real experience with women except for the near disaster in high school. Naina made it easy. It seemed as natural as could be with her. He'd never come across a woman more beautiful or sensual; even more so than the nude he'd attempted to draw during the summer art lessons that Rudy had persuaded him into attending, the woman who'd been responsible for giving him a few sleepless nights.

It was Naina's first time, too, he realized. Shy at first, she slowly lost all her inhibitions and participated wholeheartedly in the act of lovemaking.

He followed his instincts and they all seemed perfectly right as she moaned and writhed and arched under him.

He paused for air, having reached the end of his tether. "Naina…?"

***

Naina opened her eyes hearing the low, strangled growl of anguish. Desperation was clearly evident in Rihaan's glazed-over eyes, in the primal expression on his face, in his steamy breath and the rough pressure of his hands marking her hips. It didn't frighten her, rather made her flesh vibrate and tingle with an equally frenzied craving.

She surrendered completely and her body bucked back in a shock of pain. Her cry was cut short by his deep, bruising kiss.

She whimpered, holding him tight, as he thrust deeper, knocking her head against the bed frame. She cried out his name as he came in a rush.

Her tears made him look at her in anxious inquiry, but she smiled. It was all right.

They were going to be all right.

Ache

The last vestiges of sleep drifted away. Rihaan blinked awake, as broad shafts of sunbeam warmed his naked skin and that of his companion, who was in a similar state of undress.

He remained still, his head resting on her silky mane, relishing the moment. No day could dawn more sublime than the one when he woke up in the arms of his beloved, especially someone who has given up her all to him.

She was a work of art, a masterpiece made only for his exclusive viewing. He held her close. She felt so good beside him.

Soft breath fanned his chest. Hunger stirred again.

Thumbing the curve of a golden breast, he dunked his tongue into the salty hollow of her throat. It sent a low moan rumbling up her neck. He grunted, "Is it a good morning?"

"It's a wonderful morning," she retorted, rooting brazenly for his mouth.

They kissed—the simplest, purest, most profound expression of love. Hearts reaching out, bodies melting into one another, all the angst and turmoil, emptying, purging, and then refilling with love.

With her hips crushed against his, she tasted the full brunt of his disease. And with her air sucked dry, she quivered like a giddy puppet in his arms. He had his way with her flesh, toying and teasing, laying out extensive trails of moist heat. She gasped, in shock and delight, and lay panting, like a wild animal in heat, as her brain got pulverized with sensations of the most alien kind. He cavorted inside her. It was love at its most raw; a heady mix of perspiration, body fluids, entangled limbs, and living dreams.

***

Sweet exhaustion. Blessedly sweet and all the more decadent as it was sinful. Yet she felt no remorse. Not even a tinge.

It was close to noon, but Naina wanted to remain in bed and savor his lingering presence while it was still warm and fresh. But after a few more moments had passed, she sighed and got up, and took a slow turn around the apartment, naked except for a sheet, hugging *her Rihaan,* her husband and lover to herself, and the memory of the passion they'd shared.

Skimming her fingers over the counters and shelves, she gazed out of the window at the bright, sunny skies. Everything looked and felt so different today, so welcoming and warm. And one night had changed it all. It had given her all that she'd ever wanted and more; a man to love, a sense of permanence.

She found a stack of magazines on the coffee table. The one on top lay open to the page that displayed her latest work. Her eyes welled up with unshed tears. "My darling. You may wish to call it biology. But I will call it love, because that's what it is."

'We'll bring back your stuff. You're staying with me and never leaving again. Got it? Can't wait for tonight,' he had said before kissing her goodbye.

She closed her eyes, sliding deeper into his recliner, and shuddering at the notion of being in his arms again. "I can't wait either."

But the relative peace was disturbed by a repetitive buzzing sound.

She discovered it to be his cell phone. He had forgotten it in his hurry to leave. She smiled and shook her head. *Poor Dr. Mehta, your wife has completely messed up your equilibrium.*

***

"Hi Mrs. Mehta! Can you excuse me for a moment? I just need to forward this call. The phones have been ringing off the hook since morning," the receptionist at Central Neurosurgical Associates said as soon as she saw Naina walk into the office.

Observing the flurry of blinking lights on the terminal, Naina smiled and nodded sympathetically. Mrs. Mehta—she'd never been addressed as such before. Might as well get used to it.

After a moment, the receptionist turned back to her. "Yes, how may I help you?"

"Uhm. Dr. Mehta, is he available?" Naina asked.

"He's in the OR, assisting the chief. The case was supposed to be his, but since he didn't get here on time, the chief had to be called in. Do you know what happened?"

"I…I'm afraid I don't," Naina said feeling perturbed.

"He was also on call last night," the receptionist continued, now in full flow. "He didn't respond to any of his pages. The chief had to cover for him. He had to field calls from angry patients, as well as frustrated hospital staff. This morning he even attended a long meeting with the hospital administration, all because of Dr. Mehta."

Oh no! Naina screwed her eyes shut.

The receptionist's chubby round face looked bewildered. "It has never happened with him before. And all of us here are having a tough time believing it's all true. Few are more dedicated and conscientious than Dr. Mehta. Was he incapacitated in any way? Was he sick? He should have at least notified us."

"No, yes… He was sort of incapacitated…" Naina admitted recalling Rihaan tossing away his pager while carrying her into the bedroom last night. She had thought nothing of it at the time, being in way too much of a hurry to give herself to him.

"We did try contacting him by phone. But there was no response."

Naina flushed pink. Of course there wasn't any response. Their passion had reached such thundering heights enough to drown out all extraneous sounds.

"And, he was late for surgery."

Naina pursed her lips as she recollected pulling Rihaan back when he was about to slip out of bed that morning. He had resisted, albeit very slightly, before giving in. Yes, *she* had incapacitated him.

"Dr. Mehta may be in for some trouble. The chief, he didn't say anything, but he was wearing his mad face."

"I'm so sorry you had to go through so much trouble," Naina murmured.

The woman smiled. "It's not your fault. These things happen sometimes. They are unavoidable. Let's be happy that a major disaster was averted. That'd have been terrible indeed."

Naina turned away and walked out slowly in a daze, unable to check the flood of tears that had begun streaming down her face. *I'm sorry Rihaan, my darling, I'm so very sorry.*

Torn

Spring was in the air. Soon the cherry blossoms would be in resplendent display all over the city. The warblers were already creating a ruckus in the trees and the squirrels and chipmunks were running amuck in the backyards and open spaces. New Yorkers were out and about, taking advantage of the brilliant sunshine, flaunting their brand new shorts, Ts and tank tops, even though the temperatures barely grazed 50. Never mind, they said, it was the spirit that mattered. And the spirit was so strong that it touched everyone, from the naïve infant, to the old and infirm, and it was so pervasive that it seeped into the tiniest nook and recess of every dwelling; all except for one, where winter and its attendant gloom still prevailed unscathed.

Rihaan sat in the living room of his apartment with the curtains drawn and his weary eyes closed, wishing for some kind of miracle, invoking all the various supernatural forces out there to bequeath him with at least a few hours of blessed sleep. Odd for a man who prided himself on his mental agility, to pray for senselessness. But he was beat. Wiped out. His mind had been operating on overdrive for over six days now without any respite in sight. It was as if he'd been confronted with a particularly confounding case, that he, as a physician, was supposed to solve, but with the key clue missing. And it was driving him insane as he asked himself over and over again: *Why? Why had she left?*

Six days ago, on the night after that fateful Valentine's, he had made his way back to his apartment—late. He knew Naina would be getting edgy. He had asked her to wait for him so they could go to her place together to get her things. He planned to apologize profusely for his rude behavior. And to supplement it, he was going to present her with a bouquet of fresh spring flowers as well as a sumptuous take-out from their favorite restaurant.

No cooking tonight my darling, just making love...wild inebriated love. As for your stuff, we'll get them tomorrow. He was sure she'd understand.

Prior to leaving work, he'd had a long talk with his chief. The man had taken him aside—Rihaan had been preparing all day for it—and demanded an explanation for last night's fiasco. And Rihaan, not knowing what else to say, had told him the truth.

But instead of reprimanding him and throwing him out of the practice or giving him the dressing down he deserved, his boss, to Rihaan's surprise, had simply smiled.

Perhaps, Rihaan thought as he mulled over it, the older, more experienced man had dealt with something similar in his life. He let him off with a mere rap on the knuckles and then switching gears, had thumped him on the back, even giving him a couple of days off. *What bloody luck!*

But when he didn't find Naina in the apartment, all the exhilaration he felt was blown away. And when none of his calls or texts seemed to go through, he struck out, on a mad dash across town to her place, triggered by a sense of tremendous urgency, as the letter she'd left on the kitchen counter made no sense at all. It read like some cryptic puzzle.

She'd written—

Rihaan,

I don't know how to say this. I've pondered over it for a long time and this is how I feel. I don't think it's a good idea for us to move in back together. You've always said how much you value your independence...well, so do I. I'll get in your way and you'll get in mine. It's bound to happen, no matter how hard we try. We shouldn't rush to fritter away the rest of our lives, just on the basis of one night of passion. Let it remain a sweet memory. As for our marriage, I'm sure you will agree that it was an unfortunate accident.

Goodbye,

Naina

The sucker-punch delivered by the cold and calculating letter had left him nearly breathless. But not for one moment did he believe those words. They weren't at all like the woman he'd come to know; who, that very morning, had flipped over his chest and admonished him playfully when he'd expressed the need for a larger bed.

"No Rihaan, we don't. Because I want every excuse to hold you close." She wouldn't have said so if she hadn't meant for them to be together. The candor in her eyes was undeniable. Then what had happened in the interim?

"Never mind!" he told himself. "Whatever it is doesn't matter, because when I see her, I'm going to drop down on my knees, beg for her forgiveness, pour my heart out, declare my affection, clear all the differences, talk about the future, our lives, children, pets, etcetera. I'll reassure her that she can rely on me; I'll be there through thick and thin. I'll never let her down, or leave her to face the world on her own. She can nag me as much as she pleases. I wouldn't mind at all...at least I'll try my best not to."

He was sure they could hash out a reasonable agreement. Naina was by no means an idiot and neither was he.

Thus galvanized, he jumped out of the car as soon as it drew to a halt and sprinted up the stairs, taking them three at a time, then knocked hard on her door, shouting, "Naina open up! It's me, Rihaan! Get off your high horse and stop whining like a baby! I know that you love me and guess what, I love you, too."

Silence.

"A lot!"

More silence...

"Oh c'mon already! Enough's enough."

But as the minutes ticked by, the affected bravado was supplanted by grave anxiety and the demands by desperate cajoling. He sank down to the floor, head down between his knees, puzzled and bewildered, unable to understand what in the world was going on, or what he was being punished for.

He wasn't sure how long he sat there. He must have fallen asleep for the very next thing he knew, it was 4 a.m., when he heard the loud THWACK of the newspaper landing in the neighbor's front yard.

Cursing and berating himself loudly for precious time lost, he made his way back across the East River. But instead of going home, he headed straight to her workplace where he camped outside the building waiting for some sign of activity.

In the meantime, he analyzed, reanalyzed, and worried about her.

Perhaps she was put off by his selfishness. Yes, he was an incredibly self-centered guy. She was scared by his intensity. His possessiveness made her nervous, he could see that. He was going to try his best not to encroach on her space. She could dictate the terms of their relationship. He was willing to give up anything as long as she didn't insist on them living apart, because now she was a part of his life—she was his missing link. And he wanted her in it at all costs.

But when the office opened, he discovered that she'd left yesterday as part of a group touring the war zones of the Middle East and Arab states over a span of several weeks, the middle-aged secretary reeled out as if she was reading the six o'clock news. Naina had been the last to join though, taking the place of someone who had dropped out at the last minute.

And when he inquired about the itinerary, the woman pleaded ignorance. The trip was for the most part an unplanned one, not atypical for journalists visiting foreign countries who often find themselves at the mercy of their local contacts. And the same held true for communication as well.

"Usually they'll call me first, but only when and if they choose to. Can't force them, they are all adults, you see," she said with a knowing smile.

"Yes they are," he agreed. "Independent adults."

The woman, appearing to sense his unusual level of agitation, promised to call him as soon as she had more information.

On the way out Rihaan stumbled upon Maria. She appeared shocked by his despondent appearance.

He asked her if she had any idea about why Naina could have left.

"When I saw her last she was very happy that we were going to be together." He didn't tell her about the note.

She didn't look very concerned. "You know that she loves you?"

"Yes."

"And you her?"

"Of course!" *Though I haven't declared it in so many words.*

Her smile was genuine. "Then trust in your love. Support her. Sometimes there are things we've to deal with on our own, things that need time and shouldn't be hurried. But ultimately everything clears up."

But nothing had cleared up, despite nearly a week having gone by.

Rihaan sighed, *If only I knew why.*

He was startled out of his reverie by a loud knock on the door. It was his mother, the last person he wished to see.

"What's with that beard and long hair? You look like a hippie, Rihaan. I hope you're not smoking hashish."

"Why didn't you call me first?" he asked as she ducked past him into the hall.

"Because you would make some excuse as always not to see me. Anyway, my business is with my *bahu*. Where is she and why isn't she answering my calls. I want her to organize a grand Sai festival at our house."

He rolled his eyes. "She isn't taking your calls because she is not here. She's out on a tour."

"Tour? For whom?"

"Work. She'll be gone...for several weeks."

Shobha didn't look convinced. "Did she inform you?"

"Yes, of course she did." He avoided her eyes.

"Then why do you look so miserable? And just look at this place! When did you start reading international newspapers?" she demanded, catching sight of the dailies strewn everywhere. "What happened to your diet? Is this all you're eating?"

She held up a power bar wrapper. "I don't understand. You weren't like this before. What's wrong between you two? You're keeping something from me."

"There's nothing wrong."

"There is something fishy, about your marriage, and about Naina. I can feel it. If you don't tell me now, I'll call Rudy and find out. He's your best buddy, isn't he?" She began rummaging in her purse for her phone.

"*Was.* He was my best buddy. Not anymore," Rihaan said stopping her. "I will tell you everything you need to know."

And he did...about the whole snafu, stressing on his own role in it; about his makeshift marriage with Deepika and then with Naina (sparing the sordid details) in a most lucid and succinct way.

His mother listened quietly, her expression waffling between shock, dismay and disbelief.

"And that's that," he said, feeling a tremendous weight lift off his shoulders.

"Oh my poor Rihu. How you've suffered!" she cooed, rushing to his side and clutching his head to her bosom. "Good riddance!"

He disengaged himself. "What did you say?"

She smiled. "I said good riddance. I knew it from the beginning. She looked too good to be true and I was right. She's nothing but a gold digger and a sly opportunist. She used you to get here. She and her friend, Deepika, plotted it somehow. Anyhow it's over. Forget about her and start over. She's not even your wife."

Rihaan was taken aback. He couldn't believe his mother had harbored such thoughts. "I can't forget her. She *is* my wife. And it's legal. I just got back the annulment papers I'd mailed to Deepika weeks ago, signed and sealed."

"Then divorce her." His mother seemed unmoved. "Our family solicitor will draw up the papers. My son, I assure you, there'll be no trouble." She stroked his face.

He pushed her hand away. "For godsakes, Mother, don't you get it? I love her! Besides, marriage is not a ritual or a sheet of paper, it's a meeting of hearts." He couldn't believe he was repeating Naina's words, but he was determined to tell his mother how he felt. "A convergence of two souls and I've lost mine to Naina. It's just a matter of time before we'll be together again. Now please leave me alone!"

***

Several days later...

The secretary at *Landscape*, true to her word, kept Rihaan updated regarding Naina's movements as often as she could. She also provided him with a number that he could call in order to get through to her, but cautioned that it was likely to become nonfunctional without notice— 'the fickleness of modern communication,' she'd said.

He found himself stuck in an unusual predicament, a situation that offered no simple or straightforward solutions and it was frustrating to say the least. Immediate instinct clamored for prompt action—call and ask her to come back. But thinking it over made him hesitate.

He tried composing several letters where he declared his affection and attempted to reason with her, but then chose not to mail them. He didn't want to clip her wings or stifle her, neither did he want to impose his will upon her or restrict her independent spirit—just as he wouldn't want his own restricted. All he wished to convey was that his affection was real and unconditional, even though he was certain there was some other reason behind her leaving. He wanted to let her know he would be here, waiting, and that she could put her trust in him.

Finally, he wrote a letter telling her exactly where he was coming from. Leave her in no doubt whatsoever. He handed it to the secretary who assured him it would reach Naina.

His restive spirit settled to a degree, he walked back to work, mulling over what the woman had just told him: "Naina is in Kabul, and she'll be there for several weeks."

An idea began to take root in his mind and the more he thought about it, the more plausible it seemed. *I should go there myself. Not to ask her to come back, but to stay. To be with her, observe her work and to work myself. There's bound to be no dearth of opportunities available.*

He became excited as he thought more. *I can volunteer my services at the local hospitals and share my expertise. Perhaps even set up or help improve their Neurosurgical departments.* It was a thrilling prospect and he was sure he'd be welcomed with open arms.

He had confined himself so long within a very narrow definition. Only Naina had given him a glimpse of what life could really be like; here was an opportunity to learn more. He wanted to see the world through her eyes, delve into her intellect, and meet her on neutral ground. It would do him a world of good to expand his own knowledge, too, and may also help them build a firmer foundation for their relationship. A smile tugged at the corner of his mouth. Finally, there was something he could look forward to.

Infidelity of Hope

Kabul

Naina tucked her camera away in her satchel along with the several packs of gum she'd bought from a little boy on the street. Then fixing the black hijab around her head, she started on the long trek back to the hotel where her tiny group was located with several other journalists. She had spent most of the morning taking aerial shots of the city from a vantage point she'd found yesterday during her visit to the refugee camps. She had come prepared to spend most of the day there, hoping to capture the harsh landscape in the soft warm tones of dusk, but her intentions were interrupted by a familiar cramp in the lower reaches of her abdomen signaling the onset of her monthly cycle.

Thankful she had chosen to wear a long, shapeless dark shirt and loose black pants, she paused as another spasm gripped her, much more painful than she was used to. Or was she perceiving it to be so due to the state she was in? Feeling the disappointment that she wasn't pregnant, which had been her only hope for consolation.

She fought back a sob. *Naina, stop, it's too late now. You have to learn to live with it!*

It had been hard, very hard, the pain so sharp, almost visceral in its intensity. And she had struggled with it, with her need to go back. Rihaan might come to detest her after reading the callous note she left for him. But that maybe just as well. She'd hate it if his career was ruined because of her. It was not just a job for him, it was a gift he had, a wonderful blessing that'd benefit so many. It'd be a crying shame for him to lose it.

Yes, she had been a wimp for leaving without meeting him and telling him the lie to his face. Because she couldn't, just the sight of him would have made her weak and broken her resolve. She would have forgotten everything she wished to say. She loved him so much it hurt. That was the reason why she had run away. She couldn't bear to stay in the same town without wanting to see him every day. Her heart, her body would crave it constantly.

Their love making, her last memory of him—a parting shot. Every act as fresh as yesterday and so beautiful. The sorrow she felt was immense. Almost every night she had cried herself to sleep trying to fill the deep bottomless pit that had formed inside her. Yet, it seemed like he had accepted their separation without reservations. She hadn't heard a word from him.

Her only distraction and consolation had been her work, into which she plunged with gusto.

Their small group of eight journalists had flown to London and then to Turkey, where they had split into teams of two and three before dispersing in various directions. She, along with her friend, Adamma, and a male journalist, Adam (Maria had chosen to stay behind), had proceeded to Kabul. Why she had chosen to come to this place, Naina wasn't exactly sure. But she recalled a certain curiosity after hearing stories from her father when she was very young (when he was still fond of her) about *kabuliwallahs*—hefty, tall and imposing tradesmen of a very genial temperament who were particularly fond of children though were rarely seen around anymore. Ever since, she had nourished hopes of seeing a real live *kabuliwallah* one day and a better opportunity couldn't have presented itself.

Naina paused at a street corner to take some pictures of a shop selling bales of colorful cloth and yarn. It was packed with haggling customers, mostly female. The landscape here was similar to her homeland yet different. There was a definite sense of déjà vu, especially when she saw the chaos on the city streets, as traffic of all kinds vied for space on the narrow roadways and in the permanent din created by the honking and the loud blare of afghan songs. One had to be on constant watch or run the risk of being mowed down.

Also familiar were the low brown treeless hills and the mud-walled huts, but not the uniform-like *burqas* that almost all the women wore.

After her arrival, Naina was inevitably drawn toward her favorite subject—children. And what she saw appalled her. Because the kids not only had to fend with the squalor and abominable living conditions that prevailed in the refugee camps as well as the poor tenements, but also had to work and forage daily for food. And these were not just street children but those with parents, too. They were out washing cars, combing the garbage for paper and rags, scrubbing dishes, selling trinkets and gum in the streets, and the girls suffered the hardest as always.

But it's not as if the parents don't care, Naina thought, *they do. They are just too bogged down by poverty, by war, by misogynistic pressures and fears of retaliation and lack of education.*

She was trying hard to get the adults, especially the women, to open up but success was slow because all foreigners were eyed with suspicion. However the children were like children everywhere—innocent, trusting, carefree and with dreams of a bright future.

She adjusted her black headscarf. It had taken awhile to get used to, but now she knew how to keep it in place without fiddling with it. And even though her appearance and coloring was very similar to the natives and should have offered her a sense of anonymity, she was plagued by a constant feeling of insecurity, of being discovered and punished for something she hadn't done. Of how she used to feel as a child, being picked on and admonished for anything and everything. And when she dared to defend herself, she would be declared too *haazir jawab* and impudent and be soundly reprimanded. *"No boy from a good family will be ready to marry a girl like you."* Naina broke into a hysterical laugh at the memory which prompted quite a few heads to turn her way.

Finally, having safely made it back to the hotel, she ducked into a tiny room that served as their makeshift nerve center. Adam, who was sitting at his desk, looked up and smiled. He had the most startling pair of blue eyes. He was going through the mail. "Were you out visiting Zeenat again? Seems like you've found a permanent fan in her."

Naina smiled. Zeenat was a little girl who'd found a special place in Naina's heart. An orphan at seven, having lost her parents and brothers to war, she lived with her uncle, his wife and six cousins in a one room tenement in one of the most squalid sections of the city. As an unwanted child, besides dealing with what most children generally had to, she faced further abuse and the danger of being bartered as a child bride to repay unpaid debts of her parents'. Yet, despite a horrendous future, the young girl displayed a bright outlook.

"Things will get better," she told Naina. She also said she wanted to get educated and become a nurse, or a doctor or a teacher. "Will you take me with you when you leave? I want to be like you when I grow up."

Naina would sadly reply that she wasn't sure, as more likely than not she wasn't returning to the United States. The idea of seeing Rihaan again simply tore at her heart.

Maybe I'll go home to India and find a way to get Zeenat there somehow, she thought, quickly wiping her dripping nose with the back of her hand.

Naina cleared her throat. "She has chicken pox and today is her last day of quarantine. She's thrilled because she's going to get a haircut and will soon look like a boy and confuse her aunt!"

Adam laughed. "I'd surely like to see her." And when Naina turned to leave he stopped her, pointing toward the mail. "I haven't sorted through the entire stack but there's something there for you."

"I wasn't expecting anything..." She stopped at the door, holding her breath. "Who is it from?"

"A Rihaan Mehta?"

She moved to the table in an instant and snatched the letter from his grasp. She stared at the envelope. It was true. It was from Rihaan.

Adam looked at her curiously.

Quivering with emotion, Naina whispered a soft thank you and turned away. She wanted to read it in private and savor it, whatever he had written, words of hate or words of love—it didn't matter. At least he hadn't forgotten about her. She brought the envelope to her mouth and kissed it but imagined it was his lips she was kissing.

She hurried across the narrow courtyard to the flight of stairs that led to her room on the second floor. A young boy shot out suddenly from nowhere and stood blocking her way.

"Excuse me..." she said, then stared at the child for several moments. "Zeenat! Is that you?"

Her young friend grinned cheekily. "Would you have made out I wasn't a boy, if you hadn't seen me before?"

Naina smiled, and shook her head. The young girl continued to chatter as she followed her into her room. Naina laid her precious cargo down carefully on her bed and turned to her. She had never seen Zeenat talk so animatedly.

"I want to test it. I want to go outside and roam around and see how everybody reacts, especially my cousins and I want you to come with me."

"But Zeenat," Naina said, "I want to rest a little and I also have a letter from home to read."

"You can do that later. I can't be away too long before I'm discovered," Zeenat insisted, pulling at Naina's hand so she reluctantly agreed.

***

The bazaar was densely packed as evening set in and the sun fled from the sky. Naina tried to keep an eye on her charge while taking care to skip over and walk around the several muddy puddles of water that had gathered after the short spell of rains that afternoon. There were rows upon rows of bustling shops selling anything and everything from fresh food to cheap imported furniture. It vaguely reminded her of Delhi's Chandni Chowk though she hardly saw any women around.

Zeenat suddenly squealed and tugged at Naina's long *kurta*. She pointed down the street at a tall, thin boy. "There's Amir, my cousin. Follow me!"

Naina had to hurry to keep track of the child as she ran ahead. And while doing so, she looked curiously at the young man whom Zeenat had called her cousin. He was standing outside a leather goods store and looked very ill. His eyes were shifty, he had a fevered appearance and as she drew closer she saw his face shining with sweat which was unusual for the arid climate. There was also an unusual bulge on his chest.

A sudden terrible dread filled her. A horrific premonition.

After barely a moment's hesitation, she rushed ahead, pushing through the crowd indiscriminately, shouting at people to disperse and get out of the way.

"Zeenat... Stop!" Naina screamed, reaching out and grabbing the back of the little girl's shirt. She then pulled her around, and shoved her in the opposite direction.

The last thing Naina remembered was the perplexed look on the child's face before a deafening blast rang out and shook the air. Then darkness closed in.

A Victim of War

Emergency Care Center for Victims of War, Kabul

"The impact of the blast was so severe that she was lifted and thrown back several feet...she has sustained severe head trauma...blast lung, deep penetrating wounds to the abdomen, compartment syndrome of the left lower extremity, burns over 15% of her body... She has undergone multiple surgeries and will likely need several more in the coming few days to weeks...any questions?" The Afghani surgeon turned and looked at Rihaan who stood at his side, listening, as he read out the laundry list of injuries from the clipboard, without so much as batting an eye.

Rihaan simply continued to stare at the bed. He was in a state of shock. The only thing he could see was his beautiful wife lying confined to a hospital bed in a faraway remote land, unconscious and utterly helpless, swathed in bandages, with tubes traversing in and out of every cavity and orifice, her vibrant young body damaged and disfigured, fighting for her life with every ounce of her battered spirit.

All of a sudden, Rihaan sprang into action. Diving down to the side of the bed, he gently gathered his wife's broken body in his arms, then bending forward, kissed her on the edge of her swollen lips, and whispered into her ear, "I'm here, Naina. Your Rihaan is here." After which he collapsed, breaking down into violent sobs that raked his entire frame.

The surgeon slipped out, closing the door quietly behind him.

***

Over the following several days, Rihaan spent every possible moment with Naina, fearing that if he let her out of his sight, she might vanish forever. The severely critical nature of her condition gradually sunk in, yet he didn't allow it to pitch him into an overwhelming depression. He dealt with it the only way he knew how, by fighting the inertia through intellectualization. He took it upon himself to oversee every aspect of her care, reviewing the tests and standing by during all procedures and surgeries. They couldn't throw him out, he was a doctor after all.

He actively engaged with the team of physicians, questioning and challenging their decisions, but he found them at no fault. They were doing a commendable job under the toughest of circumstances. Indeed, it kindled in him a deep sense of admiration, which conflicted with the immense rage he felt for all those who he thought responsible for committing his beautiful wife to her present condition. She, who bore nothing but kindness in her heart, didn't deserve the pain, nor did any of the other countless innocents out there.

But when he saw Naina making steady progress, his spirits soared. She was responding remarkably well. Her wounds were healing, her vital organs recovering appropriately and she was requiring minimal life support. Yet she remained on the ventilator under deep sedation, and this was a source of constant irritation to him. He worried about the obvious complications but even more, he was impatient for her to wake up, so he could make her aware of his presence. He wanted to assure her that she wasn't alone and that she was safe. That there was no reason to fear or be afraid. "Everything is going to be fine," he wanted to say.

But most of all, he wanted her to know that he loved her. It had been so long and he couldn't wait to say the words to her.

He fired his concerns at her neurosurgeon, an elderly Brit, who listened to him patiently wearing a fatherly smile on his face. In his long career he had seen many smart young docs like Rihaan, who transformed into petulant teenagers when it came to one of their own on the sickbed, though this brilliant young neurosurgeon—Rihaan's recent paper had created quite a furor in the community—had to be credited for exhibiting extraordinary restraint under these particularly trying circumstances. And given his singular devotion to his wife, his demands were legitimate.

"Son," the surgeon said, "given the amount of trauma she has suffered to her brain, it is our general approach to keep patients like her under sedation for some amount of time, to allow the brain to heal and to prevent further injury. A few more days and she'll be ready. I'm sure you understand."

Rihaan nodded, agreeing reluctantly. Of course he understood. Perhaps he was in denial, unwilling to accept how serious Naina's injuries truly were, even though all her scans and tests he had personally reviewed several times over told him so. He was losing his objectivity and that wasn't good. He had to toughen up if he wanted the best for her.

Two days later, news of another horrendous terrorist attack rocked the city. Rihaan, despite his existing anxieties, rushed to the scene to volunteer with the already overburdened medical personnel.

When he returned, thoroughly drained, he was met by Naina's trauma surgeon, the same who had acquainted him with her situation, upon his arrival.

He addressed him in his heavily accented monotone. "I'm sorry, but we have to transfer your wife out of this hospital."

Rihaan was shocked. "But why?"

"As you can see, this place is very small. We don't have enough beds to handle all the cases. Your wife's condition is stable."

"What do you mean 'stable'? She needs specialized care, at least a couple more surgeries, and she still remains heavily tranquilized."

The man's lips curved into a trace of a smile that was perhaps meant to be reassuring, "All of that can be handled elsewhere. Tomorrow she's going to the best private hospital in Kabul. Sorry, but my hands are tied," he said stepping out of the room and closing the door on further protests.

Rihaan sank into a chair beside Naina's bed. Nothing could be more terrible. He had tolerated everything so far; the outdated equipment, slipshod hygiene, even the poorly trained nursing staff, as there weren't other options. Her progress had filled him with optimism and driven some of the cynicism away. But now they wanted to throw her out, cast her away in her fragile state, send her to some place else where there was no assurance of proper care, where she could possibly lose all the gains she had made and forgo any chance at being well again.

"I'm not going to let it happen, if I can help it Naina. You can be sure of that my love," he said, reaching over to squeeze her limp hand.

Hope and Faith

Rihaan tracked down the surgeon in his office and tried to reason with him, even beseeching him to reconsider his decision. But when the man appeared unmoved, he resorted to the next best thing he knew. He threatened to sue him along with the entire medical facility for negligence.

The Afghan laughed to Rihaan's bemusement. "This is not America. No one sues anyone here, because no one has the time or the money. We are all busy fighting to stay alive." He wrote something down on a prescription pad and handed it over to Rihaan. "I understand how you feel. Here, go and check out this place. I'm sorry, but it's the best I can do."

Rihaan thrust the paper in his pocket and rushed from the building in urgent need for some fresh air, but also to check his impulse to punch the doc on his jaw. He was practically seizing with anger.

That will be of no benefit to Naina, rather it is bound to be counterproductive. Under no circumstance whatsoever do I want her to pay for my poor judgment. I have to curb my frustrations and try to think clearly, he brooded as he passed through the lobby. He had always found it filled to the brim, with people in varying degrees of grief and mourning. As he tried to push his way through a wall of cops blocking the entrance, his gaze fell on a television monitor that hung close to the door. It was tuned to *Al Jazeera* news. Images of the recent bomb blast flashed across the screen, followed by those of American soldiers who were soon to be withdrawn from the area. One of them, upon being interviewed, said that he couldn't wait to get home.

But of course! Why didn't I think of it before? Rihaan berated himself.

He spent the following several hours on the phone, talking to a series of people, explaining and re-explaining his plight, negotiating, even cajoling and making appropriate arrangements, so that it was morning before he was able to head back to Naina's room.

He bent down to kiss her gently on the forehead and then whispered in her ear, like he had so many times before, hoping his voice would register somewhere in her subconscious.

"Darling, as I said before, you're going to be fine. Tomorrow I'm going to take you home."

***

A few days later in the Neurocritical care unit of a premier NYC hospital...

"Naina..." Rihaan sat on the edge of her bed, waiting.

"Mrs. Mehta, can you open your eyes?" a nurse said on the other side of her bed.

"Naina, wake up, it's me, Rihaan."

She opened her eyes. He felt a thrill rush through him. *At last.*

Her head turned toward him. But her eyes...they didn't see him. They saw through him.

"Naina...?" he asked again.

Her gaze veered away.

"Naina!" He grabbed her face, in the process dislodging a couple of monitor leads that set off a chorus of loud beeps. But he didn't care. All that mattered to him right now was her. Her knowing him. "Naina, look at me. It's Rihaan, your husband!"

Her glassy eyes remained blank.

"I love you. Please say something, anything." He bent down and kissed her lips, but felt no returning pressure. She whimpered, indicating her discomfort.

"Dr. Mehta..." The nurse urged, pressing gently on his arm.

He released his wife and withdrew into a corner and watched silently as the staff went about their business.

You're reacting prematurely Rihaan, he thought. *You have to allow for the drugs to wear out of her system. You have to be patient. You have to give her time.*

After consulting with Naina's neurologist, Rihaan had discontinued all but her anti-seizure medications. In response, she seemed more alert at times, but then during others she appeared to revert back to a blank glassy stare that rotated aimlessly across the room. She also seemed to have lost all purposeful movement. The staff had to move and position her like a mannequin. She rarely spoke, and when she did, her speech was unintelligible; a garbled mish-mash of words that Rihaan couldn't make out even when he strained very hard.

But he didn't give up hope, sure that it was a transition period. *Time, Rihaan, give her time!* He reminded himself of it over and over again.

But Naina wouldn't eat, and she was losing weight by the day despite the tube feeds, which was worrisome. He discussed his concerns with her gastroenterologist who suggested instituting a special tube into her stomach as a better way of supplementing her nutrition.

"No," Rihaan said with a cringe. He had seen feeding tubes turn many individuals into permanent invalids and he didn't want the same fate for Naina. He wanted her to have every chance at a normal life. He left saying he needed some time to think about the decision.

When he returned to her room, he was taken aback by the sight of both his parents, his mother in particular, who had always maintained that she hated hospitals, including the very sight and smell of death and disease. He saw her standing and staring aghast at his wife, who sat propped up in a bedside recliner with the nurse fussing about her. Naina seemed restless for some reason.

"Dad," Rihaan said, turning to Shashank. "I asked you specifically not to bring Mom here. She doesn't get hospitals. And I don't want anything to upset Naina at this time."

"I'm sorry, son, but she insisted. She went to the temple this morning and brought some *prasad* for *bahu.*"

"Naina is not in any state to take *prasad*," Rihaan said, glaring at his mother, but she didn't appear to hear him.

"What is wrong with *bahu?* Look at her! So pale and thin. I can even see her bones!" she exclaimed, raising a hand to her mouth in a show of horror, which infuriated Rihaan even more. "Look at the big dark circles around her eyes and where is her beautiful long hair? And why is she staring at me like that...as if she hates me or something?"

Rihaan turned to look at his wife. Indeed, her gaze had become vehement and fixed, and her movements were increasingly agitated. Naina was pulling at everything; her face, the hospital gown and IV lines. The nurse couldn't keep her still.

All of a sudden Naina's lips curled back and her face turned into a horrible fiendish mask. And from in between her clenched teeth started pouring out a torrent of bizarre nonsensical speech.

"Naina!" He rushed to her side, but she wouldn't calm down. Her nails dug sharply into his flesh as her body grew rigid like a board. He recognized the malady for he had seen it happen several times before. Her eyes rolled back into her head, the muscles in her neck stood up in painful tense cords and she began thrashing violently and choking on her own saliva. And while his mother screamed hysterically in the background, Rihaan along with several other hospital staff tried to hold Naina down and sedate her again. She packed an amazing amount of strength in that tiny, little frame.

An hour or so later when Rihaan emerged exhausted from the hospital room, he was surprised to see his parents still there, waiting in the lounge. He managed a tired smile at his father who came up to him bearing a face full of anxiety and concern. "Naina's fine. She's sleeping now. You can go home."

"Fine?" His mother cried out from her perch in the corner. "You call behavior like that fine? When one rants, raves, and curses and exposes herself in front of her in-laws? I call it shocking and offensive!"

"Mother! Please understand. Naina wasn't aware of anything that was going on. She was having a seizure!"

"I don't believe it. She did it because she hates me. I saw it in her eyes!" Shobha shot back.

"Naina can't control her..." Rihaan began to explain, then cut his sentence short. He quietly turned on his heels and left. Convincing anyone, least of all his mother regarding her daughter-in-law's lack of malice didn't figure anywhere on his list of priorities.

And Naina wasn't fine. She began having recurrent and violent partial complex seizures, which to control she had to be kept under a drug cloud, in a semiconscious state. Rihaan felt at once helpless and frustrated. He couldn't handle the sight of seeing his wife committed yet again to a state where she was barely alive and utterly dependent on others for even the most mundane of her bodily functions. He wanted her back, like she'd been before, vibrant and wonderful. He wanted his Naina back. But the options to help her seemed to be running out.

***

Late the following evening, after having reviewed and discussed the results of a battery of tests with his boss, Rihaan began to see a glimmer of hope. Naina's case was going to be discussed by a panel of experts and his chief had assured him that a solution was bound to be found.

"Have faith, son," he had said, clapping him on his back. "Good things happen to good people. And your wife is one of the best."

Rihaan hurried back to the hospital. He hadn't seen Naina all day. Besides, he wanted to tell her about the developments, whisper into her ear, like he'd been doing all along. Talking to her made him feel good.

He was intercepted in the lobby by his mother, an occurrence he'd least expected. He smiled at her, "Are you here to see your *bahu?*"

"No, I'm here to see my son and bring him some home-cooked food," she retorted, handing over a large bag.

"Well, if that is the only reason, then I don't want to see you. You can take back the food. I've lost the taste for it." He turned away.

"Rihaan! My son! *Hey Bhagwan!*" she cried, pulling on his arm. "What has that girl done to you?"

"That girl has a name…Naina."

She ignored him. "She has turned you into *Devdas.* I see a haunted look in your eyes. Where has my carefree, go-getter son gone to?"

"Stop being melodramatic, Ma. It doesn't become you," he said with a short laugh. "And the carefree go-getter son you talk about was a rudderless, selfish bastard. Naina, who's my wife by the way, has changed me for the better. I know where I'm headed now, and she's going to be with me all the way."

"No, she won't. Not the way she is now…" Shobha said, her voice loaded with skepticism.

"She's sick, that's all. But she'll get better soon. I'm confident."

Shobha let out a dismal sigh. "She'll never get better. I remember a neighbor we used to have in our village. I was very young then. This girl, who used to be my friend, had attacks just like Naina. She'd be walking on the street when suddenly she'd fall to the ground, start pulling her hair, and begin screaming like a madwoman… They said she was possessed by

148

the devil. But the *ojha* couldn't do anything. Her attacks grew so bad that she had to be kept chained up in a solitary room. I don't know exactly what happened to her. Someone said she cut her throat because she had lost her mind. I can see Naina in her place."

"Dangerous superstitious nonsense!" Rihaan exploded. "Your poor friend needed a good doctor, not an exorcist! Mother, I'm surprised that you allowed yourself to believe in such crap. Naina hasn't lost her mind. She just needs some help."

She gave him a look. "You've already helped her a lot, don't you think? She's taken enough advantage of you."

"What do you mean?" Rihaan scrutinized her suspiciously.

"I mean what I say," Shobha said, looking at him with a strange light in her eyes. "I can't see you wasting your future for a girl who left you. She abandoned a loving husband, for her own selfish motives. Naina has become a vegetable and will remain like that for the rest of her life."

"So what do you expect me to do? Leave her?"

"Yes." His mother nodded, continuing earnestly as Rihaan stared at her in horror. "I want you to leave her. Marry another girl and be happy. I'm sure Naina would want the same. Unfortunately she's not in a state to say so."

"I'm glad she's not in a state to say so and even if she was, I wouldn't listen to her. Because she's my wife and I love her... I love her like a crazy madman! She's the only one who can make me happy. And she won't be able to get rid of me, either, no matter how hard she tried. Got it Ma? Let's forget that we ever had this conversation," Rihaan said getting up from his seat. He'd had enough of his mother's uncalled for advice.

As he walked away with a renewed determination in his step, he recalled the conversation they'd had in a café not so long ago, when he'd told Naina about his patient; about a young man rendered totally incapacitated by an inoperable brain tumor, and his wife who wouldn't give up. Naina had uttered plainly that he would know why she hadn't given up if he found himself in a similar situation.

Now he understood what her words meant. Hope and faith kept them going through the toughest of times. And he had plenty of both.

***

Rihaan waited impatiently outside the conference room where a group of consultants had gathered to discuss Naina's case. He'd been asked to participate, but had declined, because he'd let emotions cloud his judgment. That wouldn't be fair to her.

The meeting ended and the doctors dispersed, nodding with encouragement at him. A couple of them even gave him the thumbs up sign. He turned to his boss who'd headed the meeting, "So Chief, what's the consensus?"

"It seems surgery is the only way."

Rihaan nodded solemnly. "I guessed you'd say so. So who's going to do it?"

"You."

"Me?" Rihaan laughed nervously. "You've got to be kidding. I can't... Why not you? Or Dr. Garrett. I'm sure he wouldn't refuse."

"Rihaan, my boy..." the chief gently squeezed his shoulder. "You are a master in cutting edge focus resection surgical technique. You've even presented a paper on it. Besides, would you be able to forgive yourself if someone else did it and there was a complication?"

Rihaan shook his head. His boss was right. He would never be able to forgive himself and Naina would never get another chance. He looked down at his hands. It was going to be the toughest job he'd ever undertake. His ultimate test. And he had to take it if he wished to get her back in his life. And she was going to make it...for herself, for him, for the both of them.

Rebirth

Rebirth—of a body buried before it had taken its final breath.
A mistake discovered before the flame of life had flickered and died.

Heavy lids cracked open slowly like those on an ancient coffin. Naina was rousing from a deep, deep sleep. Few perceptions could be more terrifying. What lay in wait on the other side?

She was emerging from an endless pitch black tunnel. The tiny spot of light was growing larger and larger and so bright that it hurt. Her eyes clamped shut, then opened again, slowly, with caution.

Someone spoke at her side—a man's voice, warm, gentle and caring—one she'd heard before, instinctively letting her know that he was friend not foe.

***

Rihaan had been waiting restlessly for this moment. For his Naina to wake up. The light of life was back in her eyes. They were as beautiful and clear as ever. Dark, luminous pools. And she was looking at him, returning his smile. He was ecstatic, overcome by immeasurable relief and joy.

"Darling! Thank heavens! Welcome back!" He scooped her up gently into his arms. "I've missed you so much!"

But he felt her resist his embrace. His joy faltered. "Naina?"

***

Naina pulled away, disregarding his plea, and slowly scanned the rest of the hospital staff gathered in the room. Her bewilderment intensified.

She looked down at herself, surveying her skimpy gown and her much bruised and punctured arms from which trailed an assortment of wires and lines, then demanded in a rough, cracked voice. "Who... Who are you all? And what am I doing here...like this?"

They all looked as one to the man who'd been sitting on her bed and talking to her.

He was now standing up and regarding her with a perturbed expression on his nice-looking face. But he spoke with a voice that was calm and steady. "You were in an accident, a very bad accident. That's why you're here, in the hospital. All these people have been working with you, helping you, trying to get you better. Naina, don't you remember anything?"

"Naina?" Her eyes narrowed. "Why are you calling me that?"

***

"Because that is your name. Naina Rathod Mehta. And unfortunately you've lost your memory," Rihaan said. Then at once turned on his heels and strode out of the room, and out of the hospital and away.

Away from the flurry of emotions that threatened to overwhelm him. Away from the incredible dejection and gloom that, like a pair of invisible hands, had come clamping down on his throat and were squeezing so hard it felt as if his torso would split wide open and expose his poor, pathetic heart at any moment.

In a rush to exit the building, he lost his footing and stumbled, pitching headfirst toward the icy pavement. As the ground rushed to embrace him, he succumbed gladly, giving himself up to oblivion and to the yawning quagmire of self-pity because he had been betrayed. His immaculate dream had been destroyed. And, as luck would have it, some damn do-gooder chose to yank him up. Destiny wasn't prepared to let him off the hook that easily.

So he continued to walk, his eyes burning with tears of bitter regret. They spurred him on, goading him to walk faster. With his long frame stiff, head bowed and hands thrust deep in his pockets, he stood at the crosswalk waiting for the lights to change, craving to be just another anonymous, inscrutable face headed for some obscure destination.

How long he walked or how far, he wasn't aware, just that it was critical for him to keep his body in perpetual motion. When abruptly, amidst an enclosure of several tall shiny buildings, he was forced to come to a standstill. It was as if the looming giants had all ganged up and were hell-bent in fencing him in.

Alarmed, he glanced around, searching the faces of his companions, but none appeared to share his uncanny experience. *It must be in my head,* he thought, closing his eyes and taking in several slow, deep breaths.

Then he looked up warily.

The mammoth structures of concrete and steel, they towered so high it looked as if they were scraping the sky—reflecting man's eternal quest for the ultimate. And they were all beckoning to him, urging him to join them in their quest. Rihaan responded by drawing his hands out of his pockets, reaching up, craning with every fiber of his being. Yes, if he tried hard enough, he too could touch the sky. Nothing was impossible.

I should be grateful that my Naina is fine. That she is alive and with me. I've all the time in the world to help her get to know me again and love me, just as I love her. Yes, nothing is impossible.

***

He returned to find her refusing to eat or take her medications.

"I won't do anything until someone tells me what's wrong with me. Why can't I remember anything?" she asked.

An indulgent smile lit his face and he nodded reassuringly at the flustered nurse. Seating himself on the bed next to his wife, he took the bowl of soup in his hands and looked directly into her eyes.

She was scrutinizing him with suspicion.

"Nothing's wrong with you. The reason why you've lost your memory is because your brain has suffered a tremendous amount of trauma. I know that can be very frightening. But don't worry, everything will come back to you soon. I'm damn sure of it."

"How can you say so and with so much confidence? Who are you anyway?"

"I say so because I know so," Rihaan said. "I am one of your doctors and I also happen to be your husband, Rihaan Mehta." He scooped up her hand and gently kissed it.

She trembled before snatching it away and concealed her hand under the bed sheet. "And...I'm supposed to take your word for it? I'm no fool!"

She looked taken aback when he burst out laughing. "No, absolutely not. I don't expect you to take my word for it, for then I'd be committing the unpardonable offense of insulting a woman who's not only beautiful but also very intelligent."

Her cheeks grew warm but her steady gaze told him that he wasn't off the hook. A few moments passed before he smiled again. He removed his cell phone from its clip and held it in front of her face. "This is our wedding video. No better proof than that."

Naina observed the ceremony silently. "But I can barely see the girl's face, it's hidden by the veil. How can I be sure that's me?"

"You're right," Rihaan agreed. He'd never attended to that glaring fact. Maybe because for him, the girl in the video had always been Naina.

Yet when he saw her continue to look at him expectantly, he knew he couldn't let this vital moment go by. It was a chance to establish his sincerity.

"Here," he said, exhaling with relief, "look at these." He handed her his cell phone again. "They are some pictures taken by my Uncle Rajbir on the day after the wedding. I didn't realize I had them."

Her face assumed a flustered expression as she scanned the pictures quickly; most of them showing an uncharacteristically stiff and awkward bridegroom standing next to a demure and shy bride. "But this girl isn't me! She's so beautiful! Whereas I'm ugly! I know because I've seen myself. I made her brinng me a mirrrorrrr..." She looked at the nurse, who acknowledged guiltily.

Then Naina started to scream. Her faint slur becoming prominent as she got more and more worked up. "Youuur all init togetherrr, deceivinn me an tellinnn me horribbbbl liessss!"

Rihaan folded her in his arms and tried to calm her as she continued to stammer incomprehensively. "No, darling. I'm not telling you lies... No one is. It's you in the pictures. Believe me. And you're not ugly. You are beautiful, more beautiful than anyone I've ever met. Everything is going to be fine. Trust me."

***

Raising her tear-stricken face to his, she examined him keenly with red-rimmed eyes. She wanted to believe in him, desperately. *Why would he lie to her? What did such a wonderfully patient and handsome man have to do with an ugly girl like her, unless he was telling the truth, that she was indeed his wife? Maybe it was worth the risk.*

She capitulated and ate the soup.

Missing

Naina sat next to the window and scanned the scene slowly with her eyes. Hospital Room - bland, white, synthetic.

Clock reading - 11:03 a.m.

Faded print of Van Gogh's Starry Night on the wall.

White board stating today's date - 5/2/2014—the month written before the date in the American way (she did recall that) along with the name of her nurse—Stephie. She'd had her yesterday, too. Pretty, young, auburn-haired and nervous, whom her so-called husband had in his pocket, just like he did so many others.

She had been moved to this room on the 6th floor from the ICU exactly four days ago Naina had taken to keeping close tabs on every excruciating detail of what was going on, ever since she had become aware that her memory was suspect.

The reason for the move she was told was that her condition had been downgraded from 'critical' to 'stable' which was apparently excellent news. Also, because it was a quieter and more secluded location with VOILA! Not one, but two large windows! Though no one cared to elaborate that the only view she got to stare at every day was of city streets full of normal, healthy people, very much unlike her, but she didn't grumble. Her doctors intended well, Rihaan in particular.

She directed her attention on a pair of pigeons roosting in the eaves while trying to swallow the lump that seemed to form in her throat every time she thought of him. What a horrible plight for a man to be in! If she was really his wife...

She craned to get a better view and winced. Stephie rushed to her side immediately. She fussed around, attempting to rearrange her pillows so it didn't chafe the raw area on her back which had been freshly grafted that very morning with skin harvested from her thigh.

Stephie asked her anxiously, "Are you hurting? Can I get you something for the pain? You haven't had anything since you came back from surgery."

"No." Naina declined with a determined smile, even though every inch of her body throbbed like it had been pounded by a wrecking ball. She'd have loved an opportunity to escape to some weird and fantastic world that looked and felt so much better than the one she was in right now. But she couldn't, because she had persevered to hold on to her mind; at least what remained of it.

They'd all informed her (the experts assembled by the man who'd adopted her as his wife) that she suffered from a profound case of dissociative amnesia. They'd arrived at this general consensus after subjecting her to a staggering number of tests that involved spending harrowing eons inside claustrophobic chambers, getting her brain mapped with weird probes plastered to her scalp, plus countless hours of interrogation, during which she was repeatedly posed the same questions, tested on her reading and writing skills, and made to perform silly tasks like counting backwards and drawing clock faces which any fifth grader could accomplish. In conclusion, she was informed that her brain was in excellent working order except— they looked at her with uniformly grim faces—somewhere in the course of events she had lost sight of herself. She had buried herself deep inside her brain and omitted to mark the spot.

Bewildered and frightened, she had turned to Rihaan, who was holding her hand while sitting beside her throughout the whole sermon. Deducing her turmoil right away, he said, "Not to worry. All they mean to say is that part of your memory has taken a vacation. It should be back in no time."

Thus, he had allayed her anxieties with a smile he seemed to reserve only for her.

And while she tried to come to terms with her 'temporary' deficiency, he gave her information about herself—something to build upon, as he put it.

She was a young Asian woman, born and brought up in India—she had gathered as much, going by the color of her skin and that she was fluent in three different Indian languages. She was well-educated (a PhD student of English, no less). And while working in New Delhi, she had met Dr. Rihaan Mehta, and within a short period, got married to him and emigrated to the United States.

"A whirlwind romance?" she had questioned dubiously.

In response to which he had hedged a little before nodding, "Yes, you could say so." But then he hadn't chosen to elaborate further.

"What about my parents? I want to talk to them," she had demanded.

"Your parents are no longer with us," he told her after some hesitation. "It's been several years since they passed."

But when she inquired about the rest of her family, he wasn't quite as forthcoming. Nor was he about the circumstances that had led to her accident.

"Don't get flustered, Naina," he had said. "Think of it as a game of trivial pursuit that you're playing with yourself. The picture will become clearer as your brain builds on bits of new information."

She had taken him for his word. But the picture continued to remain as elusive and abstruse as ever.

"Time for lunch!" her nurse chirped.

Naina was snapped out of her morose musings by Stephie, who placed a tray of sterile hospital food in front of her.

"No, take it away," instructed Rihaan, as he breezed in, looking suave and handsome as ever. "My wife's having none of that junk today. She's going to eat something I've made especially for her." He opened a brown paper bag from which emanated a mouthwatering aroma.

"It's the very same that you fed me, when I came hunting for you at your apartment the day after we met." He placed a spoonful into her mouth. "I didn't realize it then, but I think that's when I fell irrevocably under your spell. Remember, Naina?"

Naina tried to nod and smile as she chewed on what felt like sandpaper on her palate. But her husband was no fool.

"I'm so sorry to be such a disappointment!" she burst out, reaching for his hand. "Frankly, I don't remember anything at all!"

"It's okay, darling. How can I blame you for my abysmal lack of culinary skills?" He laughed, grabbing a tissue and dabbing at her tear-stricken face.

Later, to make amends, he snuck her down to the lobby for a delicious sundae, then as an added bonus pushed her wheelchair around the moonlit courtyard until she fell fast asleep.

Of Spells and Guardian Angels

It was the darkest of nights in the middle of nowhere and it was cold, *so very cold,* with a bitter, biting wind. And in the midst of this hell, Naina found herself running as fast as her broken feet would allow her. She was fleeing from something unseen, something more terrifying than anyone could ever imagine.

The wind began to howl, pushing her back, smacking her on the face with her own hair. Her limbs were heavy and weak, like stumps of dead rotting wood and the numbness began creeping up her torso. But she wouldn't give up. She just couldn't.

Up ahead on a low hill she thought she saw some flickering lights. They emboldened her to get moving again. But she had barely progressed a couple of feet when the ground under her started to slide. The asphalt had turned into a bed of loose gravel.

She fell forward and began to crawl, using her nails as talons, seeking purchase on the steep incline which had abruptly transformed into a river of slime. It poured into her nose and her mouth, extinguishing her screams for help.

The thing had almost caught up. She could perceive its putrid burning flesh. The heat seared her skin. She closed her eyes and prayed for a quick end.

Just then the earth tore apart and she saw herself plunge into a gaping hole. She plummeted, gathering speed as she dropped, further and further. But she wasn't alone, there were others with her, falling, too. And they were laughing in great merriment.

Astounded, she looked around and saw that she was seated on top of a gigantic Ferris wheel, high in the sky, floating among wisps of soft cotton.

"Naina!" Someone called her name.

"Here!" She responded earnestly seeking the source.

The voice belonged to someone she knew, but hadn't seen in ages. She finally spotted her. A beautiful woman with a face radiant like the sun. And she was smiling at Naina while eating ice cream. Rocky Road. Her favorite kind.

"Mama!" Naina screamed, reaching out with both her arms.

But the woman drifted away, waving cheerfully as she disappeared into a dense bank of clouds.

"Mama!" she called again.

"Mrs. Mehta!" Someone tapped on her shoulder.

"No," Naina grumbled, burying her face deeper into the pillows, desperately attempting to reassemble her dream. But it wasn't to be.

"Good morning. I'm Cara. Your new nurse," announced a woman with an incredibly bright smile on her perfectly done supermodel face.

Naina decided right away she didn't like her. "Where's Stephie?"

"She has the day off," the supermodel nurse replied, the corners of her mouth straining to reach her ear lobes and almost succeeding. She maneuvered a tray table close to the bed.

"It's way past breakfast time. But Dr. Mehta insisted to let you sleep through. He said you had a…"

"Dr. Mehta? Rihaan?" Naina exclaimed eagerly, struggling to sit up. "Is he here?"

"No. But you have other visitors," Cara said.

Naina became aware for the first time of the small crowd gathered in the room. Her beautiful, dark eyes, the most prominent features on her thin, pale face, grew wider as they darted from one person to the other.

"You know who we are, don't you? I'm Rima, Rihaan's sister," voiced a pretty young woman dressed in a becoming yellow and pink spring dress.

"Yes. I do. How are you?" Naina answered slowly. She did recognize them from the pictures Rihaan had shown her. Yet it felt odd seeing them in the flesh, in a most surreal way. The fantastic fable had finally come to life, filling her both with excitement and fear.

Her gaze first rested on a gentleman (who was apparently more than slightly fond of his *paneer tikka* and *tandoori* chicken) whom she recognized as Rihaan's father. The smile he wore on his ruddy face was so frank and genial that it instantly caused her to relax. She judged him to be a kind-hearted and down-to-earth individual, a person who invited trust and confidence.

She smiled back at him before moving on to his wife—a short, thin woman wrapped in a grey-black sari. She was examining her keenly with hazel eyes, which were just like her son's, though hers weren't smiling.

Seized by a peculiar sense of unease, Naina looked away and spotted a strange man standing right beside her bed. He wore the saffron robes of a priest. His bright, jet black, beady eyes made her skin crawl. She desperately fought the urge to pull the covers over her head.

"You're looking very good," Rima said, breaking the uncomfortable silence.

Naina, thankful for the distraction, looked gratefully at her, though she knew she was lying. How could a pale sickly alien wearing a chemo cap to cover her shaven skull look good? But Naina forgave her for she believed Rima bore no ill will in her heart.

Her sister-in-law placed a large bouquet of painted daisies on the bedside table along with a box of chocolates. "Rihaan told me there are no dietary restrictions. He said I could bring anything that'd encourage his picky, little wife to eat."

Naina smiled nervously, all at once realizing how desperately she missed him.

"Maybe we should come back later. Let *bahu* have her breakfast," her father-in-law suggested, and began hustling his wife toward the door, much to the woman's annoyance.

"No. Please stay. I'm not hungry," Naina pleaded, though wishing quite the opposite.

Her mother-in-law finally spoke, but not to her. She shared a knowing look with the priest. "Guru*ji*, do you see what I see?"

He nodded, continuing to stare at Naina with his eerie eyes. "Yes. I do. This young woman's life is in great danger. She is haunted by malevolent spirits. She needs help or else she'll take everyone with her to hell."

Naina looked on helplessly, wanting to but unable to push him away, as the priest anointed her forehead with vermillion and ash. Then digging into his cloth bag, he brought out a white powder which he blew into her face, making her sneeze loudly.

"Shobha, what are you doing?" Naina heard her father-in-law yell from somewhere in the room. "I thought you brought this man here to bless our *bahu* and pray for her quick recovery!"

"Her condition calls for more than just blessings and prayers," her mother-in-law said. "Guru*ji* knows exactly what she needs. Let him do his job. It's for her own good and for our son's, who happens to have turned into a big hard-headed fool!"

There were more voices raised in argument. Someone fled, shouting from the room.

Meanwhile Naina stared in horrid fascination, as the priest sat down by her bed and began intonating in a loud and fervid tone. She wanted to look away but couldn't. She was trapped; ensnared by some strange force in a dark, mystical realm.

And then to her alarm, she began to break apart. Her head separated from her torso and so did her limbs, detaching themselves one by one before drifting away. And she couldn't do anything about it. It was a conspiracy, a vile plot hatched to annihilate her very soul. Her mouth opened to protest, but the words were rammed back into her throat. Her heart screamed vainly inside her chest. She fought feebly, raising her hands in front of her face, but the voice only grew louder.

Fortunately at that very moment her guardian angel walked in. "What in hell is going on here?" Rihaan shouted.

He ousted the wicked man from the room and admonished everybody to be silent and stop irritating his wife. He even ticked his mother off and sternly warned her against committing such foul acts again. "Enough is enough. There's nothing wrong with my Naina, absolutely nothing! Understood!"

My Naina. She closed her eyes and reveled in the sensation of being his.

Beacon of Light

"Something's brewing in that little mind of yours and it's potent enough to overcome the soporific mix we feed you. Care to put me in the loop?" Rihaan remarked feigning surprise one afternoon, when he came upon his wife engrossed in a task other than the one she was usually in—her post lunch siesta.

"It's nothing. Nothing that would be of any interest to you," Naina retorted sharply, snapping shut her notebook and shoving it deep inside the folds of her blanket.

"Hmm…that makes me even more curious," he said casually sauntering over to the window, from where he pretended to regard the buildings across the street, before turning back to her with a sly smile in his eyes, one designed specifically to unnerve her.

But she hung tough, gripping the book even harder. It'd certainly not do for him or anyone else for that matter to become privy to her incoherent ramblings which were bound to lay her wide open to ridicule. These were her very own, brand new, untried thoughts and feelings and she chose to guard them with ferocity.

It had been only a few days since she'd been involved in her new hobby. The journal, a gift from one of her therapists, had come with specific instructions: "Write in it every day, anything, as long as it is positive."

In other words, it was a prescription for pragmatism, or to put it plainly— "Drink your poison and stop complaining!"

It had irked her immensely to the point of indignation. She had scoffed at the idea, finding nothing to be even slightly perky about. Until lately.

"Your lips are cracked, they are dry as a bone. Where's your nurse? Let me get her." Rihaan, who'd been examining her face closely, frowned with concern.

"No, please…don't. She's busy." She reached for his hand. "Besides, it's just a minor thing. See, I can fix it," she said gaily, swirling a moist tongue over her lips.

He burst into a loud guffaw. "Gosh! You are one smart vixen. Nonetheless an adorable one." He stared at her, looking as if he wanted to say more. She waited eagerly, but his pesky little pager ruined the moment.

"Seems like we're running late for your therapy session. Shall we go?" he muttered rather brusquely.

She sighed, nodding a grudging assent while trying to swallow her disappointment. He helped her transfer to the wheelchair, taking care her bony behind was cushioned well. *Work! Work! Work! That happens to be his only mantra and getting me well his sole mission!* She silently fumed.

A gentle smooch landed on her forehead making her smile and instantly easing her tensions. It was just a benign token of appeasement. But for her, it was a moment of bliss, to be treasured and locked away in the empty spaces of her heart and permanently etched onto the leaves of her memory book. Pity, how starved of love she felt.

"Anything wrong?" he asked.

"No, nothing," Naina said, turning a bright face to him. Yet she had to suffer his keen scrutiny a bit longer. Fortunately, he didn't touch on it again.

The shaky foundations of their relationship had found firmer ground. They had successfully waded past the preliminary hang-ups and progressed to the next phase—the more than just friends phase—or so she hoped. That brought with it a different kind of intimacy—the reading of minds kind; the instinctively knowing without breaking the silence kind.

There was something about him that instilled a confidence in her, like in the way he spoke while looking in her eyes. It was a calming, reassuring connection that made her feel safe. So much so that sometimes she panicked when he wasn't around.

After the unfortunate incident with his mother, Rihaan proceeded to impose strict restrictions on all visitations, except a few. No one could meet her without his prior approval. And he insisted they did so in his presence, so he could send them packing at the slightest hint of trouble or irritation.

It was a bewildering throng that flitted in and out of her room, overwhelming her with flowers and gifts. She was surprised she knew so many people and that so many people knew her. And if what they said was really true, she gave them credit for controlling their reactions when they saw her. But it wasn't difficult to sense that they weren't pleasantly surprised. They introduced themselves as friends and acquaintances, a few coworkers even—yet none of their faces triggered even the vaguest recollection which plunged her into deep discontent.

They told her that she was a photojournalist of some stature. *They've got to be fibbing,* she thought looking to Rihaan for confirmation. But he didn't validate her suspicions, which perturbed her even more because he was the only one she trusted.

None of her visitors stayed long, except Anna, Rihaan's stunning blonde secretary, who devoted an entire lunch hour toward giving Naina a luxurious makeover, then actually broke down and sobbed over her hand. But even she didn't make any useful revelations, merely provided noncommittal responses to all of Naina's questions.

This piqued Naina's curiosity. Was Rihaan trying to protect her by keeping her in the dark?

"With time, darling. You'll know with time," was his resolute, almost stubborn reply.

Nor was he open about what had transpired between him and his mother that was grave enough to stop her from coming by to visit Naina again. She could only hope it wasn't something irreparable. Rihaan's intensity sometimes frightened her.

Yet, despite it all, Naina looked forward to seeing him every day. This guy, with his heady mix of stern and charm, cared for her. This extraordinarily handsome guy, who claimed to be her husband and showed her stuff to prove it—videos and pictures of a beautiful girl who shared the shape of her face and the color of her eyes. And even though she didn't doubt him anymore, she didn't tell him so. His enthusiasm was infinitely endearing.

Though he did still perplex her at times, like the day when he dumped a camera in her lap and demanded that she take pictures of him, as he required them for some odd chore. And when she did, manipulating the complex controls without hesitation, he whooped as though she had won the Olympics! Maybe there was some truth in the photojournalism rumor after all.

Yet he was the only one who, when she wailed in frustration and despair, spoke to her with extraordinary patience and deposited chaste kisses on her head.

He oversaw every step of her care, insisting on changing most of her dressings himself, his touch ever so soft and gentle.

He took her on rides around the hospital campus and sometimes snuck her out for treats to the neighborhood patisserie, all the while treating her like a princess and discounting all the strange looks they attracted.

He coaxed her and egged her on during her therapy sessions, but at the first sign of discomfort he was at her side, tending to her as if she were a fragile infant who was just learning to walk.

He would bring her books to read, talk to her or simply sit by quietly, watching her while she slept. She knew because often when she woke, she'd find him dozing with his head resting on the side of her bed. She wondered how he found the time to spend with her, as he was without question a very busy man, a much sought after neurosurgeon she'd heard someone say.

One day, she overheard the nurses talking outside her room. "The only reason why Mrs. Mehta is alive today is because of her husband and the courage he showed in undertaking such a difficult procedure."

Naina was stumped and overcome with awe. How could she even begin to repay such an enormous debt to Rihaan? The least she could do was gather up the tenuous strings of her sorry life and buck up and assist him in his goal, even though every step took a mountain of effort.

But eventually her hard work paid off. Finally, the day had arrived to escape the bland confines of her hospital room.

But she wasn't going to Rehab as her therapists had recommended. Rihaan had persuaded them otherwise in his usual forceful manner. He was taking her home with him.

And she couldn't wait…

Home

Rihaan gently deposited his feather light charge on the balcony and watched as she hung onto the railing and look around, hungrily lapping up the sights and sounds of mundane city life. Seeing her like this filled him with a sense of relief and achievement. *I can breathe a bit easier now,* he thought. Yet, he couldn't dispel the nagging irony of the situation. He had her, his wife, back where she belonged, in their home, by his side. Yet she failed to recognize him. He was still a perfect stranger to her.

"How does it feel?" he asked once several minutes had passed.

"It feels wonderful. Everything looks so...normal. Thank you, Rihaan," she said, turning to him with such a beautiful and brave smile that his heart surrendered at once.

"Don't thank me, darling. I've done nothing at all. Even if I had, no one deserves it more than you," he said, pulling her enthusiastically into his arms.

But almost instantly he noticed her splinting her breath. Her color had turned ashen, though her smile still remained very much in place. He realized that the pressure from his embrace was aggravating a fresh wound on her back, the spot where a failed skin graft had just been revised.

He released her while cursing fervently under his breath. "Sorry Naina. I should've known better."

"It's all right."

"No. It's not. Don't make excuses for me," he said picking her up briskly and striding inside the apartment.

Her wheelchair had been abandoned at the hospital since she had graduated to crutches. But she was still learning to use them and he didn't mind carrying her. She felt lighter than a grocery bag even though she appeared to have recovered most of her appetite.

Meanwhile, he continued to rail against himself. *How can I be so mindless when I'm supposed to be familiar with every detail of her condition? Besides, I'm her caretaker and her health is my first priority! This is inexcusable!*

It was because he had taken leave of his senses. Seeing her in his apartment again had sent his emotions on a wild spin, rekindling all the bittersweet memories of the times they had spent together, in particular those final hours of incomprehensible bliss that he'd been so desperately trying to stonewall.

"Rihaan," Naina said, "put me down please."

"What?"

"I said, put me down. You don't plan to carry me around all day, do you?" she asked with an amused smile.

"I could carry you around all my life, if I had to," he retorted. But then relented and set her on the bed before squatting down on the floor in front of her.

"I don't want to be a handicap," she mumbled.

"A handicap? What are you trying to say?" he demanded sharply.

She looked down at her lap where her fingers twisted and untwisted the fabric of her cotton dress which hung like a curtain over her thin frame. "I've been thinking...for a while about various things. About what could have happened..." Her eyes restlessly panned the room. "...that no one wants to speak about. It must have been something really big to have put me in this state. And I must have surely brought it upon myself, my gut tells me so."

She stared directly into his eyes. "Yet you've been so wonderful. Never expressed outrage or a word of complaint, always been cheerful no matter how tired and frustrated you probably felt. And you gave me my life back. But I wonder..." She paused, looking down again.

"Wonder about what, Naina?" His hands gripped the edge of the mattress. He loathed suspense other than in the movies.

"What if all your efforts come to no end. What if I don't remember anything and what started as a blank page remains as one. What if *I* fail you?"

"Fail me? Stop this nonsense immediately, Naina!" he thundered, springing to his feet. "Yes, I do want you to remember! I want you to remember everything! Your home, your family, and most of all me! And it will happen someday. Maybe tomorrow, or the day after. In a month. A week. I don't know. Regardless, everything I'm doing is not with that end in mind. I want you to get back to where you were with your confidence and independence restored. I'm doing it because you're my wife, and *I love you, damnit!"*

"I'm so sorry, Rihaan. I didn't mean it like that."

"Yes you did. You meant to hurt me!"

"No, please! You've misunderstood me!" Her face crumpled in dismay.

All of a sudden he began to laugh. "C'mon! I was just kidding. *I* was being mean. Don't you see?" Dropping to his haunches again, he grabbed her hands and gently massaged them, speaking in a more somber tone. "You would never willfully hurt anyone. It's not in your nature, unlike me. But I'm working on it."

"You...hurt?" She stared at him with her mouth slightly ajar. "I don't understand. You are so cryptic sometimes, Rihaan." She looked thoroughly befuddled.

"Am I?" He cocked an eyebrow and regarded her thoughtfully. *Perhaps the memory loss was a blessing in disguise, an opportunity for me to start on a clean slate.*

"Rihaan...are you okay?"

He blinked, then smiled and shook his head. "Naina! Now this won't do at all. I almost made you cry. This isn't how I wanted your homecoming to be like. Please say you forgive me."

Her smile resurfaced. She nodded. "Yes I do."

Rihaan breathed a sigh of relief. A certain disaster averted. *I'd better buck up or prepare to get my ass fried!*

Then he grinned brightly. "Enough of *bakbak* and time for some *petpooja,* as dad would say. As a welcome back treat, I have prepared for my lovely wife a sumptuous all *desi* repast that's sure to blow your mind. I'll have it ready in five minutes flat!" He jumped to his feet and headed toward the kitchen, then suddenly stopped, and turned around. "You married an idiot, Naina, an absolute bonehead! How can I be so remiss? You must be dying to freshen up. Let me help you to the bathroom."

He crouched down to lift her up again.

"I can get there myself. Just hand me my crutches."

"But you may fall. Don't forget you still have your cast on," he persisted.

"No I won't," she said with a cheeky spark in her eyes. "Didn't I hear you mention 'independence' not too long ago?"

"Okay, I give up lady. Suit yourself!" He threw his hands up in mock surrender and stood by as she braved the several feet of wooden floor on her own. Abruptly, he found himself smiling. Naina—his little firecracker of a wife who at every turn had left him dumbstruck with awe, was now telling him in her own quiet little way— *'Fragile I may be, but a weakling I'm not!'*

How could he forget all the adversities she had overcome throughout her life? How could he do disservice to the creature who had changed him into a man from a machine? A woman like her needed an anchor, not an impediment. He had to give her room and not just say it. And there were no two ways about it. Having lost her once already, he wasn't planning on losing her again.

Healing

The dinner was a disaster.

Naina had barely swallowed a spoonful of the delicately spiced *dal* soup when she began to splutter and cough violently. The spasms lasted so long that Rihaan was nearly persuaded to summon the ambulance. And he wouldn't be pacified, even though she pinned it squarely on her wretched digestive system. Instead, he berated himself repeatedly for being overly ambitious and lacking in foresight, and swore never to expose her to such abominable experiments again. He was a horrible cook.

When she woke up the next day, from the longest and most relaxing slumber she'd ever had, and found the curtains drawn even at ten o'clock, she realized the true benefits of this new phase of her life.

There were to be no more annoying vital checks and bed alarms. No more having to save her pee and assuring the nurse that yes, indeed she *did* have a BM. No more embarrassing skin checks and position changes. No more constant poking and prodding. No more threadbare gowns that exposed more than they covered. No more having to wake up when she just got to sleep. No more bland food on regulation tableware, and most of all—no more beeping IV pump jam sessions. The silence was unbelievably melodious and Naina just couldn't get enough of it.

Her husband had rescued her from hell and she didn't even know it!

"Rihaan, did you know that you're such an adorable sweetheart!" she declared aloud to the empty room before bursting out into a fit of embarrassed giggles.

"And look at me, I haven't even thanked him properly. Poor guy. He must be feeling so awful, especially after last night."

She sat up and reached for her crutches that leaned conveniently alongside the headboard and hobbled slowly toward the living room, leaning to her left as her right side still felt awkward and weak, from when she had taken a fall and strained her shoulder during one of the therapy sessions. She broke into a wry laugh. "What a mess I am!"

"Press down, hop forward, press down, hop forward." She repeated the words like a mantra. They were Dave's—her astounding, patient physiotherapist.

"Rihaan...?" She called out, breathing heavily, the short trip proving to be quite an exertion.

But of course he isn't here, she thought, gazing around the empty space. There are so many more who demand his time. I'm not the only patient he has. She smiled, "Never mind. I'll make it up to him later when he gets home. But first, some *petpooja* as he would say."

She shifted her feet in the direction of the kitchen, then paused and began laughing. "No. I need to freshen up first. Stephie and Cara aren't going to be here to remind me anymore."

She hesitated at the door of the bathroom. It had been easy at the hospital to ignore her reflection, because she was supposed to be sick and sick didn't look good. But that wasn't the case anymore.

She stared at the mirror. Her reflection appeared as aghast as her. What does he see in me? Except maybe those eyes?

For a brief instant, the girl in the pictures became real—the beautiful, clear dark eyes, glowing smooth skin, brilliant lovely smile. Recalling images of her long lustrous hair, Naina slowly peeled off her turban cap—it had become her most endeared accessory; so much so that she even slept in it. At last, her scalp was beginning to show signs of recovery—a thick black mop now covered it completely. Still, not for a moment would anyone mistake it to resemble the pictures. She pinched her bony cheeks and pursed her pale lips to tease some color into them and then smiled, imitating the girl. She could have very well not made the effort.

She flipped the lights off and finished brushing her teeth in the dark. It'd take a while for her to summon the courage to face herself again.

She slowly made her way into the kitchen, wondering if there was anything edible in the refrigerator. The appetite she'd woken up with had disappeared. But she had to eat, if not for herself, for Rihaan. She owed him that much.

But a surprise awaited her there. Sitting on the counter she saw two large brown bags, each stacked to the brim with cartons filled with an array of fresh mouthwatering and wholesome food catered from god knows where.

It is probably someplace special because they certainly know how to cook for delicate constitutions like mine, she thought, rolling her eyes back in ecstasy as she bit into a juicy chocolate-covered strawberry.

Rihaan, forgive me, but I've lost count on how many things I owe you so far.

A sudden buzzing noise woke her from her trance. And it steadily grew louder. She followed it warily to the bedroom, wondering if she'd tripped on some kind of alarm. It wasn't. It was just her brand new timed pill box, reminding her to take her medicines. Rihaan had explained it to her while setting it up the night before.

"Now, I'd have surely forgotten that," she grumbled. She screwed her eyes tight shut and gulped the pills down in one big swallow trying not to gag. She didn't. But in a few minutes she collapsed on the bed and fell into a deep sleep.

And so she remained until…

"Rise and shine!"

"Whaaat?" She cracked her eyes open to find Rihaan bending over her with an anxious look on his face. It took her awhile to orient back to her surroundings.

"Whaat's the time...?" she asked groggily.

"It's seven in the evening, darling. Have you been sleeping all day?"

She propped herself up, flustered that he'd found her like this, disheveled and still in yesterday's bedclothes. Swinging her feet off the bed, she got up and would have toppled over hadn't he caught her.

"I feel sooo...dizzhhy..." she moaned, holding her head as he sat her back down.

"It is not at all unusual when you've been sick and confined to bed for the length of time that you have. Your reflexes get all messed up. You have to take it slow." He said the words with a smile, not appearing in the least concerned.

"But it wasn't so thish morning. I felt good. I think its thossh medicines I took. They knocked me out compleetly...and I still...feel drugged. Look...I can bare...ly shpeek!" she said, peering at him from under droopy eyelids.

His smile broadened into a foxy grin. "It's because you're way too excited to see me."

"Nooo!" She shook her head. "I mean yesss!" She colored a deep scarlet, furious at being taken in by his banter. Then slowly enunciating every word, she said, "I just don't think I need them anymore...now that I'm fiiinne."

"You're fine because you are taking them. They are keeping you seizure free," he explained to her patiently, as if to a child with his eyes twinkling with amusement.

"But so many? I don't think so," she argued heatedly. "They are enough for a meal! Do Checkk themm. *Pleease!*"

"Okay madam, I will!" He surrendered with a laugh, then picking the bottles up one by one from the nightstand, turned them slowly over in his hands. "Hmm, maybe the dose of this one could be reduced. You're aware why Dr. Beg prescribed them for you?"

Naina nodded. They were her 'calm down pills'. 'They will reduce your anxiety levels and keep your mind running on an even keel,' the beautiful young Turkish psychiatrist had advised her.

"They weren't doing a good job at the hospital, but now they seem to be working way too well. From tomorrow, take only half-a-pill instead of a whole. I'll tell Dr. Beg that my wife commanded me to change the dose. Then she might sympathize with my plight." He grinned playfully, then pretended to howl and collapsed on the bed with her, laughing when Naina came at him with her tiny fists.

"Rihaan I...I want to tell you something," she said out of breath from the exertion. Her complexion had suffused to a healthy pink and her eyes sparkled. She felt almost normal again.

"Yes?" he asked with a hint of trepidation in his voice.

"You are...the best husband a girl could ever have," she said solemnly. "One day I hope I can make you a worthy wife."

"But darling, you already *are* a very worthy wife!" he exclaimed, his face lighting up with surprise and delight. He enveloped her in his arms and hugged her (more gently this time). You've made me the luckiest bastard in the world. I can't tell you how happy I am tonight."

Pillowing her face on his broad chest, she let his solid warmth seep into her tired bones and let herself relax, feeling for the first time utterly free and unburdened since setting foot in this world again.

Visible Signs of Progress

The following day was slightly better. Naina felt less groggy. Her head felt normal and not like an inflated melon. Still, she slept through the afternoon. Though that didn't seem to bother Rihaan at all. "Sleep is good. It heals. I prescribe at least a couple of hours of siesta every day."

But I'm sleeping for more like five hours! She wanted to argue, but quelled the urge. She had caused him enough headaches.

Therefore, as an expression of gratitude, well, not only that; in order to show him that she was really committed to being a good wife, she planned on cooking a proper meal for him—a four course *desi* dinner complete with all the trappings.

But how could she go about accomplishing the ambitious task when the simple act of hustling together a regular breakfast wore her down?

When he came home that Friday evening and found her tottering around a messy kitchen, almost on the brink of tears, he put an immediate end to her endeavors.

"You're a phenomenal cook Naina, I know that from experience," he said, staring sternly into her eyes. "But this is not what I want to see you doing now. All I expect from you to try to concentrate on is getting better. Everything else will automatically follow."

So Naina took his advice, and did just plain nothing. She idled around the apartment, dividing her time between the solitary bed, the living room couch, and the balcony, where she would lounge under the oversized umbrella, and either read, snooze, or stuff her mouth with delicious food. She was pretty sure that she must have put on at least half her weight in three days, though the scales in the bathroom indicated a measly two pounds.

It was a situation she found she could easily get accustomed to, except for one vexation—there was no Rihaan to share it with. She considered herself lucky if she got to see him at dinner time. Though one evening he arrived early enough for them to have tea and cookies on the balcony. An uncomfortable silence settled between them once she'd finished responding to his usual barrage of questions about her health.

"Naina, I..." he began then impulsively reached for her hand and kissed it. There was a soft, wistful look in his eyes which prompted her own to instantly tear up.

She didn't know what he made of her reaction but it was awhile before they enjoyed tea together again.

Yet, no matter how late he got home, he didn't spare her a thorough head-to-toe once over. This daily ritual would fill her with intense confusion, making her protest with a nervous laugh, to which he'd retort tersely before resuming, "Am I the doctor or are you?"

Naina awoke on Day #5 of her overindulged new life. In a couple of days her therapy sessions would resume.

She shuffled around the apartment in abject boredom, having run out of books to read, and with nothing on the telly to hold her attention. Anyhow, she felt too restless to take the nap that her dear husband had ordered. To be truthful, she didn't want to. His taunt the previous evening had hit her on a sore spot.

She stood by the living room window and marveled at the brilliant blue sky. There wasn't a cirrus in sight. "It's going to be a gorgeous balmy day!" The fat, black weather man on NBC had said that morning, substituting his umbrella with a sun hat.

"Why not?" Naina muttered, suddenly seized by a reckless urge to venture out on her own. Not far, just a block, maybe two. The overbearing Dr. Rihaan Mehta wouldn't approve but then why did he need to know? The idea of putting one past her shrewd spouse filled her with an unfamiliar excitement. *She could go on walks, bus rides, even take the subway! The possibilities were endless.*

In a hurry to begin her new adventure, she swung away from the window and started forward and tripped; her foot catching on the edge of the Persian rug. Unable to stop her momentum, she went crashing onto the floor lamp causing it to nearly topple over.

With silent tears coursing down her cheeks and her toes throbbing from where she'd stubbed them, Naina watched the heavy brass fixture dangerously wobble a few times before righting itself. Her crutches lay in disarray on the floor. They had bypassed her mind entirely as had the dreaded cast that still clung to her leg like a leech. There was no way she was going to get anywhere with these in tow. At least not in her current shabby state. And the thought made her mad. *Really mad.*

"How much longer is this supposed to go on?" she demanded of the bookcase that lined the wall nearest to her. "How much longer are we supposed to continue like this, me and him?" She cried as her eyes erratically scanned the over-crammed shelves in a vain bid to find the answer.

She was about to turn away in a frustrated huff when her gaze was caught by something glinting in one of the lower shelves. Eager for distraction of any kind, she sat to investigate and discovered the object to be a camera, the same that Rihaan had presented her at the hospital.

"He probably dumped it here after bringing it back," she murmured, carefully retrieving the instrument. "And for some reason he didn't download any of the pictures he made me take."

She smiled. By now she knew him well enough to deduce that he had undertaken the exercise with only one purpose on his mind—to convey a message to her in his usual direct and no-nonsense manner—that she held a special gift with the lens.

Maybe I should put his claim to the test! she thought, her interest sparked.

She clicked a few practice frames. Again, the ease with which she operated the controls surprised her. Getting bolder, she hobbled to the balcony and began shooting at random. And soon became engrossed, discovering that not many things remain innocuous when viewed through a camera lens—be it the fluid lines of an arched doorway, a pair of dark and mysterious old windows, an ivy draped trellis gate leading to a narrow flight of stairs, or even a solitary child's bike lying abandoned on the sidewalk—everything had its appeal and a story to tell.

A yellow taxi drew to a halt in front of the apartment building, distracting her from her preoccupation. She was startled to see Rihaan jump out.

What could he be doing here at this time?

He cut a remarkably dapper figure in a short-sleeved checkered shirt and olive green khaki slacks, a fact he seemed completely unaware of. Her camera was irresistibly drawn to him, zooming in on his stirringly elegant profile as he stooped low to chat with the cabbie, one hand casually propped on the roof of the vehicle. A shock of thick, black hair glinted blue in the sunlight while lush eyelashes formed inky pools of mystery on his cheekbones.

Suddenly she drew back, her pulse bouncing around like a yoyo. She had seen the image before, but with the hair worn longer, plus a thick blue scarf and a warm wool coat...and the surroundings had a uniform grey white tone. She leaned back in the chair and closed her eyes. *What did it all mean?* She was too scared to think.

"Naina?"

She jumped, probably a foot in the air.

He was standing in front of her, sporting a clever grin on his mug, as if to tell her he knew exactly what was passing through her mind. She colored, opening her mouth to defend herself, but then just as quickly closed it.

He wasn't alone. There was someone with him. A woman.

"This is Mrs. Alice Croaker, your new nurse and companion. Mrs. Croaker..." His smile shifted to the woman, "...this is Naina. My wife."

"Nurse?" Naina repeated dumbly, her heart plummeting to her feet.

"Yes." He nodded somberly. "She's going to take charge of your care since, unfortunately, as you've seen I'm terribly restricted by lack of time. And I don't want you to lose out. She's the best there is in her field and she has very graciously agreed to come out of retirement on my request. I trust her with my eyes closed." He winked at her.

Nurse? Companion? Take charge? Best in her field? So he wants to wash his hands of me and hand me over to this...this... Creature who he trusts with his eyes closed!

Naina hated the woman, despised her for disrupting her paradise, her pristine little sanctuary.

She critically examined the subject of her husband's gushing admiration, as she puffed up like a peacock under all the praise. Mrs. C was a black woman who looked to be in her sixties. She was round all over—round body, round face, round calves, and she draped her roundness with a prim old-fashioned, high collared dress that reached well below her round knees. Her salt and pepper hair was pulled back into a severe round bun and she wore bright red lipstick and glared at Naina with her severe round eyes.

It took Naina all her strength to stop from breaking into a vexed sob. Nothing could be more humiliating than to be attended to by someone more than twice her age and to have her stick around all day.

"Are you going to stay with me twenty-four/seven?"

"No," Mrs. C said, speaking for the first time. Her voice had a surprisingly pleasant resonant quality to it. "Dr. Mehta asked me to arrive at nine and leave at six."

"Did he?" Naina said relaxing slightly. Rihaan wasn't being so terrible after all. Maybe she could even like this *nurse* he had thrust upon her. She could definitely give it a try.

Just then she noticed her husband staring quizzically at the camera lying on the patio table. But before he moved to pick it up, she'd snatched it and slung it around her neck. "I was fiddling with it as I was bored but couldn't get it to work," she told him with a wry shrug, then turned and smiled brightly at Mrs. C. "How about some chai?"

***

The next day Mrs. C arrived promptly on time. She was 'clocking in' apparently, hence effectively putting an end to Naina's relaxed and laid-back mornings.

Unusually sprightly for her age, the woman was a cleanliness freak. She sprayed and wiped down every surface in the house at least five times a day. Her excuse—bugs are taking over the earth and invalids like her, Naina that is, made for particularly attractive petri-dishes.

She was unlike any other nurse Naina had come across (and she had quite a repertoire). She was rigid like a wooden pastry board with a comparable charm quotient *and* she lacked the essential empathy ascribed to her profession. Actually, she was more like a boot camp director whose only agenda was to whip Naina in to shape and do so in the shortest time possible.

And did she take charge!

She began by planning out Naina's entire day. Everything was set by the clock with a start and end time. When to wake up. When to bathe. When to eat, what to eat—she even prepared all of Naina's meals 'sensible home-cooked nutritious food' (the good Doc is crazy to waste hard-earned money on fancy, useless junk!) When to exercise (she was a trained physical therapist). When to rest (siesta was only one hour, not two)…and if that wasn't enough she also managed to squeeze in the few hundred doctors' appointments that Naina was supposed to attend, now that she was out of the hospital. The woman was exhausting. She left Naina no room to pause, brood or even breathe. It was like running to catch a train that had long left the station.

And whenever Naina gathered enough courage to complain, she received the same stock response—"I'm just complying with Dr. Mehta's instructions."

Or so it appeared. For when Rihaan returned in the evenings, he seemed greatly elated with the *visible* signs of progress he saw in her. So much so that Naina began to wonder if this was his way of getting back at her for her 'independence' jibe.

Well if that was so, then he was in for a big surprise.

It wasn't easy for Naina to curb her growing resentment or subdue the deep-rooted instinct she had been born with; that of a rebel. But she accomplished it. She tagged along Mrs. C's dictates, and played 'the good soldier' so to speak. She sweated it out, straining with every ounce of her eighty-five pound frame, because, as Hemingway had said somewhere: 'A man (or woman in her case) could be destroyed, but not defeated.'

A few days into this intense game of wills, Naina realized that indeed she was starting to feel better. The days had begun to dawn brighter, her mood was up, and the need to break and rest at every juncture didn't seem as urgent as before. Mrs. C's secret smirks weren't as malevolent, nor was Rihaan, her husband, out to get her.

Hence, one golden spring afternoon, when Mrs. C was busy fixing lunch in the kitchen, Naina decided to approach her. She stood in the doorway waffling for several minutes, watching as the woman bustled around humming a happy tune, before summoning the guts to put thoughts to words.

"Mrs. C, I mean Mrs. Croaker..." She blushed, then spoke rapidly to cover her slip. "I want to thank you for all you've done for me and I sincerely apologize for mistaking your intentions. You really aren't as bad as I thought."

And much to her bewilderment, her nurse broke into a loud guffaw—a very rich sound, emanating from somewhere deep inside her rotund body that blossomed out and around the tiny space like the weighty notes of a church bell.

It took a while for her to calm down. Then she said still chuckling softly, "Lady, you don't have to say sorry at all. Indeed, I'm honored to be chosen to work with my favorite doctor's wife. It gives me great pleasure to see you doing so well."

Thereafter their relationship evolved into what Naina termed as a cordial companionship. At her behest, Alice (they had switched to first names) agreed to relax the rules slightly, and spend some time in other gainful activities.

One of them amounted to accepting Naina's assistance in the kitchen, where Alice gave her some simple, stress-free pointers in order to get her closer toward her goal of preparing a meal for Rihaan. Alice in turn acquired some *desi* tips on how to jazz up her Cajun recipes.

***

One evening, after Alice had left for the day and she was alone in the apartment, she received a surprise visit from Rihaan's father and his elder sister. The timing, it appeared, had something to do with Rihaan's not being in town. (He had left earlier that day on urgent official business.) And though sorely dismayed at the absence of her mother-in-law, Naina was gratified to play the proper host and offer her guests some tea and snacks. Rihaan's father, seemingly moved by the gesture, gently smoothed his hand over her head, before folding several hundred dollar bills into her palm.

"*Beta*, don't refuse. Consider it as a *shagun* for your new life. My son is a very lucky man."

Naina wondered what he meant, wishing he had elaborated further. But the money left her utterly stupefied. *What do I do with it?*

Still unsure what to do, Naina mentioned the visit to Alice the next day.

"Spend it, that's what!" Alice said, smiling and shaking her head incredulously. "You really could do with some new clothes. Tomorrow I'll take you to a place where they sell real good stuff for dirt cheap."

Naina agreed. Her wardrobe was indeed sparse. All she had was a long kaftan-like robe she'd worn home from the hospital, a couple of halter sundresses Rihaan had bought that she'd never dared to try on, and a couple of PJs that she generally spent all day in. None of her old clothes would fit. The prospect of shopping was exciting.

The next day, soon after entering the store, when she was confronted with row upon row of bewildering array of apparel, she became riddled with anxiety. "Let's go back, Alice. This place isn't for me."

But Alice wouldn't hear a word. "Stay quiet, woman. I know exactly what you need," she said and marched right ahead, leaving Naina with no choice but to follow on her heels.

True to her word, within minutes, Alice had assembled a pile of clothes. Among them, a couple of lightweight jeans and cotton skirts that enhanced Naina's slim figure without making her look scrawny; a few soft, cotton fitted shirts and a couple of beautifully embroidered blouses that she could wear on special occasions. A fluffy scarf draped around her neck was an indispensable accessory—to add color and flair, but more importantly to camouflage the many scars that she had accumulated.

Later, Naina took a nervous peek at the mirror, and was surprised by the image she saw. It was something she could live with. She felt human again, someone who could step out into the world without fear of prejudice or ridicule.

Alice, who was standing behind her watching, said, "Now you know why the Doc loves you? Because you're one helluva beautiful girl!"

"You probably tell that to all your patients," Naina retorted, yet deep inside she was pleased.

Growing Pains

The days rolled by as life slid into a new pattern. A week passed, then three. Naina considered herself healed except for her memory.

On a sultry May afternoon, with the entire city reeling under sweltering heat, Naina and Alice chose to call it a day. They decided instead, to camp out on the balcony and sip chilled glasses of minty lemonade and watch the languorous citizens parade by.

"It's high time the clouds made up their minds and gave us a good old downpour," Alice said, fanning herself vigorously with the frilly bottom of her apron.

"It's high time *my* brain made up its mind and gave me my good old memory back," Naina muttered.

"Do I hear a note of bitterness in that sweet voice, Mrs. Doc Mehta?"

Naina glanced sharply at her friend. She had the irritating habit of switching to formal terms whenever she didn't see eye to eye with her.

"Maybe you do," she replied, leaning back in her patio chair and gazing unseeingly at the shade umbrella. "But my memory, rather its absence I should say, has become a wound that won't stop festering. I remain a stranger to myself. Who am I? What am I like? Do I have a family, if so, why don't they look me up? Why does my mother-in-law refuse to have anything to do with me? What could've I possibly done to grudge her? Is it because of something between Rihaan and me? Why is he so tight-lipped about everything? I know he pretends to brush it under the carpet, but I can't! There are way too many questions that need to be answered!"

Alice scrutinized Naina silently. That she harbored a far deeper malady hadn't escaped her, Naina knew. Yet, not wanting to intrude, she seemed to have waited patiently for the revelation.

"I do understand what you're going through," Alice began, weighing her words with care. "I was born an unwanted child, who spent nearly all her life shuttling between foster homes. Don't get me wrong! I've nothing against the system. It's the reason why I'm here today," she said emphatically. "But there've been more than a few times when I've wished to confront my mother, just so I could ask her why she gave me up? Was it because she didn't want me or did kismet make her do it? I don't blame her, I just want to clear my mind. But now I know I'll probably never meet her."

"Are you meaning to imply that I should simply stop harping over the past and get on with it?" Naina quipped.

"No, not at all." Alice shook her head. "What I'm trying to say is that there are certain things in life we have no control over and dwelling over them just causes more pain. Take for instance Tommy, my foster brother," she said, her eyes taking on a distant look. "I loved him like my very own. Not just me, everybody did. We kids employed him as our bodyguard because he was *big* with lots of muscles, yet, the gentlest and kindest of creatures. But the bullies didn't know that." She tittered, tickled pink at her revelation, which made Naina smile.

"Tommy was a slow learner. He struggled a lot at school, but he worked really hard and it paid off. He got a scholarship to college. He was also an ace athlete. Music, art, you name it, there was nothing that was out of bounds for him. He was always willing to learn and that was inspiring. For us kids, he was our brightest star. He gave us hope, showed a way out of the drudgery." Her face brightened at the memory.

"Then all at once, this beautiful life was delivered a cruel blow. Tommy was struck by a blinding disease. An irreversible condition, the doctors said. His world began to slowly fade away. He told me how one day he could read the words on the billboard across the street, but on the next it had dissolved into a messy blur. He lost his job. His driving license got taken away. And then when we thought things couldn't get any worse, Karen, his beautiful wife, left him taking the children with her. That broke him completely. He was devastated. Life had lost its purpose. He tried to kill himself and almost succeeded." Alice grew quiet.

But Naina's curiosity was piqued. "What happened to him? Tell me please," she urged Alice.

Her friend complied. "A dramatic change came over Tommy after his brush with death. What happened? No one knows. According to Maya, my romantic little sister, he had some kind of otherworldly experience while lying comatose on the hospital bed. We joke about it even now." She chuckled. "But it's true, he woke up a changed man. There was this new energy about him that's hard to describe."

Her unblemished ebony brow wrinkled into a frown. "He was caught up in some kind of frenzy. He went to school again to train to be a counselor and now spends all his time helping people with developmental issues and other disabilities to better themselves. And I understand he's very good at it."

Naina didn't know how to respond. She stared down at her arms where the veins made a lacy network under the skin. The bruises and blotches she'd brought home from the hospital had long since disappeared. She felt at once humbled and deeply mortified by Alice's account. Her own predicament seemed innocuous in comparison, and her anger irrelevant. "You must be so proud of your brother, Alice," she mumbled.

"Yes. But so am I of you, sweetheart," Alice effused, leaning forward to encase Naina in a comforting hug. "Not many can achieve what you have and in such a short time."

"But I couldn't have accomplished anything without either you or Rihaan," Naina muttered in protest.

"All we did was stand by while *you* sweated and slogged," Alice insisted. "You're a woman of rare courage and I'm privileged to know you!"

"You are very kind, Alice. Your words give me confidence," Naina said, hugging the woman back.

"Good. I'm glad," Alice said, pulling back.

Suddenly she looked very solemn. "Because I think the time has come for me to leave."

Naina stared unbelievingly at her. *"Leave?* Did I hear you right? You can't say that! That's insane! How will I make it without you? My life will fall apart. How will I survive?"

Alice laughed, reaching to run her fingers through Naina's short curly hair. "Don't panic. You will survive. You aren't a child anymore. Though you look very much like one." Her tone turned wistful. "You have to learn to take care of your life and your husband. God bless him! I know you can, because your spirit is strong and it shines brighter every day. Besides, if you need anything, your nasty friend is just a phone call away."

Naina smiled, choosing not to argue. She could tell that, Alice too, was hard-headed just like her. Yet she couldn't help but seek one last reassurance. "My memory, do you think I'll ever get it back?"

"You will. Most people do. Try to titillate your mind. Don't be afraid."

Yes, Naina had been afraid, wondering what she'd dig up. Her past seemed not just mysterious but also dark and sinister. *What if she found something she didn't like?*

Later, with Alice out on an errand, Naina set about in search for clues. Pictures, letters, a laptop perhaps? She found none except Rihaan's PC and the tablet he liked to carry around. Eventually she zeroed in on a scuffed up brown leather bag that lay hidden, deep in the rear of the bedroom closet. She'd seen it before but it'd been too heavy to pull out, or maybe she hadn't tried hard enough. This time she had no trouble.

Inside it, she found some clothes just like the oversized ones hanging in the closet. They were of no interest to her. What caught her eye was a beautiful silk sari, tie-dyed in a rainbow of colors with decorated elephants marching along the borders and tiny shiny mirrors that caught the light and sparkled like diamonds. She flung it around her neck like a shawl and felt deeply comforted by the strong fragrance of sandalwood.

Underneath was a finely inlaid wooden box, inside which on a bed of tissue, lay several glass bangles in red, green and orange tied together with a string. Slipping them over her hands, she wondered if they were a gift from Rihaan. Instinct told her they were, thus filling her with a warm glow.

Trembling with excitement she dug deeper, and at the very bottom, found a large album. She flipped the pages over, only to find random black and white shots, of people and children on the streets. Nothing else. No blissful wedding pictures, in particular no family portraits, as if she'd severed all ties before coming here.

Feeling utterly wretched and frustrated, she tore the bangles from her hands and sank sobbing to the floor.

***

The following evening, Alice proposed her intention to leave.

Rihaan considered it for several moments, though he didn't seem much surprised. He wrote her a check, apparently a very generous one, because it stimulated a spurt of happy tears as well as a resounding kiss on the cheek that made him blush pink.

She requested them not to accompany her to the street. "Then I won't be able to go." She slipped out the door and left.

The tears that Naina had been holding back came pouring out. She scrambled to get to the balcony.

"Wait Naina. Let me." Rihaan ran to her assistance and to her surprise took her crutches away.

But she remained silent, not uttering a word of objection when he carried her outside, and then, propping her against the low railing, wrapped a solid arm around her waist. She remained so because she didn't want to be alone at this moment of loss. Alice's absence already made her appreciate Rihaan more.

Setting her qualms aside, she flung her arms around her husband's broad chest and embraced him, springing a pleasant exclamation of surprise from him.

He whispered into her hair as he stroked her gently on the back. "Everything's going to be fine, Naina. I shall see to it."

Alice looked up just before climbing into the taxicab and broke into a broad grin on seeing them together.

Naina smiled and waved cheerfully. She wanted her friend to leave in peace.

Whole

As Alice had predicted, Naina had no difficulty adapting to her absence. She kept herself occupied, sticking to the regimen her friend had drawn up, as it left little room to sulk over the palpable void she had left behind, along with her own persistently nagging insufficiency.

She worked on her exercises, prepared quick and sensible meals (much to Rihaan's delight) and rode the taxi alone to all her appointments, though often she found her husband waiting there ahead of time, perhaps indicating a lingering lack of trust in her decision making capabilities. It irked her immensely yet she didn't begrudge him, because she wasn't prepared to trust herself either.

Despondent thoughts like these continued to plague her periodically. At such times she'd consciously recall Alice's wise words and try to comfort herself.

Alice had said: 'The secret of happiness is very simple. Just count your blessings. You'll see that you have more than you think.'

Naina couldn't do anything but agree. She had her health. She had her life. And most of all she had her crux—her husband. He was her blessing.

There were days when her endurance was rewarded and hope made an ungainly resurgence. Flashes, tiny frames, teasing glimpses, of people, scenes and events that didn't string together in a neat logical sequence sorted themselves in her mind.

Such as when Rihaan took an entire weekend off and chose to spend it taking her around the city. "We need to spend some quality time together. Just you and I."

She didn't realize until later that it was his way of dropping hints without making blatant suggestions, thereby relieving her of considerable anxiety.

She accompanied him to the corner bagel shop for a late morning breakfast, where the young proprietor greeted her by name. She smiled to shield her embarrassment, not having any inkling whatsoever of ever being there before, let alone eating a bagel or meeting Gil, or his Indian wife Uma, who had just delivered their first child.

Yet, she didn't hesitate when asked to place her order. "Toasted pumpernickel with jalapeno," she said, then stood back perplexed at her not so conventional choice.

Rihaan, on the other hand seemed quite amused.

"Do you know something I don't?" she demanded, looking at him.

He responded with a grin as he pulled her aside. "Rest easy sweetheart. It's what you usually order. Things are looking up, shall we say?"

So it appeared.

They took a cab around the city, stopping briefly at various spots—Wall Street, United Nations, The Met, St. Patrick's cathedral, Tiffany's… Naina's face drooped as the skyscrapers rushed by—her mind drawing a continuous blank and all the razzle-dazzle only making her nauseous and dizzy.

Her husband probably read her mind, for within the space of five minutes (more likely fifteen, but it always seemed so much quicker with Rihaan) they had boarded the subway for a ride across the river. And soon after getting there, they drove to a café oddly called Happenstance where Naina sat trying to hustle a Key Lime shake while Rihaan stared fixatedly at an obscure apartment block across the street.

Why had he brought her here? Was it to trigger a specific memory? Was he disappointed that she hadn't jumped up screaming: Yes! It's all coming back to me!

Her perturbation on a steady upswing, she wanted to cry out—*What do you expect from me, Rihaan?* But she couldn't get the words to her mouth. She didn't want to risk provoking him. He was all she had—her past, her present and her future. Without him her life would become tenuous. She would cease to exist.

"Shall we go?" he asked her after what seemed like forever. His mint julep remained untouched.

She nodded vigorously, not trusting her speech. Maybe it'd been a long day, maybe she was simply worn out, maybe she was just tired of trying to remember all the time—a perfectly valid explanation. But all she wanted to do now was get back home, curl up in bed, and go to sleep.

The train jerked as it hugged a sharp curve. She went sliding across the plastic seats. Rihaan caught her and they both broke out laughing. He held on. She snuggled into the open V of his shirt, seeking much needed solace. The contact stirred something deep—a surge of emotions—of gnawing pain, unrequited love and a smoldering all-consuming passion. She retracted, trembling with fright, leaving him utterly bemused.

***

The cast came off. Finally! She was free! And there was no need for continued use of the crutches.

Naina danced a little jig in front of Rihaan. "Now I'll be able to come biking with you."

"Yes," he laughed, "but let's first celebrate with a walk."

She sensed an undercurrent of excitement in him, and she felt it, too. It would be her first outing as an emancipated woman.

They took a cab to the park. "This was a bad idea. I've no muscles to speak of. Let's go back," she exclaimed, frustrated after trudging only a few yards.

"No. I won't let you goof-off. We shall finish what we set out to accomplish!" he declared, dismissing her demand.

The resolute brute! But his cheer rubbed off on her and somehow she made it to the lake where they sat down on a bench to rest. It had been well worth the effort.

"Close your eyes. Do you see anything?" he asked.

She closed her eyes. After a few moments she smiled and nodded. "Yes. The color of the water, I remember it was much darker and the geese—they created such a din that I…"

"Let's go, Naina." He stood up abruptly. His face darkening with anger and also apparent pain.

"But why…?" she asked, puzzled.

"It doesn't become you to lie. The last time you were here was in the dead of winter and the bloody lake was frozen," he said tersely and strode off.

"But…but, Rihaan!" She hobbled after him, forgetting that she could walk just fine. "I was just trying to please you…"

He swung around. "Don't Naina, don't ever do it again! I can handle anything but I cannot handle untruths, no matter how innocent they may seem!" he snapped.

She bit her bottom lip to keep it from trembling. It took all her self-control to avoid bursting into a loud frustrated scream. What had she done to upset him so much? Had she deceived him in the past?

They returned home and soon after he left, saying he needed to attend an urgent call. He was providing himself with a convenient excuse to flee and walk away from her questions.

It was hopeless. They were hopeless. She locked herself up in the bedroom and cried herself to sleep.

***

The following two days were spent deliberately avoiding each other. They were not unlike a couple of rash and impetuous teenagers after a particularly fierce spat. It was quite a comical situation and if Naina hadn't been party to it, she'd have probably died laughing.

But then something happened to interrupt the silent brouhaha.

Rihaan was lounging in the living room, in his favorite recliner, when Naina approached him.

"Your mother's on the phone," she said. She held a cordless phone.

"Tell her I'm not here," he muttered quietly, continuing to scroll on his cell as if his life depended on it.

"It's not you she wanted to talk to, it's me."

His head came up sharply. "Whatever for?"

Naina faltered. It was clear that the situation between mother and son continued to remain grim. "Uhm… She has invited me along with you, of course, to the house tomorrow…a sort of welcome back party for me—her *bahu,* she said."

A myriad of expressions crossed her husband's face—from shock, to frank incredulity, to wonderment.

Naina was growing impatient. "What should I say? I told her I'd let her know after asking you."

"I'll go with whatever you want," he replied evenly.

"But…I…" Naina was thrown by his words. How could he leave it to her when thus far he'd been the one who had been making all the decisions? She wrung her hands. "I guess I cannot say no. She's my mother-in-law after all. God, I'm so nervous."

His expression softened into a smile. "Don't be. She's not going to eat you alive. Besides, I'll be there with you. Consider it your coming out ball, Cinderella."

Inconsistent Life

Silk and summer don't go together, Naina brooded regretfully, as another rivulet of sweat trickled down her side and drenched her sari-blouse. But her sister-in-law had insisted. "Mom will be absolutely bowled over. She's a tradition junkie!" And now, even though she wished she had opted for the more sedate *salwar kameez*, Naina was glad she had sought Rima's help. Who'd know better about a woman's likes and dislikes than her own daughter?

Besides, her skills as a couturier had come in very handy when she expertly refitted Naina's blouse for her and offered valuable advice on the best way to drape her sari, so as to conceal the worst of her scars and wear makeup to highlight her beautiful eyes and draw attention away from her hollow cheeks.

As a bonus she even provided her with a shoulder length wig, which boosted Naina's confidence tremendously, though Rihaan didn't look very impressed.

Naina turned to glance at her husband. She found him in a pensive mood, gazing out of his side of the cab. Now there was someone who'd never need a morale booster of any kind. Even in the casual jacket he'd hastily shrugged on after returning from work, he managed to look breathtakingly suave. Even despite a six o'clock beard.

Naina frowned. She'd rarely seen him miss out on that aspect of his grooming. Undoubtedly, he had something serious playing on his mind.

Suddenly he leaned forward and tapped the cabbie on the shoulder. "The address is at the end of the street."

Naina's grip tightened on the door handle. She didn't want to do anything to further upset her mother-in-law and damage their relationship forever. If nothing else, for Rihaan's sake. He seemed a lot more affected than he let on.

She took a deep breath and gave herself a pep talk. *I can do this.*

***

From her perch on the edge of the flagstone path, Naina stared warily at the secluded suburban villa, anticipating a turmoil of some kind. But the vibe counter was registering a dismal zero.

Backing onto lush green hillside, the red tiled, ivory-washed stucco house, and it's tastefully landscaped grounds dotted with an abundance of shade trees, evoked nothing but a sense of blissful serenity. Adding to the rustic appeal, a profusion of summer color sprang artfully from every direction—it was by no means an ominous vision.

The fluttering in her chest settled down a little, but sped right back up when she spotted Shobha standing at the front door with an *arati thali* in her hands, her expression in complete variance with the surroundings.

"Let's get this over with." She heard Rihaan mutter under his breath at her side.

Yes, might as well suck up and face the music, Naina reasoned wryly and pushed forward. Though at the same time, she struggled to draw the sari's edge over her head, in a show of modesty and sound upbringing, but the wretched thing wouldn't stay. It kept slipping from her fingers.

She lingered wordlessly, as the metal plate with its oil lamp, circled the air, encompassing both her and her husband, keeping with the ancient tradition of warding off all evil. Then dutifully, she bent forward to accept the red *kumkum* dot in the center of her forehead, thereby awakening the third eye.

Here it comes! Naina braced herself and waited for the ax to fall.

But Shobha, having honed her skills on a steady diet of *desi* soap operas, seemed intent on prolonging her daughter-in-law's agony. She smiled, rather sweetly at her, though her words were directed at Rihaan. "At last…you think of bringing your wife to visit your mother. *Meri aankhen toh taras gayi thi. (My eyes had grown weary.)* When did a son need an invitation to visit home?"

Naina glanced at her husband in confusion, but his features revealed nothing. They seemed set in stone. And whether her mother-in-law was expressing genuine sentiment, or was it all a part of some grand scheme, Naina didn't have the luxury to ponder it over because she was swept away in a whirlwind of festivities, set up apparently in her honor—the daughter-in-law who had defied Yama, the God of death himself.

The Mehta residence was much larger than its exterior belied. But the wide open floor plan which allowed for plenty of natural light, plus the ample use of marble everywhere, endowed the place with a soothing ambience rarely seen in large houses. And even though one could tell it wasn't filled to capacity, the crowd present wasn't meager either—quite unlike the intimate gathering that Shobha had mentioned on the phone.

"My mother is very gregarious as you can see. She never lets go of an opportunity to socialize, much to the chagrin of the rest of us," Rima explained in a regretful aside coming to stand next to Naina.

Naina silently acquiesced to being exhibited like a trophy acquired after great battle, disguising her fears and mortification with a smile. She was determined to give Shobha no reason to find fault with her—not if she could help it.

Yet as the hours passed, Naina felt more at ease. Everybody seemed so nice and mindful of her sensitivities. They introduced themselves, sometimes more than once, and treated her no different from the rest of the clan. Though of course, there was the usual sprinkling of unavoidable characters with shady intentions, but that didn't concern her, because her husband, as promised, stayed by her side with a hand parked firmly on her hip—alert for mischief and icy sharp with his repartees.

Indeed, he appeared to have assumed the role of her unofficial bodyguard, that too with an exceptionally cynical sense of humor. And though it appeared many were put off by his apparent fierce possessiveness, she reveled in it.

It was close to ten in the night before Naina concluded that the grand showdown with Shobha had been deferred to another day. Better still, it seemed the woman had forgiven Naina for her mistakes and secretly reconciled to all their differences. Even if she was doing so for her son's sake (who unfortunately seemed to cut her no slack) it was to her credit. She was at least trying.

Rihaan, having perhaps realized the same, relaxed visibly and stepped away to mingle with his own set. His full-throated laughter that boomed forth from time to time imbued Naina with pleasure and satisfaction—her decision to confront the lioness in her own den hadn't been in vain.

The evening was in its final laps. Gossip with coffee and *chai* was winding up in the reception lounge. The ladies were ferreting their men from their various hideouts and saying their goodbyes. Naina stole the opportunity to stifle a yawn, but nothing escaped Shobha's eyes.

She looked legitimately concerned. "You look tired. *Mein toh bhool hi gayi* (I almost forgot) you are still an invalid. You need your rest."

Though Naina didn't entirely concur with the opinion, she agreed to retire. But when Rima offered to take her to Rihaan's room, she refused politely. "Thank you, but I think I can find my way." She desperately wanted to spend some time alone.

"It's isolated at the end of a long corridor in the west end—a large room swimming with books on gross topics—you can't miss it!" Rima said with a laugh.

Naina couldn't suppress her excitement as she headed down the aforesaid passage—like a child on an illicit mission of discovery.

And illicit it was. Though not in the way she wanted it to be—

She heard voices. Ugly, nasty whispers that filtered through the door hinges, ricocheted off the walls and poured directly into her ears. They belonged to the same people who had conversed with her hours ago and wished her well.

"I know I shouldn't be saying this, but I really feel for Rihaan. The poor boy. Look at his wife... How she was and how she is now."

"And totally clueless..." This was followed by a hushed snicker.

"Never seen anything uglier."

"But he appears so devoted..."

"Sab dikhawa hai. (It's a mere pretension.) He must be cursing his luck. I don't get why he sticks with her. Someone should thrust some sense into him.

187

My Sushmita...she is ready even now, if he would just..."

Naina clamped her hands over her ears and snuck into a darkened alcove. She had heard enough.

Her husband—young, virile and very much a man—had been leading the life of a virtual saint. Deprived of his needs because of her. And she...a fool, had been blind to it all, or had simply refused to acknowledge it. Maybe because in all this time he hadn't touched her. Not in that way... And why would he? Her ugliness repelled him.

Hot tears of pain came gushing down her cheeks. Everything was falling into place. Her husband's distance. Shobha's reservations. Everything. Her daydream was over.

Finding an unlocked side door, she yanked it open and rushed outside. But what she saw there brought her to a sudden halt.

Under cover of the heavy blooms of the Wisteria tree, was a couple shamelessly making out. But there was no mistaking their identities. She remembered the man from introducing himself to her earlier. It was Rudy, Rihaan's perpetually smirking friend, in his stand-out stark white suit, with a girl in a white and gold *lehenga*—who did not happen to be his wife in the terminal stages of confinement, but her teenage cousin.

Choking back a cry of disgust, Naina turned and fled the other way.

She made for what looked like a gazebo, brilliantly white and surreal in the moonlight—a perfect place to escape and tally her woes.

The night air was scented with the cloying fragrance of jasmine. She squatted on the low wooden bench and listened as the crickets, frogs and other nighttime creatures performed a raucous symphony; as dancing fireflies went off like tiny flashbulbs in the bushes, and somewhere faraway, a lonely house pet let out a mournful howl.

She heard the muffled sound of footsteps approaching and hurriedly wiped her cheeks.

"There you are!" Rihaan's voice sounded almost angry, but he instantly moderated his tone. "I was worried."

"Why?" she said, continuing to stare into the distance. "Am I not allowed to spend time alone?"

"Of course you are. But..."

"But what?" She turned around and saw him standing with his shoulder slouched against the trellis, slightly inebriated.

"I..." he hesitated.

"Thought that I'd have a seizure? I haven't had one since I was released from the hospital. Please Rihaan...!" Her voice was unintentionally gruff.

"Okay. Sorry. My bad." His mouth relaxed into that familiar lopsided grin.

"You're forgiven," she responded indulgently.

His beautiful face was etched in silver, but his eyes—they shone like burnished fields of gold—warm, benevolent and sensual. A man like him would be no stranger to receiving love notes and sundry messages of undying devotion from his patients—his naïve victims. He probably took them in his stride. They were to him but a clinical curiosity—to be examined and dismissed, before moving on to the next.

Was she too—one among his umpteen transiently interesting subjects?

He looked uncomfortable under her scrutiny. "Anything bothering you? We can talk about it."

She stood up abruptly. "I don't want to stay here anymore. Can we go home...please?"

Us

Naina stood in front of the floor length mirror and began to slowly unwrap her sari. She called it her reality check mirror because it helped keep track of her scars, both old and new, and monitor them, as some faded and others took their place. Of late, she had even begun to find some resemblance between her reflection and the girl in Rihaan's video. But now she knew it to be a delusion.

She sneaked a glance at her husband out of the corner of her eye. Having just walked out of the shower, he was vigorously toweling his hair. His white T clung lovingly to his damp torso.

She yanked her eyes away and said, clearing her throat, "Can you help me with these pins? My hand isn't cooperating again."

"Are you all right?" he asked, flinging the towel away at once and rushing to her side.

"Yes I think so. Just tired."

But he wouldn't believe her as usual, going through the ritual of examining her arm, and asking her to follow simple commands to reassure himself. When he was done, he smiled, appearing satisfied and chided her gently while unpinning her sari. "Why did you have to wear this?"

"To please your mother," she said watching him in the mirror.

But he looked intent in his task.

"You have to please no one," he said, tossing the long end of the garment down on the bedroom floor. She sensed his finger run down the spine of her shoulder blade and shuddered, closing her eyes.

"Fabulous," he murmured softly, as if he was talking to himself. "I must congratulate Dr. Rivers."

Her eyes sprang open. "Who is Dr. Rivers?"

"Your plastic surgeon," he explained, meeting her eyes in the mirror. "She's done an excellent job. The huge scar on your back is almost invisible." He grinned.

"Oh…right." She turned around and took a deep breath. Time to come clean. "Rihaan, I appreciate your sacrifice…but…"

"Sacrifice? *What* sacrifice?" He stared blankly at her—that innocent I-don't-know-what-the-heck-you-mean stare. Why was he making it so difficult!

She tried to compose herself. "I release you from your obligations. You're free."

He continued to watch her. "Obligations? Free? Stop talking in riddles, Naina!" He stepped forward, making her stagger against the dresser.

Her hands scrambled for support. The look on his face was sapping her of her courage. Maybe this wasn't the right time but she couldn't postpone it any longer. She had to get it out of her system.

She bit her bottom lip to stop it from quivering. "I've compelled you all this time to lead your life with a selfish and mean woman, who isn't even a tiny bit attractive," she said looking down. Her head sagged weighed down by grief. "I never thought of you. Not once…about your wants, your desires. And I know what you'll say. You'll say it doesn't matter, but I can't. I can't let it continue like this. Because…I love you so much!" She broke into a sob.

"Naina…"

But she couldn't stop crying. The feelings she had suppressed for so long had chosen to revolt. "I really do love you, Rihaan and that's why even though the very thought kills me, I will let you go."

"No." He propped her up as she swayed tipsily on her feet. "No Naina. No! Please. My love. My poor darling. Stop." Grasping her tear-soaked face in his hands, he kissed it. "Stop crying and listen to me!" He admonished her, but she ignored him.

"I'm an invalid. Damaged goods. Scarred and ugly. You cannot but abhor me. It's plain as day!" she wailed.

"HUSH!" His lips covered her mouth. "There now."

She stared insensibly at him.

"Now that I have your attention," he said, smiling tenderly. "I love you, all of you, every tiny scar. The way you slur your words when you get excited, your ungainly walk. Even your annoying little tantrums." He tapped her chin with his forefinger. "They make you the most complete and beautiful woman that I've ever known in this world, or ever will know. And unfortunately… you can't let me go."

"Why?" she asked dumbly.

"Because I am stuck to you, stupid girl! Like a limpet, with waterproof glue or whatever you may choose to call it! You can't get rid of me no matter how hard you try! Because I belong to you. Only you. Always have!" He yanked her into his arms so fiercely that her breath expelled with an audible whoosh.

"My love. My only love." He kissed her tear-soaked lashes. "I want to cry with joy when I hear you say that you love me. No words have ever sounded more sweet and pure."

With her hands held up against his chest, she scanned his face rapidly, and was surprised by the earnestness she saw there. Her doubts and misgivings began to gradually evaporate. "But I've displeased you by telling you lies. It's okay, Rihaan. You can leave. I can take care of myself. I'm capable now. Alice told me so."

"It's okay!?" he exclaimed, throwing his head back and roaring with laughter. Then he clutched her even tighter. "It's not okay! Because you haven't, you *didn't displease me*, as you so sweetly put it. It was just an innocent way of showing me how much you loved me. And I pounced on you viciously for it. I'm so terribly sorry. Forgive me, darling. Won't you? Please?" He supplemented his plea with a disarming smile.

She shrugged. Was it that easy? "All right. But…"

"But what?"

"You don't love me…not in that way…" she said, her eyes fluttering bashfully.

"I do. Love you…very much in that way," he grunted, dipping his head closer, the smoldering flames in his eyes bringing the blood rushing to her cheeks.

"But…" she gasped. Her heart had gone berserk, pounding so hard it was ready to explode. "You haven't ever…"

"Shown it?" He completed her sentence. "Yes. I accept I'm guilty and I've a confession to make. I was pressuring myself to keep my feelings in check. I was afraid of making a mistake that I'd never be forgiven. I didn't want to appear to be taking advantage of your situation and add to all the trauma you've been through. That is the reason why I didn't share your bed or sleep in the same room. I simply didn't want to give in to temptation which seems to multiply with every moment that passes. I know you've accepted me as your husband, but I wanted to gain your affection and trust beyond any doubt. I was just waiting for the right moment…"

"Oh Rihaan… My darling," she said, her eyes glistening again, but this time through a pool of joy. "Don't you see that I love you? I don't remember anything of how we got together but I know it must've been beautiful. We must've been in love and I still am. My feelings have never been stronger and that's the only truth I know."

They gazed mutely at each other. Their hearts, having suffused to the brim with love, tottered and spilled over, engulfing them both in a sea of sensations that had no parallel. Silently, he scooped her up in his arms and walked to the bed, leaving a trail of silk as the rest of her sari unraveled on the floor.

Laying her down gently, he reached with eager fingers to unhook her blouse.

"Stop!" she said, gripping his hands. "You first."

He grinned foxily. "Shy, are we? Fine." He got rid of his shirt in one swift movement.

She sat up, sucking her breath in sharply. With eyes wide open, she skimmed in wonderment at his finely chiseled flesh, the pads of her fingers brushing across his well-defined pectorals and down his strong, sinewy arms.

A muffled groan escaped him. The look in his eyes made her rush to hide her heated face in the crook of his neck. But he drew her out and locked his mouth onto her trembling lips. Long and hard. Tasting her, as if he hadn't had a meal in ages. She knotted her fingers into his scalp and kissed him back, while he lay her down removing the rest of her clothing.

Tugging at her hairpiece, he sent it flying to join the rest of the pile on the floor. Then they were bare and pristine, lying side by side, skin to skin, staring boldly at each other.

She experienced no shame. Not even for a moment. They were like two lovers who had known each other all their lives, just hadn't met yet.

There was no mistaking his desire as his hands launched themselves on an amorous journey all over her body, lingering on her curves which had finally filled back up and were hungering for his touch.

Something clicked, kindling a deeply buried memory for Naina. The lock to a hidden door snapped open. He reached inside and grabbed her soul and took her to a place somewhere far beyond this world. Kissing, coaxing and caressing her wound-tainted flesh, he applied the final healing touch. The scars—they vanished into thin air. Her heart leaped out of her chest wanting to scream and announce aloud to anybody who could hear—Yes! I am the most beautiful and desirable woman in this world, if not for anyone else, to this man, who gives me definition—slowly, intimately, and with love.

The mystery had unraveled and the dust from the storm finally settled. Yes, he was her love, her husband, the only man she'd ever known or wanted to know. And he was loving her just like before. Nothing remained that needed to be proved or disproved.

She gazed up at him. An all-consuming need awakened deep in her body, forcing her to throw her arms out and reach for him.

***

"Naina. My most adorable, beautiful wife." He took her in his arms and wept.

She was finally *his*, completely, and he was loving her and begging her forgiveness for his reckless misdeeds. Her arms tightened around his neck and she whispered his name, over and over again. He choked with joy. "I love you so much, my sweet darling."

They made love, explicit and irrefutable in every way, moving together in smooth synchrony—a glorious culmination to a long and painful journey. And they savored every moment.

Not Just Biology

Naina deposited her purchases on the small flight of stairs leading to the entrance of her apartment building, then sat down to rest herself. She needed it badly, having been on the go since early that morning.

And by 'on the go', she meant exactly that. She'd begun by baking a batch of cookies—her very first—and taking them over to the hospital where she shared them with a surprised staff, all of whom were uniformly thrilled to see her doing so well. Then, instead of stopping for a bite she'd embarked on an impromptu bus ride and unsuccessfully attempted to draw a mental map of the route. Subsequently, after disembarking right in the middle of downtown she'd proceeded to hike several blocks of teeming city streets, gawking at the sites, even stopping intermittently to take snapshots of some colorful hobos. Following which, she'd spent nearly an hour at the grocery store buying things she didn't need!

Yet, it just wouldn't quit! Her gears seemed stuck in perpetual overdrive, making her head spin and her body cry with exhaustion. She stared dolefully at her scuffed up soles. *How much longer am I supposed to handle this torture?*

Forever, Naina, a little voice said.

Forever? But of course! She smiled. And I won't have it any other way, even if it implies that I'm prematurely headed for the grave. Because I possess the most precious thing in the world that'd remain absolute even if I paint myself black and blue or get myself locked up in jail—my husband's love. Nobody on earth can take it away from me. And if that's driving me insane, so be it!

Naina colored, recollecting what had transpired just a few hours ago...

Morning had broken. The sun's shadow had gradually crept up over the edge of the bed. Naina lay there like she did every day, in silence, waiting for the fog to lift, so she could take some more pills and summon it back. But not today.

Today, unlike any other day so far, there was no sign of any fog. Only blue skies and brilliant sunshine, making her mind and body feel beautifully fresh and clear and...*naked!*

Thrown into a tizzy, she scrambled for the sheets.

"No, don't. I like you a lot better this way," her husband's voice rang out smooth and loud and she was yanked back down only to be spooned onto his bare torso and have her rump lodged firmly against his growing hardness. Then draping an arm possessively across her chest, he began nibbling on her left ear with his sharp teeth, sending tiny shocks of pleasure down her spine.

Shuddering uncontrollably, she flipped over and pressed her lips hard against his.

He was the reason the fog had cleared and for that he deserved anything and everything she could give him. *And why not?* Wasn't he the man she had loved from the beginning of time?

Yet she couldn't suppress the moans and cries and gasps as he toyed with her flesh and made a meal of her. Last night's gentleness was gone. It had been replaced with love which was impulsive, forceful and fiercely passionate. These were all the characteristics she'd come to associate with the man, the secret of his charm, his energy and vibrancy that was making her fall deeper and deeper in love with him.

But he wouldn't let her quietly rejoice over her fate. He wanted, *demanded* her participation. And she gave it willingly—for her man was endowed with not just a beautiful mind but an unbelievably sexy body. Joyful laughter gurgled in her throat but no! That excited him even more!

Shackling her arms above her head, he imprisoned her with his mesmerizing gaze, then without any further ado thrust into her deep and hard. Her startled cry disappeared into the roomy cavern of his throat when he kissed her with the utmost tenderness, yet continued to slam into her establishing an unearthly rhythm.

She was pulled down along with him, plunged into a vortex of unequal ecstasy. They had attained their goal, two beautiful souls finally locked together. As she sank down, her head exploded with flashes of brilliant color she had never seen before. She was in the center of the universe, weathering the strongest typhoon. Then she was riding an invisible roller coaster, ferried to dizzying heights from where she fell free into empty space, before hurtling through galaxies at the speed of light. The stimulation was relentless, incessant, and she could only take so much. His affection had dragged her to the edge of survival.

But just as her batteries were about to run out and she shut her eyes preparing for the waters to close over her head, she was suddenly rescued, and was off riding the crest of a gigantic wave, higher and higher until the darkness was pierced by the purest, sweetest and most serene, white light. She believed she had glimpsed heaven.

Later lingering in the aftermath of ultimate togetherness, Naina shivered as the perspiration evaporated from her back. He drew her closer, flush against his chest, where his respirations still carved a ragged course.

Emitting a happy little moan, she snuggled deeper into his warm and toasty neck waiting for the pleasant numbness to spread through her body and shut down her brain. But just then he murmured in her ear, "I have to go."

The words jolted her like a thousand watt lightning bolt. "What did you say?"

195

His response was a dramatic sigh of regret. "Darling, I've decided to grant you your wish—independence. I'm leaving you."

"What? No! You're lying!" Her eyes were filled with agitation and disbelief.

He laughed and dropped a kiss on her curly mop. "My love, it isn't what you think. That'd just kill me. I'm going away for a few days, four to be exact."

Now fully awake, she brooded silently over the information, while his hands smoothed her bare back before localizing suggestively over her butt cheeks, setting her ears aflame.

"Stop playing with me!" she exploded, elbowing him away. "You can't leave me! Not now, not ever! I won't let you!"

"I don't want to go, either," he said in a more sedate tone. "But my boss, he asked me to. He called yesterday and requested me to present your case at a conference in Rio. I couldn't refuse, though it's something I'd rather not do."

"But if that's so, you must!" she said earnestly. "There are bound to be so many others like me, who could benefit from your experience. You cannot deny them the chance, Rihaan."

"Guess you're right. And you make it sound so noble." His lips curled into a fond smile. "I wish I could take you along but…"

"I know why you can't. Because you aren't yet prepared to divulge to me the circumstances of my accident. Will there ever be a time when you will?" she asked not seeming particularly perturbed.

"Yes, and it'll be very soon. I promise. I love you so much, my darling! Thank you!" He pulled her again into a tight embrace.

She hugged him back, loving him for protecting her with such a fierceness, even though she felt it may be a bit too excessive.

"I've asked sis to take you to her place every night and drop you back off in the morning, so you can enjoy your *freedom* most of the day."

"You trust me to take care of myself?" she asked cheekily.

"I trust you only to a point. And if you don't behave…be warned," he murmured gruffly, smothering her giggle with a kiss. "So, what will you give me for a farewell gift?"

"How does a hearty breakfast sound?" she suggested brightly.

His eyes glinted with mischief. "Plenty of time for that. Right now I'm in the mood for sustenance of a different kind." He bent down and closed his mouth around her aroused flesh.

***

Naina shivered despite the eighty degree heat. Her entire skin had erupted in goosebumps. She'd heard about the power of love and all the wonderful things it could accomplish, but this? She sighed. *I better load up on calories if I want to keep up with him.*

She was in the process of gathering her bags when she heard someone call her name. She glanced up and saw a young woman looking earnestly at her.

Naina bit her lips in frustration. This hefty creature with a white-blonde mane and explosive vocal cords couldn't exactly be termed forgettable. Yet, she couldn't place her at all. She chose to play it by ear. "Rihaan...I mean Dr. Mehta is out of town. Could I deliver a message?"

"It's not him I've come to see, it's you." The woman smiled. "I'm Maria, your colleague from *Landscape* magazine. I understand why you're having trouble remembering me."

"You do?" Naina said, detecting an undercurrent of excited anticipation.

"Yes." Maria's expression grew solemn. "I'd have come to visit you earlier, if I hadn't been away on a sensitive assignment in Africa. But I heard about your accident and everything else."

A prolonged pause followed as she appeared to grapple with what to say next, then just chose to blurt it out. "What you've been through is...is unimaginable. I just can't begin to say how terrible I feel."

Naina smiled genially. She found Maria's earnestness captivating, and the empathy that radiated from her required no validation. "Thanks. I'm doing much better now. Why don't you come in?" She removed the apartment keys from her purse. "We can talk over some tea and maybe you'd like something to eat? Rihaan says I make a mean pita sandwich."

"That sounds fantastic!" Maria accepted the invitation with a bright smile.

While Naina put the kettle on to boil and set about preparing a small meal, Maria hovered in the vicinity, peeping through windows, picking up random books from the shelves and placing them back right away, simply pottering around aimlessly, looking distracted and preoccupied. And though Naina was bursting at the seams with questions she'd been long seeking answers to, she maintained her peace. Her friend's visit appeared to have a specific purpose.

Later, as they munched in silence, Naina noticed her guest looking her over. Automatically, her fingers rose to the small cluster of scars on the side of her neck. Her hair was still too short to cover it. She looked Maria directly in the eye, "Would you be honest and tell me something?"

"Cross my heart and hope to die."

"I'm ugly, right?"

Maria looked startled. "Of course not. You're beautiful. More so now. There's something in you which wasn't there before."

"Yes, the scars."

"No," Maria took Naina's hand. "I meant to say *resilience*, a charming vitality, which adds an earthly vibe to your ethereal beauty. A deadly combination."

Naina burst out laughing and pulled her hand back. "Words! Just words from a journalist's repertoire."

"Maybe you don't believe me. But your husband. Doesn't he make you feel beautiful?"

Naina flushed a deep red. *He makes me feel a lot more than beautiful.*

"There." Maria grinned. "What else could you ask for? I've never seen a man so madly in love. I cannot forget how distraught he looked, when he discovered you'd left without telling him. I remember it very clearly."

"I...left him?" Naina echoed.

"Yes. You quarreled or had a misunderstanding of some kind. Didn't he tell you?" Maria spoke casually while reaching for her satchel.

"No he hasn't." Naina murmured softly. She could sense her unrest returning.

Maria pulled a large manila envelope from her bag and handed it over. "These are yours. Your laptop and camera were stolen I was told, but not the prints fortunately."

Naina removed the contents of the envelope with trepidation. Her hands started to shake just a little.

It was a magazine along with a few other things. She glanced at the cover. It featured the picture of a girl. A young girl in a plain brown kaftan, standing in the middle of a mud caked street, surrounded by filth and garbage, smiling at the camera, her grey green eyes startling in their beauty.

Naina's breath hitched in her throat and a tension rapidly expanded inside her chest, locking it. She doubled over, clutching her twisting stomach and broke out into a cold sweat.

Her friend grabbed her shoulders. "Naina! What happened? Are you okay?"

"That girl! I know her! I know her, Maria. Her name's Zeenat!" Naina gasped as food rushed back up to her throat forcing her to retch, then throw up all over the beautiful carpet. She began shivering uncontrollably, her face turning into a haunted mask as terrifying images from a day long past swam in front of her eyes.

Maria embraced her and held her tight. "Yes, you're right. Zeenat. You saved her from the blast."

***

Later that afternoon Naina sat amidst her spoils, with the pictures of Kabul she'd taken spread around her. They told the story of her fateful journey very well, yet strangely she felt no regrets.

"Thank god you're okay," she said, picking up one of Zeenat's pictures. "I'll talk to you soon. I promise." She caressed the image before setting it aside, then turned to inspect the remaining contents of the envelope. There was a journal with some random notes; a rough draft of the article she had begun to write; a few trinkets, and an unopened letter addressed to her from Rihaan.

Her hands were now shaking uncontrollably. The past had started to unravel in her brain; the images flickering rapidly like a stop motion movie with several of them featuring Rihaan, a very different Rihaan. She was hesitant to press the pause button and examine the scenes fearing what she might see.

After considerable hesitation, she removed the single sheet from the envelope. The words were printed in bold as if to convey he meant every word he'd written—

NAINA,

I DON'T KNOW WHY YOU LEFT, BUT I CAN MAKE A GUESS.

YOU AREN'T SURE ABOUT WHERE I'M COMING FROM

SO LET ME GET THIS OFF MY CHEST: IT'S NOT BIOLOGY.

IT NEVER WAS!

She closed her eyes. 'Biology'—the word evoked a memory. Of a certain place with large glass windows and an OPEN sign…also of an intimately entwined couple, the smell of food and Rihaan's unmistakable droll voice making a statement.

She continued reading…

IT'S A LOT MORE THAN THAT.

IT'S TWO SOULS MAKING ETERNAL LOVE

THAT EXTENDS THROUGH LIFETIMES.

THAT'S HOW WE BOTH ARE—YOU AND I.

AND I CONFESS I CANNOT GO ON WITHOUT YOU.

I NEED TO SEE YOU SOON.

I'M GOING TO MAKE IT HAPPEN SOMEHOW.

WAIT FOR ME.

TILL THEN,

LOVE,

R.

She set the letter down on the table and the tears just flowed… Life had come full circle. She now knew all that she needed to know.

Epilogue

A few months later…

Naina heard the door of the room down the hall close softly. Then waited patiently as the light measured footsteps covered the distance to the master bedroom (she and Rihaan had a much bigger place now) and the mattress gave as he quietly slipped in beside her. She sighed and snuggled into his nourishing warmth.

"Is Zeenat asleep?" she asked.

"Yes, but only after I'd read *Goodnight Moon* close to a hundred times! What's it with kids and bunnies?" he muttered.

"You were no different according to your mother," she retorted with a teasing gleam in her eyes. "The only distinction was that you were hooked on Peter Rabbit instead."

He laughed. "Seems like the skeletons are gradually trickling out of the closet. Mom was never one to keep her mouth shut."

"Your secret is safe with me," she said, nuzzling into his neck. "Thank you for being so patient with Zeenat and getting specialized therapists to work with her."

"You don't have to thank me, Naina. I'm her dad, just like you're her mom. We are both in this together, remember?"

"Do you think she'll be all right? Be a normal child ever again?"

"Of course. She's going to be fine. You and I are going to make sure she is. So stop worrying!" he chided, tapping her lightly on the jaw.

She smiled and the worry creases vanished from her brow. Everything would be okay as long as she had Rihaan.

***

He perused her in the semi darkness. Her hair had grown. She wore it shoulder length now, in soft waves that bounced about her delicately boned face as she walked, giving her a smart chic look. Her eyes—startlingly brilliant, sparkled with humor, candor and an incredible amount of love. In them, he could see his future and it looked fantastic. They had become his inspiration, a sight he had to see every day. And to know that he'd almost come close to losing her… He tried to shake the thought from his head.

"So how was your first day at school? Were the students able to concentrate on their work or did they find the teacher too hot and distracting?"

"Jealous?" she asked.

"A little," he admitted.

She shook her head. "They are all innocent eight and ten year olds, Rihaan."

"I can never trust a Y chromosome around you. None besides mine! Understood?"

"Understood," she replied demurely.

He grinned. "Good. I'm glad we're both on the same page. Now let's talk about our other little one," he said slipping his hand under her Betty Boop night shirt. "I wonder how she managed to sneak in despite all the precautions we took."

"Precautions?" She laughed. "Are you sure?"

"Well, most times." He smiled, not in the least contrite.

He lovingly caressed the barely discernable bump of her womb and saw her eyes glaze over with pleasure.

"This baby has inherited her rash and impulsive genes from her dad," Naina whispered. "You should know by now accidents do happen."

"Agreed, they do," he murmured, smooching her firmly on the lips. "But none more wonderful than that which happened to me…my accidental wife."

Glossary

Terms are in Hindi or Urdu unless otherwise specified.

Aap: You
Aap yahaan: You here
Aashiqs: Admirers
Amanat: Property
Arati thali: A special tray used for offering prayers during religious ceremonies and for welcoming guests.
Bachu: Kiddo
Bahu: Daughter-in-law
Bakbak: Chitchat
Bechara: Poor thing
Beedis: A thin Indian cigarette, with tobacco wrapped in a special kind of leaf.
Beta: Child, son
Bhai: Brother
Bharta: Dish of mashed vegetables
Bhoj: Feast
Bhoots and daayans: Ghosts and witches
Bhabhi: Sister-in-law
Chaat: Savory Indian snack
Chachi: Aunt
Chal phatt: Get lost
Chalo: All right; let's go
Chaloo: Sly
Charpai: A traditional light woven bedstead
Crorepati: Millionaire
Dal: Dried pulse (lentil, pea or various types of bean) that has been split
Damaad/Dammadji: Son-in-law (formal)
Desi: Indian
Devdas: In popular Indian culture, the name of a fictional character who squander's his life away pining for the love of a woman he can't have.
Devi Ma: Goddess mother or Durga
Dhurrie: Thick woven rug
Didi/Di: Elder sister
Dimaag ka doctor: Head doctor

Dost: Pal
Dupatta: Shawl
Durban: Doorman
Ek aur: Another
Filmi: Related to movies, movie like
Ghoonghat: Veil
Gyan: Knowledge
Haan: Yes
Haazir jawab: Witty and always ready with an answer
Haveli: Mansion
Hogi meri jooti: My foot
Honhaar: Smart, Astute
Jaldi: Quick
Jharokhas: Windows
Joru ke Ghulam: Wife's slave
Kadak chai: Strong chai tea
Khattara: Ramshackle
Kheer: Indian style rice pudding
Kumkum: A red powder used ceremonially and cosmetically, especially by Hindu women to make a distinctive mark on the forehead.
Kurta: Long loose collarless shirt
Lattu: Nuts, crazy
Lehenga: Long skirt, embroidered and pleated
Mami: Aunt (maternal uncle's wife)
Mandap: Sacred tent used in Hindu wedding ceremonies
Mangalsutra: Auspicious thread knotted around the bride's neck
Manmaani: Wish
Mannat: Wish, prayer
Marad: Husband
Masala: Spice
Mein ek imaandaar aadmi hoon: I am an honest man.
Miya biwi: Husband wife
Moksha: Liberation from the cycle of death and rebirth
Muh-phat: Outspoken
Munimji: Accountant
Naamkaran: Naming ceremony
Ojha: Exorcist
Pagris: Turbans
Pakoras: A deep fried Indian snack
Paneer: Fresh Indian cheese
Papaji: Papa or father, ji is added at the end of a word as a form of respect.
Parda: The tradition of wearing the veil by married women.
Pet pooja: Feeding the stomach
Phataphat: Quick, instant
Poojas: Prayer Ceremonies

Prasad: A religious offering in the form of food in Hinduism, consumed by the worshippers.

Rotis: A type of Indian flatbread

Ruko: Halt, stop

Saas/Saases: Mother-in-law/mother-in-laws

Saat pheras: Seven sacred vows taken by the bride and groom during the Hindu wedding ceremony.

Salwar kameez: A dress consisting of a pair of loose, pleated trousers tapered to a tight fit around the ankle and a long loose shirt worn by women from South Asia.

Sasuma: Mother-in-law

Shagun: Auspicious gift

Shandaar: Awesome

Sherwani: Knee length coat buttoned to the neck worn by men during weddings and other formal occasions.

Sindoor: Red vermillion powder worn by married women along the parting of their hair.

Tandav: A divine dance performed by the Hindu God Shiva. It is considered as the source of the cycle of creation, preservation and destruction.

Tanga: A light horse-drawn carriage

Tangawallah: Driver of the Tanga

Tez: Fast

Uncleji: Uncle, ji is added at the end of a word as a form of respect.

Upma: Traditional South Indian breakfast dish made from semolina.

Vadi: Nuggets made from lentils

Waah: Great, superb

Yeh lo: Look here

Zamindars: Aristocrats in the Indian subcontinent who held large tracts of land.

Zanana: Pertaining to women

Zaroor: Definitely, absolutely

About the Author

S imi K. Rao was born in India and has been living in the United States for several years. The Accidental Wife is her second novel. The inspiration for her stories come from what she has seen transpire among and within the immigrant community. Some of the experiences included are her own; some have been garnered from friends and casual conversations with acquaintances. She also writes poetry, is an avid photographer, loves to travel, and is a practicing physician. She currently lives in Denver with her family. You can connect with the author and read more of her work on her website at www. simikrao.com, follow on twitter @ simikrao and on Facebook: https://www. facebook.com/simikrao.